POOR DEAR CHARLOTTE

'An acute observer of the Battle of the Sexes
. . . she exploits her real life position as a
teacher in a smart girls' school by writing
with unnerving accuracy about the
adolescent psyche and the lethal bitchiness
of staff-room intrigue . . . She has a cool
satirical vision, real wit and humanity, which
ought to make her writing appeal to a very
wide audience.

The Times

'Opens up the Pandora's Box of Charlotte's
fears with gently comical powers of scrutiny'

Company

'A merry romp'

Sunday Telegraph

'Bits are enticing . . . an attractive subject . . .
Anabel Donald wields a nifty insider's line in
waspishness among the mistresses's little
jealousies and plottings'

Observer

'The tone is lively and not unfunny'
Times Literary Supplement

'Confirms the impression that here is one of the most likeable of new novelists . . . sparkling with good humour and occasionally with malice'
Yorkshire Post

'The local colour in both Leningrad and Moscow is deftly sketched in'
Martin Goff *Daily Telegraph*

Poor Dear Charlotte

Anabel Donald

CORONET BOOKS
Hodder and Stoughton

Copyright © 1985 by Anabel Donald

First published in Great Britain in 1985
by Hodder and Stoughton Limited

Coronet edition 1986

British Library C.I.P.

Donald, Anabel
  Poor dear Charlotte.
  I. Title
  823'.914[F]   PR6054.045/

  ISBN 0 340 39644 X

Printed and bound in Great Britain for
Hodder and Stoughton Paperbacks, a
division of Hodder and Stoughton Ltd.,
Mill Road, Dunton Green, Sevenoaks,
Kent (Editorial Office: 47 Bedford
Square, London, WC1 3DP) by
Cox & Wyman Ltd., Reading.

The School

Chapter One

"This is an ill-fated trip," said Heather Noakes. Two coaches were drawn up in front of Ashcombe College for Ladies, waiting to take the school party on the first leg of its three-week tour of Russia.

"I'm sure you'll all enjoy it," said the only-just-retired Headmistress with the bracing tone of one on the point of solitary departure for the Seychelles. "A truly learning experience. Attempt to bridge the gap between East and West. Only connect."

"That's all very well," said Heather. She was the Deputy Head and looked like a golf professional, tall, grey-haired, tanned, standing assertively with her feet as close together as her chunky thighs would allow. "It's very embarrassing for Miss Bridge. She is supposed to be the party leader. She has done all the organisation and made all the arrangements. And now – the new Headmaster and his wife join us!"

"Very kind of them to offer," said the ex-Headmistress.

"But it makes for an awkward situation. You must admit that it's an awkward situation. Who is the party leader?"

"Miss Bridge remains the party leader."

"In name perhaps. But in practice – very difficult. And you know what Miss Bridge is like when her prerogatives are infringed."

"I have no patience with that woman. Where is she? Sobbing quietly in a corner? That's what usually happens when she doesn't get her own way."

"Checking the travel documents. Mr Embrey is organising the suitcases, and Miss Parker is making a last-minute telephone call. I'm so glad she decided to come with us. She is one of our most valuable members of staff. Hard-working, self-disciplined, popular with the girls, always ready to help. I do like Miss Parker. Hard to believe she's only been with us five years."

"Mmmm," said the ex-Headmistress. "Doesn't have much social life, does she?"

"That's because she's so involved with the life of the school. She's the best Head of the English Department we've ever had. Reliable, loyal, dedicated," pursued Heather, flushing slightly and breathing audibly through her nose, her habit when enthusiastic or annoyed.

"Yes," said the ex-Headmistress. "Puzzling, really."

"Puzzling? I'd say admirable. Spending her off-duty hours organising activities for the girls. Giving of herself unstintingly."

"That's all very well, Heather. If you were talking about a woman in her forties or fifties, a confirmed spinster, I'd understand."

"Like me, you mean," said Heather.

"Or like me," said the ex-Headmistress gently. "But Charlotte Parker is young, pretty, unattached."

"She has a great career before her. She'll be a headmistress before she's forty," said Heather staunchly. She was irritated by the implied slight.

"Yes," said the ex-Headmistress. "Poor Charlotte."

"I can't," said Charlotte. The telephone receiver slipped in her sweating fingers. She was in a payphone the girls used. There were numbers scrawled on the acoustic blocks lining the structure, and some comments. JULIAN IS A HUNK was printed above the phone. Her eyes dazzled with the dancing spots of the acoustic blocks. "Suki, I can't, I can't."

"Yes you can," said Suki's voice, tinny and distant on the line from London. "You can, you can. Remember, we agreed. It's the perfect chance. Travelling with a school party, so you'll feel secure, and only two men. You'll have to get used to your new boss anyway. And the other's a harmless old chap, so you said. Probably queer. Neither of them can threaten you in the least. They won't make a pass, they won't . . ."

"I'm terrified," said Charlotte. "Suki, I can't go."

"You can't *not* go," said Suki. She had a self-confident, good-natured voice. Charlotte resented her ease. PIP PIP

PIP, went the box. Charlotte fed its metal apertures with coin after coin. The longer she talked to Suki, the longer she could put off rejoining the others, starting the trip.

"We'll be such a small group. Only six escorts. We'll have to sit together at meals, and walk together round museums . . ."

"You can do it, Charlotte. Remember what you said. This is your last chance."

"Don't be silly," said Charlotte in her teacher's voice. "I don't believe in last chances. I can try again at a better time."

"There won't *be* a better time," said Suki. "You'd just be putting it off. Like you've always put it off. Ever since school. I'll try next week, you say, next month, next year."

Charlotte knew it was true. She resented the truth, and Suki knowing it. She could hear the disappointment in Suki's voice and she imagined contempt. She felt contempt enough for herself. She shifted position, looked at another wall of the booth. NEIL THINKS HES COOL, the wall informed her. Her fingers itched to insert the apostrophe.

"Miss Parker, Miss Parker," said a muffled voice. "Miss Noakes says we're ready to leave now." The willing, vacuous face of a sixth former pressed against the glass of the window.

"Thank you," mouthed Charlotte. "Just coming." After all, she knew she would have to go. She had manoeuvred herself into this position to obviate choice. To withdraw from the trip at this stage was for her unthinkable. The inconvenience she would cause, the embarrassment of explanation, were beyond her.

"Goodbye, Suki," she said. "We're just off."

Suki let out her breath in a great hiss of relief. "Oh, I am glad! Good luck! Best love, Charlotte! I'll think of you. Write to me. Please write – let me know –"

Nora Bridge was the official party leader. Already, she wore a large red badge proclaiming this. She was in her late thirties, unmarried, Head of the Geography Department. She had pale blonde hair strained back so tightly that it hurt to look at her, a lined forehead, and a narrow body with no apparent curves. In summer she usually wore shirt-waister dresses in pastel colours, but in honour of this trip she had donned a tailored trouser suit in a synthetic material that resembled acrylic porridge.

She enjoyed power and the trappings of power. She had taken roll-call of the girls, demanding, and eliciting, a formal response.

"Topham, Catherine."

"Present, Miss Bridge."

"Tromans, Louise."

"Present, Miss Bridge."

"Walden, Arabella."

"Present, Miss Bridge."

"Good. Girls, when I give the word, you may embus. In an orderly manner, please. Now." She watched the girls filing onto the buses. "Are you ready, Staff?" she called. "Miss Noakes?"

"Yes," said Heather, picking up her overnight case, settling the mackintosh on her arm.

"Mr Embrey."

"Present," said Nicholas Embrey. He was tall and bony, dressed not for a journey but, as always for summer, in worn beige corduroy trousers and a red check flannel shirt. Like Heather, he was in his early fifties: but whereas she was consistently middle-aged from her upswept grey hair to her mail-order walking shoes for the broader foot, his crumpled, expressive face looked older than he was and his angular, gawky body looked younger.

"Miss Parker."

"Yes, Miss Bridge," said Charlotte, her voice steady, her fingers tightly clenched on her leather organiser bag.

"Miss Noakes and Mr Embrey, in the first bus please. Miss Parker with me in Bus 2."

Charlotte felt her shoulders relax. She wouldn't have to talk to Nicholas until they reached Tilbury. Beside her, Heather Noakes clucked impatiently. "What's that silly girl doing? Why isn't she in the coach?"

Sophie Preston hovered between the coaches, an unconvincingly casual expression wreathing her plump and spotty face. Although it was mid-July and it had been a hot June, she was still untanned, white and bulging in an over-fussy green cotton dress.

"I can't find anywhere to sit," she said. Her voice was plaintive. It was evident already, even before the coaches set off on the five-hour journey to Tilbury, that fifty-nine girls between the ages of sixteen and eighteen had spontaneously, wordlessly decided that Sophie Preston was a lame duck. She couldn't find a partner for the coach: she wouldn't find a cabin to share on the ship, nor a table to join at meals.

"For goodness' sake, girl," Heather said in cheerful exasperation. "There's plenty of spare seats. Just sit down."

"By myself?"

"Why not?" said Heather. The fine tuning of people's feelings was a mystery to her.

"Come in the second coach with me," said Charlotte. Sophie muttered, followed Charlotte into the coach and plumped herself down beside her, arms folded defensively.

"I didn't want to go to Russia in the first place," she said.

Alone on the well-kept gravel, the ex-Headmistress waved. "Goodbye! Good luck!" Nora Bridge waved back in a regal manner as the coach began to move, following its glossy and smoked-windowed mate out of the drive through the stone gates surmounted by phoenix statues, emblem of Ashcombe College, and along the road to Swindon and the M4.

Charlotte could see herself reflected in the huge brown sheet of glass that separated her from the colossal view across the plain where Cheltenham and Gloucester sweltered in the heat, to the Malvern hills like blue whales brooding in the distance. She looked at herself, not at the view. She was pretty, she could see that; thick dark hair, regular features, a neat and well-made body, suitably dressed for a journey in beige cotton safari shorts with deep turnups that just reached her knees, beige cotton shirt, sensible brown leather sandals. Her eyes were blue, set wide apart under clearly marked dark eyebrows, and her pale skin was sharply dotted with freckles.

She looked calm and composed. This was her stock in trade, achieved, on occasions when men were present, through an effort of will that left her shaking and exhausted. At the moment, the nearest man was the bus-driver and he was absorbed in chewing gum and manoeuvring the steering wheel round his monstrous beer belly. He cared nothing for Charlotte and so she could afford to care nothing for him.

Deliberately, she relaxed her shoulders, felt the sweat drying on her skin. Russia would be interesting, she told herself. There was a full schedule of sight-seeing: she would be occupied looking after the girls. This pallid and banal reassurance receded immediately under a wave of panic as she imagined Tilbury. She would have to meet the Headmaster; she would probably have to talk to Nicholas. At this prospect she felt pain like a hand closing on her intestines and twisting. She was sweating again. Khaki cotton had been a bad idea: patches of damp were appearing under her arms, behind her knees.

She turned her head and watched the school buildings dwindle. They seemed familiar and powerfully attractive. At Ashcombe College for Ladies, she knew who she was. Painstakingly she had constructed a successful persona, Charlotte Parker the ambitious, able, conscientious young teacher: very different from the poor dear Charlotte, a victim of a family catastrophe, that the great-aunts knew; or the wretched, inept, placating daughter that her father had alternately abused and ignored.

Nobody at Ashcombe had known more about Charlotte Parker than her excellent references betrayed. She had attended a private day school in Oxford, gone on to Oxford University and then the teacher training college at Cambridge. She was honest, sober, reliable, and she filled in her lesson preparation plans. The references omitted – typically for such ritualised communications – much that would have been of interest. They certainly omitted the most important thing about Charlotte.

She was frightened of men.

Not just shy, inexperienced or unused to male company. She was frightened of men as other people are frightened of spiders, slugs, heights or enclosed spaces, with a consuming fear that paralysed and incapacitated her. There were degrees of intensity, of course. In a large group of women, one man would cause her little anxiety, though she would be constantly aware of his presence and careful to keep as far away from him as possible. Males of under eighteen and over sixty only bothered her if they were exceptionally virile. Strangers were less threatening than acquaintances. Men encountered in an official capacity – as teachers, doctors, dentists, ticket-collectors, plumbers – could be dealt with and their masculinity, if not ignored, then at least submerged in their roles. She had a special brisk manner for these situations.

She had thought a great deal about her phobia.

Until she left school she had believed that she was merely shy of boys and men, although she knew she was frightened of her father. She lived alone with him, had done so since she was ten. Most of the time he ignored her. At first she had tried to please him. It took her years to admit to herself that she couldn't. The process of discovery was slow and, day by day, freshly painful. When he did notice her, it was to criticise, in a light, detached tone. To the highly self-conscious thirteen-year-old in her first bra: "Did you know that your left breast is distinctly larger than your right?" To Charlotte ready for her first party with boys: "I'm not sure I ought to allow you to go. Most boys are lustful savages and we can hardly hope for much in the way of moderation and conduct from you. Considering that you're so like your mother. But you don't look attractive enough to get into trouble, come to think of it."

When she reached sixteen she had accepted, more or less, though sometimes it stuck in her throat like a too much chewed, ungulpable chunk of meat, that she hated and feared her father, that she could hardly wait to get away from him. Working with passionate concentration for her A-levels, keeping well away from boys because by then her father was cross-examining her about every unaccounted-for moment away from him, she would close her eyes and imagine a time when she was alone and responsible for herself. In this imagined time there were boys, her own age or just a little older. She would go out with them, kiss them, eventually marry them. Her sexual fantasies, much more insistent and powerful, coming between Charlotte and the Irish Question or Charlotte and Hamlet's incestuous feelings for his mother, never featured boys. Her partners in sex were men.

But when the imagined, fatherless time came, when she moved into a room in her Oxford college, panic seized her. Boys were everywhere and many of them imagined attractive Charlotte under her deadly tailored clothes and repressive manner and asked her out. It was then that most of her strategies developed. She worked in her own room much of the time; walked through the streets with a pre-occupied expression; gave everyone the impression she was hurrying away to a distant and significant meeting. When she was forced into conversation with men she twisted a handkerchief between her fingers to stop her hands shaking and to dry her palms; she learnt to control her rasping throat and irregular breathing by taking singing lessons with a female teacher.

Charlotte had several acquaintances – all female – to whom she revealed very little of herself: they hardly noticed, happily absorbed in their own emotions. Her only friend was Suki. Since their first meeting, in the local primary school, Suki had loved Charlotte. She thought her beautiful, clever and sad. Suki was red-haired, cheerful, plump, covered in blotchy tea-stain freckles that made Charlotte's freckles look like a scattering of fresh-milled pepper. At school she shared Charlotte's view of her future. "When you're at Oxford," she joined in the fantasy goodheartedly, "you'll have boyfriends. Masses and masses of them, standing in line."

And in the first few weeks of their first Oxford term, Suki kept this dream alive. She was popular with boys: she could call on her three brothers' friends to supplement her own resources. She brought a succession of them round to meet Charlotte. Rugby-playing engineers, hash-sodden philosophers, a poet-chemist, a male feminist she met at a bus stop. Each effort Suki made drove Charlotte further into herself. All her feelings of inadequacy, awkwardness, and plain rage against her parents for leaving her so ill-equipped for the basic manoeuvres of life, became focussed on boys.

Suki read some Penguin psychology books. She stopped finding escorts for Charlotte; tried, instead, to persuade her to go to the University counselling service, to talk about her emotions and her past. Charlotte refused. She never talked about her past. She never even thought about her past if she could help it. Each day endured was sealed away in its own little airtight bulkhead, somewhat like the system that was supposed to preserve the unsinkable Titanic.

Yet as she progressed through Oxford – working hard, doing well, never missing a lecture – she was manifestly and steadfastly failing to grow out of her phobia. So she decided to train as a teacher and apply for a job in a girls' school.

She chose Ashcombe College for Ladies because it was provincial: in the top twenty of England's girls' private schools though not quite in the top rank. Not as smart as Benenden and Heathfield, not as intellectual as St Paul's or Wycombe Abbey. It was a good solid school with nearly six hundred pupils. Most fathers were solicitors or business men or farmers or doctors, and there was a sprinkling of MPs. Its catchment area was Gloucestershire, Wiltshire, Shropshire and the Midlands, with a sizeable minority from Malaysia or Hong Kong. The parents were respectable and not young; they had often waited to have their families and they were, on the whole, a serious group, not smart. Charlotte liked that.

She was disconcerted by the smart; they reminded her of her mother, and of the woman that very young Charlotte had expected to grow into, charming, self-assured and elegant. She didn't like the academic and intellectual either;

they reminded her of her father. The Ashcombe parents were an unthreatening, moderate lot. They wanted their daughters taught enough religion to give them morals, enough morals to avoid extra-marital pregnancy, enough sense to avoid feminism and enough A-levels to get them to university.

Most of the staff were female. The few men lurked uneasily in corners of the staff-room. They tended to teach Physics and stick together. Nicholas Embrey taught Art part-time and he associated with no one. When the Head-master decided to escort the Russian trip it became necess-ary to find another male escort to share a cabin with him; the only member of staff able and willing to go was Embrey and Heather didn't trust him. Charlotte could see them sitting side by side in the coach ahead, Embrey's face contorted with boredom and Heather stiff with dis-approval.

"I said I didn't want to go to Russia in the first place," persisted Sophie, aggrieved that Charlotte was paying her no attention.

"Then why did you come?" said Charlotte, and Sophie launched into explanation. Her father insisted, he was an MEP, he had theories about education. Besides, she wanted to see the Hermitage, she did fabric design, she wanted to use the Impressionists as inspiration . . .

Sophie had the querulous delivery of one who does not expect to be listened to. Charlotte didn't listen. She watched Nora Bridge, who was muttering confidentially in the coach-driver's ear. She always muttered confidentially, putting her head next to her interlocutor and fixing him or her with conspiratorial intensity. She had an expression of constant vigilance. She had always been perfectly pleasant to Charlotte. This uncharacteristic behaviour was worry-ing: normally Nora was a seething cauldron of hostility and resentment that vented itself in little volcanic mutters and sudden gusts of unrelated laughter, often in the middle of staff matters. She was given to passionate friendships with unwary members of staff, culminating in flurries of recrimination and stony silence in the corridors.

She was ambitious. She cultivated the girls: she wanted to be popular almost as much as she enjoyed petty displays of power. Her latest enterprise, as far as Charlotte had picked up from hints and mutters, was to unite the English, History and Geography Departments in a megadepartment to be known as Humanities. Charlotte had no doubt whom Nora saw as Head of Humanities.

As soon as the new Headmaster appeared on the scene he would certainly be pursued and muttered at. Nora was probably deeply torn, Charlotte reflected with the nearest she had come to amusement that day, about the question of his presence on this trip. It was an ideal opportunity to rope and brand him even before he took up his post: but on the other hand his presence challenged Nora's central importance. If he turned out to be tactless, Charlotte could foresee a party leader alternately tearful and hysterically aggressive from Tilbury to Moscow and back.

Sophie was still talking. "I've been on lots of cruises. I went to New York on the *QE2* and I've been on a cruise round the Mediterranean. My father believes in travel, he has theories about it."

Charlotte leant her forehead against the glass and watched the comfortable Cotswolds unwind: stocky stone houses, signs advertising cream teas, rich land, petrol stations. She was already demoralised by the trip and it had hardly begun. She dreaded the prospect of enduring male company. She dreaded the prospect of not being able to endure it. She could imagine herself bolting to her cabin, locking herself in, perhaps even insisting on a flight back from Leningrad. The sympathy she would receive – genuine from Heather, gloating from Nora – was not to be borne. Whichever way she looked, fear and humiliation lurked. She had invested too much in her reputation for self-control, for reasoned moderation. Her pride was at stake.

After all, it was only three weeks. Anything could be endured for three weeks.

"I feel very adventurous," said Heather Noakes, balancing

lightly on the balls of her feet, calf muscles flexing, peering with engaging enthusiasm from under the brim of her golfing cap at the littered and grimy platforms of Tilbury Docks station. "Distinctly adventurous. The call of the sea. I wonder where the Headmaster has got to? He said he'd meet us at three."

Charlotte looked at the oily heave of the sea and hurriedly looked away. Nora Bridge noticed her face and whispered, "Here – take these –", and pressed motion sickness pills into her hand.

"Thank you," said Charlotte. She spoke louder than usual, resisting the temptation to whisper back.

"There's a bar over there," said Nicholas Embrey, approaching Charlotte confidentially. "How about a drink?"

She drew away, her heart pounding in irrational terror; then made an effort to breathe deeply and appear calm, smiled and shook her head.

"Did you meet the Headmaster on his last visit?" asked Heather. The question was directed at the whole group but Charlotte was the only one to respond.

"No, Miss Noakes," she said, and wondered at Heather's tactlessness in raising the matter now. Nora Bridge was one of the many who had been very insulted by not being introduced to the Headmaster.

The staff generally felt put out by the new appointment. Some resented the choice of a man, on the grounds that there were no signs of the appointment of a headmistress at Rugby or Uppingham. Many felt that to choose a man who had been out of teaching and in educational theory for fifteen years was unrealistic, and implicitly insulting to those still labouring away at the chalkface. And all the staff felt they would have liked an opportunity to meet the new Headmaster, if not before he was appointed, at least before he took up his post.

But the governing body of Ashcombe College was distinctly traditional and felt that the troops had no business concerning themselves with the appointment of their commanding officer. The ex-Headmistress and Heather Noakes had both gently urged the importance of public relations and in response the Headmaster and his wife had graciously offered to help escort the Russian trip to meet some of the staff and the girls in advance of the beginning of term. This annoyed Nora Bridge because she might lose the leadership of the party, Heather Noakes because she had been looking forward to the relaxation of dealing with familiar faces and would now have to be working to protect the Headmaster from the consequences of his inevitable early gaffes and to protect the staff and girls from the Headmaster, the two junior members of staff who lost a dream holiday that they had planned for two terms and whose places the Headmaster and his wife took, and all the members of staff who were not going on the trip and still wouldn't have met their new boss before he was wished on them with no prospect of relief until he reached the age of sixty-five or died or was caught having sex with a pupil.

"Miss Noakes," said a male voice. "I'm sure it's Miss Noakes."

Heather blushed and introduced the Headmaster and his wife all round.

Charlotte was first struck by his height. He was short, for a man. His eyes were exactly on a level with her own. They were washed-out blue, like distressed denim, and they surveyed her with a bland scrutiny in which a spark of appreciation (Could it be for her appearance? Panic surged up her throat and tasted bile in her mouth) danced like a firefly on a current of self-regard. He was about forty. His features were regular, handsome. He had a rather petulant red mouth, blond hair spattered with grey, and a much larger wife hanging on his arm like a hot-air balloon tethered to a post.

"Mrs Craig Stewart," said Charlotte, turning her attention to the woman with relief and taking her hand. The hand was podgy and damp, the face heavily made up in the Sixties' style with thick black eyeliner and patently false lashes.

"Here we are then," said Wendy Craig Stewart. "I am glad we can help with the dear girls. It's so important to do one's bit." She had a breathy, winsome voice. "I have a daughter of my own, you know. And a son. I understand young people. Don't I, Ian?"

The Headmaster grunted. Charlotte glanced at him. He was looking round the windswept platform, ignoring his wife. Charlotte was surprised at her own reactions. Fear, of course. The thump of her heart almost deafened her and she was sure he must see the vein throbbing in her temple. But under the fear was interest. He didn't threaten her as much as she had expected. Not that he was effeminate or unattractive – rather the contrary. She found his spruce alertness appealing. He reminded her of D. H. Lawrence, an early idol of hers. He was sleek and feral: he looked as inconsiderate as a wild mink. Moreover, he appeared totally self-absorbed.

"Headmaster," said Nora Bridge. "As you may know, I am the party leader." She gestured lightly towards her PARTY LEADER badge and waited.

"Well?" said the Headmaster.

"I have here the embarkation documents for the party as a whole. In this wallet provided by the tour company." She proffered the blue plastic wallet for his scrutiny: he looked away. "Do you wish me to conduct the formalities?"

"What about it, Miss Noakes?" said the Headmaster. "What's the form?"

"Miss Bridge is the party leader," said Heather.

"Let her get on with it, then," said the Headmaster.

Nora grinned in triumph. She clapped her hands. "Girls! Girls!" she fluted into the echoing cavernous grime of Tilbury Docks station. "Ashcombe Ladies – over here. Form a line . . . in alphabetical order."

It was neither a large ship nor an attractive one. It sported the hammer and sickle and it was white with zebra striping of rust marks down the side. The crew, all Russian, looked on with indifference as the Ashcombe College party struggled up the gang-plank in alphabetical order and assembled on deck, pursuant to instructions.

"Miss Bridge has finished the cabin allocations," said

Heather Noakes. "All female escorts are in cabin ninety-four."

"Including Mrs Craig Stewart?" said Charlotte, diverted by the prospect of the hot air balloon in a confined space, or even hovering on a top bunk. Mrs Craig Stewart was wearing an astonishing dress in a huge flower print, Gauguin reds, blues and greens splotching the curves of a body that must have weighed at least fifteen stones.

The ship was a 1930s' vessel and it smelt of oil, stale cooking and wood polish. It could have been the sister ship of the Fishguard-Cork ferry that Charlotte and her family used to take every July, from Charlotte's babyhood until the summer when her parents broke up. She walked down the broad stairs of the M/S *Tallin*, past the art deco representations of Neptune clutching a toasting fork festooned with seaweed, and remembered the last crossing with her parents and her brother Liam, seventeen years ago. An Irish steward had led them through the *Innisfallen*. No steward was helping them on this Russian ship. She had been an altogether different person: confident, impulsive, at ease. She'd been wearing a blue Aertex shirt, short-sleeved, and white shorts. She was still a tomboy, she was tall for age, her hair was short and curly and her mother kept trying to get her to wear skirts. She could remember knowing that in good time she would wear skirts, in good time she would be just as feminine as her mother. Meanwhile she pretended to be a boy and tried to keep up with Liam. Liam was thirteen and he whistled as he walked and kicked his plimsolls against the wall of the narrow corridors. Charlotte did the same. The smell of the cabin was oil and clean linen and musty air. Charlotte had a cabin to herself, Liam's was next door.

Cabin ninety-four on the M/S *Tallin* smelt of oil, clean linen and Mrs Craig Stewart's scent, expensive and sweet. It was a narrow room with four bunks on one wall, two up and two down; cupboards on the other wall and just enough room to walk down the middle. The porthole was riveted shut, just on the waterline. An empty wax carton bobbed outside and Nora Bridge stood at the end of the cabin staring at it. She was clutching the sheaf of papers in a plastic folder that the travel company had issued her with. She was clutching them so tightly that they quivered.

"Mrs Craig Stewart not here?" said Heather. It was a rhetorical question – if Wendy had been there the cabin would have been filled with her. Nora Bridge didn't answer, her usual response to purely social or friendly remarks.

"Have we decided on the bunks?" said Charlotte. "Shall I take a top bunk?"

Nora still said nothing. "Where are you going to sleep, Nora?" persisted Charlotte.

"I'll have to take a top bunk, I expect," she said. "Obviously Mrs Craig Stewart can't."

"I don't mind," said Heather. "Top bunks are rather jolly."

The ship was throbbing with the animal movement that ships have when the engines are running and Charlotte could feel the vibration of the deck under her feet when she went up to watch them cast off. Most of the girls were also on deck, mingling already with the boys from the other school party. Charlotte could see the masters roaming round, five of them, and she kept well out of their way, not meeting their eyes, pretending preoccupation when she passed them.

The whole avoidance routine had to be run through as she moved to the back of the ship along the promenade deck. The tension of the performance made her sweat and the breeze dried the sweat cool on her arms and back. She leant against the rail at the stern, looked down at the dockhands casting off the lines. She felt, as usual when she had to go through her humiliating charade, foolish and weak. Talking to men was such an ordinary thing to do. Women did it without thinking. Probably not one single woman on the ship except Charlotte would even notice whether they were talking to a man or a woman, unless they found the man physically attractive.

"Are you settled in, Miss Parker?" said Sophie Preston.

"Have you met any of the boys yet? They're from Wimborne. My cousin went there but he's left, but some of them remember him and it'll be good fun if they're with us all the way to Moscow and back, do you suppose they will be?"

"It's possible," said Charlotte.

"Oh I do hope so." Her pasty face was vivacious with excitement. "What do you think of the Headmaster? I suppose you can't say anything, can you. I'm glad I'm not a teacher, I'd always be putting my foot in it, there are so many things you can't say. I think he's rather good-looking. He reminds me of that man in *Brideshead Revisited,* the one with the teddy bear, remember you showed it to us last term in General English?"

"Sebastian Flyte. The actor was Anthony Andrews."

"That's the one, the blond one. I did enjoy watching *Brideshead.*"

Charlotte looked at the Headmaster who was standing half the deck away with his wife and Nora Bridge. She could remember the grip of his hand, wiry and surprisingly strong for such a small man.

There were two dining-rooms on the ship. The first was on A deck towards the bow of the ship, for the use of first class passengers and those travelling individually. The second, in the depths of the ship by the engines, had restricted menus, and was reserved for the school parties. On the first evening out the sea was calm and everyone was hungry. Charlotte was also very tired. She had woken at five that morning and the intense emotions of the intervening hours had been exhausting. As she showered and changed into a white cotton dress that disguised her body completely, she would have been frightened at the prospect of her first meal with Nicholas and the Headmaster, if she had had the energy; but all she could manage was apprehension. Fortunately the place left for her at the staff table was between Nora and Wendy Craig Stewart, who was now more quietly but no less massively clothed in yards of billowing yellow muslin fabric. Charlotte was opposite the Headmaster and from time to time she noticed him watching her speculatively, but he made no attempt to speak to her. He was fully occupied answering Nora's *sotto voce* questions.

The food was strange and Charlotte could tell from the restiveness and waves of high-pitched laughter from the girls that they were feeling uneasy. Great slabs of highly seasoned, unidentifiable meat and fried potatoes, syrupy fruit cordial to drink. No fresh vegetables or fruit. Hunks of bread, black and coarse white. Many of the girls were leaving their food untouched and the waiters were talking to each other in Russian. They sounded offended; but people speaking in foreign languages so often did.

"Uch," said Mrs Craig Stewart pushing away her plate, "I can't eat this. Do you think it'll be like this all the time? Ian, will it be like this all the time? Can't we ask for something else? They must *have* something else."

"I doubt it," said the Headmaster. "I don't think food will be the highlight of the journey. You must just put up with it, Wendy." He sounded detached. Not sympathetic, not hostile. Wendy looked offended and hurt. Her face quivered.

"Perfectly wholesome food," said Heather Noakes, "if a little unappetising. We must eat enough to keep our strength up."

"The food was better in Africa," said Wendy Craig Stewart. "We were in Africa, you know. Ian was acting as Education Adviser in Kenya."

"I was Lecturer in Education at the University of Nairobi, Wendy. You make it sound much grander than it was."

"It was such a gracious life we led in Kenya. The diplomatic community were so kind to us. And the white hunters."

"They aren't called white hunters any more," said the Headmaster. "Don't be more foolish than you need, Wendy." His tone was light but it was an awkward moment.

26

"I do hope the weather holds up."

"How lucky that there's a boys' party on the ship," said Heather and Charlotte simultaneously.

"And we want the girls in their cabins by eleven-thirty so we can all get to sleep with a clear conscience," Nora concluded her harangue. "Nicholas and Charlotte, will you be on duty tonight? Nicholas, tour the ship; Charlotte, check the cabins."

There was something very overpowering about so many young females washed, scented and ready for bed, thought Charlotte doing her rounds. If she had been to a boarding school, perhaps she wouldn't be so self-conscious about her body. The last person to see her naked was her mother; whereas these girls stood around in their crowded cabins, undressing, unpacking, chatting, without seeming to notice bare breasts.

Sophie had found a niche with four easy-going sporty girls and a Chinese; she was busy telling them the details of her many cruises on better ships than this one. "All well?" said Charlotte. One of the sporty girls rolled her eyes in an ironical expression Sophie could not see, but said cheerfully enough, "Everything okay."

Two girls were missing from the last cabin she checked. "Any idea where Emma and Miranda can be?" The other girls shrugged.

"Washing?"

"In the loo?"

"I'm sure they were here a moment ago . . ."

Outside, Charlotte encountered Nicholas Embrey. "I've checked the ship. No sign of anyone."

"Two missing here," said Charlotte, taking refuge in efficiency. She stuck her head back into the cabin, and addressed the girls firmly.

"I'll be back in ten minutes and I'd be grateful if you could find Emma and Miranda by then. I want to get some sleep and I expect you do too. Miss Bridge told us all after supper that she wanted to make sure everyone was in their own cabins by half-past eleven."

"Yes, but Miss Parker, we're supposed to be on holiday . . ."

"We'll discuss it tomorrow. Ten minutes," said Charlotte and began to climb the stairs to the higher decks. Embrey followed her.

"I'm impressed," he said. "They've found boyfriends, I suppose. Where d'you reckon they'll be? In the lifeboats?"

"Mmm," said Charlotte. They had reached A deck and she stopped, waiting to see which way Nicholas would go, so that she could go the other. She wanted a drink in the forward bar.

She had a clear image of a long glass of lager and herself sitting alone for the first time that evening, away from the scratchiness all round her. Some merciful Russian steward had unplugged the juke box and the bar was half-empty. She could sit at a table by the window and look out into the darkness and the sea. She could sink into herself and peace.

"Come and have a drink," said Nicholas Embrey. She was about to refuse, to make an excuse and retreat to her cabin, but he put out a hand to stop her. "Please, Charlotte. Give an old man a break. What did I ever do to you? This is going to be a very lonely trip for me if I have to cosy up to Miss Noakes and Miss Bridge."

"You're not old," said Charlotte.

"Fifty-six going on two hundred at the moment," he said ruefully. "I must have been mad to agree to come on this trip."

"Why did you?"

"I'd never afford Russia on my own. I'm always hard up," he said. "C'mon now, give me one good reason why you won't have a drink with me."

"Because I'm dead tired," said Charlotte. "Because I want to be by myself."

"And because you dislike men," said Nicholas.

His remark was so matter-of-fact, so unemotional, that she responded to it automatically. "Not dislike. Fear," she said. "I'm afraid of men."

He raised one eyebrow. "Excellent. Come and tell me about it. Are you much of a drinker?"

"What?" said Charlotte following him into the bar. She could not believe her own words, could not imagine what he now thought of her. Had he perhaps not heard properly?

"I like lager," she said.

"Tonight you can drink Russian champagne. Do you the power of good. Sit, my girl –" he pointed to a chair in the corner of the bar – "and I'll be back."

Charlotte sat. She took a handkerchief out of her pocket and wiped her hands with it. She was hardly sweating. Perhaps he was too old to worry her. Perhaps she was beyond fear. She felt stunned. If Nicholas had noticed she disliked men, perhaps this was general gossip in the staff-room; everyone at Ashcombe may have seen through the façade she had so elaborately preserved for the last five years.

He returned with a bottle of champagne and two full glasses. "Try this," he said. She gulped the drink obediently.

"I didn't know the Russians made champagne," she said.

"Judging from this, they don't," he said. "So tell me about you and men. Were you raped as a child?"

Charlotte gasped. "Heavens, no!"

"Don't look so shocked. It happens. Incest, then?"

She was beyond gasping. She looked stricken. She immediately imagined sex with her father then blocked the image. It was too frightening, too hopelessly inappropriate.

"Absolutely not," she said in her best "Miss Parker" voice.

"I'll stop guessing," he said more gently. "You can tell me something, though. Why doesn't Heather Noakes approve of me?"

This was also a hard question to answer, but this time from the diplomatic, not personal, point of view. "Possibly because you don't believe in private education," she offered. She could hardly tell him that Heather disapproved of him in every way. He was not sound. He was divorced, he painted watercolours (real men painted in oils), he always seemed to be saying "God I need a drink", he hung around the staff-room reading the newspapers and eating as many of the break biscuits as he could. Heather suspected him of trying to live on them. "The

Bursar makes a very reasonable charge for coffee and biscuits," Heather complained. "Ten pence. Very reasonable. But that is not supposed to provide packet upon packet and cup upon cup. There must be a limit. The line must be drawn somewhere."

And then there had been the episode of the nourishing soup. Embrey had called in sick and the Head of Home Economics, two years a widow and keeping an eye out for a husband, had taken round a thermos flask of soup.

Charlotte had been sitting quietly in her windowseat in the staff-room when the widow recounted her story to Heather Noakes and Paula Madders who ran the History Department. "He took such a long time to come to the door," said the widow, "and when he did –" pause – "he was only wearing a sheet."

"Where?" inquired Heather.

"Don't be silly," said the widow. She could speak to Heather as an equal because she had been at the school longer. "You know where. Around here." She indicated her waist. "Where could he have been wearing it?"

"As a kind of toga?" suggested Paula Madders, an imaginative woman. "Or over his head, like a ghost?"

"And moreover, I got the feeling that he didn't really appreciate the soup. He looked at it in the oddest way."

"Perhaps you arrived at a bad moment," suggested Paula.

"Do you mean that he might have been asleep?"

"I meant that he might not have been alone."

"But . . ." began the widow, then halted mid-remark. "But he's not married," she said slowly and reflectively, answering her own objection in her tone.

Heather raised a bristly eyebrow. "Surely not in Ashcombe?" she said. "Who would he be in bed with?"

There was a pause.

"After all he is an artist. Perhaps – an art student –" said Paula.

"It's been thirty years since he was an art student," said Heather. "Though I suppose he could have asked someone down from London."

"He certainly doesn't live with anyone regularly," said the widow. "He only takes one pint of milk a day."

"They might dislike milk," said Paula. She was amused by the incident and so had Charlotte been; but Heather had taken it seriously. It contributed to her picture of Nicholas as unsuitable.

Charlotte had always rather liked him, at one remove. She liked his sense of humour, she liked his sloppiness. He wasn't exactly dirty but he often didn't shave and his corduroys and sweaters were anything but smart. There was a Fifties' beatnik air about him.

She also liked his watercolours, surprisingly vivid for the medium and uncommonly large. She liked his elusiveness and his independence and the pointed remarks he made at staff meetings. She often wondered what it would be like to be so relaxed. She remarked on it once, to Heather. Heather's comment was "Relaxed! Huh!" She didn't like anyone who came into the school and didn't subscribe to its values. She didn't like complexity; she hated irony and thought it cheap. Charlotte didn't like irony in general; it was her father's weapon, the weapon of the educated Englishman; she never used it on the girls as a matter of principle. It would be too easy to be Miss Brodie. She tried not to cheat by pretending to a sophistication gleaned secondhand from her reading and her education and certainly unearned by experience.

But in Nicholas Embrey's case, she felt the sophistication had been earned by experience. He gave the air of one who had knocked about a bit and been rubbed smooth by life's boulders. He was entitled to subtlety in the way he saw things. But Heather thought one meaning was quite enough for anyone and if you meant something you should say so, and none of this messing about with undertones or overtones or sidetones or anything except direct statement.

"Hey!" He snapped his fingers under her nose. "Charlotte! Wake up! Where do you go to in those trances of yours?"

"What trances?" said Charlotte defensively. She hoped nobody noticed her frequent abstraction.

"Take a look at this." He unfolded a piece of paper and pushed it across the table to her. It was a pencil sketch; she had noticed him doing it earlier when the staff were drinking coffee in the bar after dinner. It was a drawing of herself: he had made her seem utterly lacking in movement or expression, like a Coppelia waiting for animation.

She was dismayed. "I don't look like that," she said and pushed it away.

"You give that impression. Tell me something else. If you're so frightened of men, why did you come on this trip?"

"I don't think I can explain."

"Try."

Charlotte looked around the bar. They were alone. She was sitting alone with a man. She wished Suki could see her. She felt warm right down to her toes.

"Originally, there weren't going to be any male escorts. Then when the Headmaster decided to come it was such short notice. It would have looked odd if I'd ducked out."

"And?" prompted Nicholas.

"And I kept promising myself that one day I would get over my aversion to men . . . it seemed the perfect chance."

"And?"

"And I was ashamed. Of being afraid. Of pretending not to be. After all, men are half the human race. It's not even as if I'm homosexual, at least I don't think I am." She stopped abruptly. "I'm not used to champagne," she said.

The cabin wasn't big enough for the four of them. It was past one o'clock and Charlotte lay awake. Beneath her, Wendy Craig Stewart lay suspiciously still. When she did shift even a little the upper bunk swayed and creaked. She was certainly awake. Nora Bridge was breathing regularly in a controlled manner that suggested she was pretending to sleep. Heather was snoring.

Charlotte thought with longing of her little house in Ashcombe, the middle one of a terraced group of Victorian cottages, thoroughly modernised and centrally heated with one large bedroom, one small, fitted carpets, sparkling clean windows that Charlotte perpetually polished in some rite of atonement which gave her great satisfaction. She did not allow herself to clean anything else obsessively; she was only too aware of the possibilities in that direction. She could well imagine herself cleaning perpetually in a routine that became more and more all-pervasive and more demanding until she did nothing but teach and clean.

But as the M/s *Tallin* creaked and rolled its way through the North Sea to Oslo, Charlotte wished herself in number 2 Mount Cottages, lying on the carpet in the living-room doing yoga in her track suit to the Beethoven violin concerto. Suddenly the thought of yoga, moving her body about with total freedom, talking to herself if she wanted to, sniffing, coughing, clearing her throat, able to make coffee or go to the lavatory or sort out the kitchen cupboards or write a letter – all the possibilities now denied her in this cabinful of disparate personalities – seemed intensely pleasurable.

She was shut up here with nothing to do but think. Tomorrow she would have to face Nicholas. She was unexpectedly sanguine about that. He had accepted her confessions as if they were the merest commonplace: interesting but unremarkable. Most of the questions he had asked about her phobia she had been willing to answer. One still remained, maggoting through her surprisingly pleasant memory of the evening. "When did it start?" he had asked. She hadn't answered, and she didn't think the question was answerable. There was no particular moment she could point to. But she knew when it had started to start: one morning during the last holiday her family had spent in Ireland.

It had been good weather, that summer, and Liam had been in an excellent humour. The great-aunts had borrowed a smart young bay gelding for him to ride and Charlotte was left to use the amiable, rotund old grey they had previously shared. She trailed around behind Liam, kicking the old pony to keep up, and the parents did – whatever it was that parents did. She hardly noticed them, saw them only at meals. It was easy to avoid adults when you stayed in Devlin's Castle. It was a rambling Georgian mansion, largely derelict. The aunts didn't have nearly enough money to keep it up.

The morning of August the eighth she came down to breakfast, proud of her appearance (new jodhpurs and blue shirt, just like a girl in the Jill pony books, her latest craze) looking forward to the morning ride. "Something's up," said Liam at breakfast. They were eating cornflakes, dwarfed by the huge, damp dining-room, perched at one end of a mahogany table that could have seated twenty-four. One pedestal was badly cracked and propped up by a stack of back numbers of the *Cork Examiner*.

"What do you mean? These cornflakes are stale."

"You left the packet open."

"I didn't."

"You did."

"What do you mean, something's up?"

"With the parents. Something's going on. They stop talking when we come near them." Liam was always more attuned to adults than Charlotte.

She wasn't interested. "Come on, Liam."

"Where?"

"Riding. Come on."

"Not this morning," he said. He had a pale face and dark hair. When he concentrated, freckles stood out sharply against his skin and his blue eyes narrowed against the light. At the moment the freckles stood out like ink spots on paper. Charlotte was impressed.

But she felt no premonition. If Liam didn't want to go riding, she felt independently and proudly, she'd go by herself, saddle the pony and ride back from the field to the house. Perhaps Liam would see her and admire her spirit.

The grey pony was grass fat and reluctant to leave his lush field. Charlotte had to admit defeat and ride round inside the field, from time to time ignominiously submitting to the pony's decision to stop for a graze. It was a warm day. Each time the pony stopped, horse flies settled, and Charlotte was kept busy brushing them away.

Lying in her bunk with only the noises of the ship all

around her, Charlotte could hear only the Irish sounds of cawing rooks and the heavy snuffles and munches of the pony. She remembered, as vividly as if she was doing it now, looking up towards the house. It was impressive at a distance, the sun glinting from the east windows, the ivy covering years of dilapidation and neglect. From this distance the ornamental lake looked ornamental. Closer to, it stank of decay and you could see the unidentifiable objects half-submerged in its boggy depths. Ten-year-old Charlotte let herself wander in one of her favourite dreams, where she grew up into a woman as beautiful as her mother (everyone said she was the image of her mother) and married a kind, handsome man who was rich enough to restore Devlin's Castle and pension the great-aunts. Henrietta would spend her money on good works and travel, Victoria would have a good time (which often meant gin and singing to the radio) and Ivy could go to the doctor as often as she liked. That was her hobby, the aunts said. She enjoyed ill health.

Conscientiously, the ride over, Charlotte rubbed the pony down though his exertions hardly warranted it, and returned the saddle and bridle to the stable yard. Batty O'Reilly, the gardener and odd job man to whom Henrietta liked to refer grandly as the groom, was lurking in the tack room. "There's the devil to pay this morning," he observed. "Isn't it the pony and trap they're wanting."

That surprised Charlotte. When her parents were at Devlin's Castle the household used her father's car. "What do they want the trap for?"

"I'll not ask. You didn't see the faces on them."

"You'd better hurry, then," said Charlotte, suddenly anxious.

When she got back to the house Liam was in his school suit. He was standing in the hall by a pile of suitcases and he didn't meet her eyes. Upstairs somewhere she could hear a woman crying. It sounded like her mother.

"Should I get changed for travelling? Where are we going?" said Charlotte. Liam only wore that suit for school or for travelling. "Have you packed my suitcase, Liam?"

Liam shook his head. "'S all right," he said. "You don't have to pack. You're staying here."

"With the aunts? For how long?"

"Not just with the aunts. With Daddy too."

"I don't understand. Daddy never stays here without Mummy."

"He may take the afternoon plane. You both may."

"But then . . . why don't we come with you?"

The crying grew louder and nearer. Charlotte's parents appeared together at the galleried first floor landing. They were side by side and at first Charlotte thought her father was comforting her mother. Then she saw he was holding her wrists twisted together and kicking her painfully about the shins. He was saying words she didn't want to recognise, and words she didn't know.

She turned to Liam and the knowing look on his face appalled her. "I don't understand," she said helplessly, and shivered in the damp of the flagged hall.

"Please don't. Please," her mother was begging, almost squealing. Her face was tear-tracked and puffy. She looked older. Charlotte was usually proud of how young and pretty she looked, but not now.

"Where are the aunts?" said Charlotte, panicking. "I want the aunts."

"Keeping out of it," said Liam. "Aunts keep out of family rows." He said this as if everybody knew it and Charlotte, never having heard it before, felt uniquely inexperienced and ill-equipped for this situation. "Aunts keep out of family rows," he repeated. He was very pale, almost green.

Charlotte's father was still kicking her mother on the landing and her mother was moaning. "Stop him, Liam," said Charlotte. "He's hurting Mummy." She had never seen her parents fight physically, she had scarcely even seen them argue. Disagreements were defused and smoothed over by her mother's charm and compliant manner.

"You stop him," said Liam. "I tried before. He's stronger than I am." Again Charlotte didn't understand. Liam was a brave fighter, a dirty one, unusually careless of pain when he lost his temper. "She deserves it," he added bitterly.

"But how can she? Tell me what's happening!"

The gardener pushed open the front door with its low brass handles and elegant, cracked panes of glass. He looked exaggeratedly serious and carried his cap in his hand. "The trap's ready, sir," he called to Charlotte's father, hanging his head and looking away as if to imply he hadn't seen the fight.

"Go on then, bitch," said Charlotte's father, and pushed her mother away from him. She stumbled down the stairs and saved herself from falling by clutching at the curved banister at the bottom.

"Come on, Liam," she said sharply, still a mother giving orders as if the scene above had never happened.

"What about me?" said Charlotte.

"You stay with Daddy."

"That's right," said her father, coming down the stairs slowly and, to Charlotte, menacingly. He looked extra-ordinary. His regular-featured, narrow face was suffused with blood and his crisp hair brushed up on end. His eyes were fixed on some object in the far distance and he had a knowing smile. "That's right, you stay with me," he repeated and gripped her shoulder. She shrank away from him and he gripped her harder as he felt her shrinking. "You're crushing my shirt," she protested helplessly. "It's my new shirt."

"Shut up," said her father, and shook her violently.

"Don't argue with your father," said her mother automatically. Liam and the gardener were loading suitcases onto the trap and Charlotte could hear the creak of springs as the trap adjusted to the unusual weight; she could hear the scrunch of hoofs on gravel and the gentle snorts from the pony. "Let Charlotte come with me," said her mother. "You don't want her."

"Never," said her father. "Let you have her? Never."

"I don't want —" Charlotte began, the word "never" echoing in her head. Never see her mother again? Never see Liam?

"Shut up. You know nothing about this, and if I can help it you never will," and he shook her again, so hard that she choked. Liam, returning for the last suitcases, met Charlotte's eyes and looked away.

Two of the aunts appeared like rabbits from a door leading to the cellar. They had been hiding within earshot and now judged it to be time for the departure. Henrietta, the bossy one, was nerving herself to speak. Charlotte ran to Victoria and clung to her. She could feel Victoria's arms clamping onto her protectively. She shut her eyes to shut out what was happening and she leant all her weight on her aunt. Victoria was usually rumpled, dressed in old woollen clothes pulled out of shape by her resentment of the world she inhabited. Victoria was the unhappy aunt. She was known within the family to have had a secret sorrow and Charlotte felt that this would make her sympathetic.

"Won't you reconsider?" she heard her mother say. "Please."

"No. You do what you like and take your scum son with you. I never liked him. God knows who his father is."

"How can you say that?" said Charlotte's mother, and Charlotte shut her eyes tighter. She could feel Victoria's heart pounding in anxiety under her ear. Victoria whispered, "It's all right. It'll be all right, doaty, you'll see." The tone of the words chilled Charlotte even more. It was the tone grown-ups used when they were lying to you, when they said "it won't be long now" and it was going to be hours and hours.

"We're going, then," said her mother and she approached Charlotte.

"Don't you touch her. Don't you touch my daughter," said her father and he picked Charlotte up. She stiffened. His grip was terrifying to her: not just hard and painful, but also impersonal. She could feel that she wasn't a person to him but a weapon for a fight.

"Please, both of you. This is very sad for the children. Why don't you go away and discuss it and leave the children with us?" said Henrietta.

"I never want to see that woman again," said Charlotte's father. He dropped Charlotte onto the flagstones. She landed on her knees and was afraid to cry despite the pain.

This can't be happening, she told herself. I'm dreaming. She felt as if her skin was being torn off in strips.

She looked up, rubbing her knees. Liam and her mother weren't there and she could hear the creak of springs again as they got into the trap. Liam clicked to start the pony and they clip-clopped off. She moved – slowly in case her father thought she was trying to follow them – towards the door.

The house had a long avenue. A mile at least of ancient elms lined the rutted road. Rain misted the air. The trap seemed to crawl along towards the main road. Charlotte felt her father's hand on her shoulder and tried not to shudder. Liam was driving the trap, she could only see the back of his head, but her mother's face was turned towards the house and Charlotte thought she was crying. Her mother stretched out her arms and the impulse to run to her was overwhelming. She stirred and her father's hand tightened its grip. "Oh no you don't," he said. "I'm looking after you now."

Charlotte couldn't move. But she could imagine, and as clearly as if it were real she could imagine pulling herself away, running down the steps and along the avenue, panting with the effort. She could see her mother's happy expression as she hopped into the trap and made a space for herself among the suitcases. She could smell the mingling of her mother's scent and the sweat of the pony. She could feel the suitcases pressing on each side of her and the jerking of the old trap over the bumps and potholes and see Liam's smile of welcome and complicity. The Charlotte her father controlled so tautly was a shell. Real Charlotte had gone: was now turning off the avenue onto the road with the others, out of sight. Escaped for ever.

"There now," said her father with a little sigh of self-absorbed glee. "That's better, isn't it? They've gone. It's just us."

Chapter Two

"Glad to see you jogging round the deck," said Heather Noakes, crisply sorting her plate of cold meat and cheese into edible and inedible. Some of the slices of sausage were solid fat interspersed with gristle and not even Heather felt any merit or benefit could accrue from eating them.

Charlotte nibbled at a slice of cheese and looked round the half-empty dining-room. Most of the girls were probably still in their bunks. No sign yet of any of the other staff. Charlotte felt hopeful. It was another sunny day. She was in a brisk, no-nonsense mood and dressed accordingly in a well-ironed white cotton blouse, a calf-length navy blue cotton skirt and Scholl sandals. Fewer memories: a sensible attitude to the Headmaster: competent Miss Parker was back in business.

She had run for half an hour round the deck, largely ignored by the Russian seamen although a middle-aged bulky officer had winked at her and Charlotte had felt safe enough behind the barriers of nationality, age and occupation to wave back.

The worst moment of the morning so far had been after her run, in the ladies' washroom. This housed ten lavatories, two showers, eight washbasins and a truly horrible smell of drains overlaid by cheap rose-scented air freshener. Charlotte sat on one of the lavatory seats trying not to breathe, trying to keep her slippered feet out of the liquid swishing across the floor this way and that in time with the wallowing of the ship, and wishing with all her being that she was in her own house with its thoroughly disinfected lavatory and its lavatory brush renewed every six months.

"You must have had bad dreams in the night," said Heather pushing away her plate. "I heard you talking in your sleep."

"What did I say?"

"I couldn't make it out. Except for one word, Liam. Is he a friend of yours?"

"No, my brother."

"I didn't know you had a brother."

Charlotte knew there would be little chance of evading Heather on this subject. The older woman enjoyed the subject of families. Her own two sisters and their numerous children were the second great interest in her life. "How fortunate you are to have a brother," she said. "My brothers were such company, such chums to play with and climb trees with. I was always a bit of a tomboy. Is he older than you?"

"Yes," said Charlotte.

"Is he married? Does he have a family?"

"Yes," said Charlotte. She hadn't seen Liam for seventeen years, eight years by her father's dictate, the rest by her own. She resented him bitterly. The aunts had kept her up to date on his activities. He had married a rich man's daughter, had started his own record company, was doing well. She expected no less. Liam was always lucky. The horses he backed at point-to-points had usually won. His two children, both boys, were probably good-looking, clever and healthy. When she allowed herself to think about Liam, she hated him. He had seemingly passed unscathed through the family disaster, leaving her behind, ridiculously damaged.

"Have you any photographs? I'd love to see some photographs." Heather leant across the table eagerly. "They must be such a joy to you, the little ones, and they will be such a comfort in later years, you take my word for it."

Never, thought Charlotte. Even in extreme old age or decrepitude, I'll never find Liam's offspring a comfort.

"Good morning, good morning," said Ian Craig Stewart. He was wearing jeans and a blue T-shirt with a little red flag under the left shoulder and Heather Noakes choked on her tepid muddy coffee, because he looked entirely unlike a headmaster. Charlotte looked at him and then looked away. She was gripped by two powerful, conflicting emotions. Fear, certainly: familiar, almost reassuring. The other, inappropriate, improper, and useless, was lust.

"My wife has decided to remain in her bunk. She's feeling rather sick."

"Good morning, Headmaster. I'm sorry to hear that," said Heather.

Charlotte smiled and he smiled back directly, as if they shared a joke, possibly at Heather's expense. Slightly ruffled, Charlotte looked away, and he said, "Any plan for today, Miss Porter?"

"Miss Parker," said Heather. "Head of the English Department."

"Yes, yes," he brushed her away. "Miss Parker, of course."

"I was going to sunbathe and read the Oslo guidebook."

"That sounds like a good plan. Have you been to Oslo before?"

"Never," said Charlotte, wishing he would include Heather in the conversation.

"I think the Headmaster fancies you, Miss Parker," said Sophie.

"Really, Sophie!" said Charlotte.

"Well, I do," Sophie flat-footed on. "He keeps following you round, and Miss Bridge keeps following him round. Whenever I wanted to speak to you, there they were. Then Mr Embrey talks to you. For ages and ages."

"Only an hour." Charlotte reflected on the time Nicholas had spent with her. She had felt mildly uneasy at first, but as he chatted inconsequentially, making no reference to the night before but assuming a community of interest between them, she had gained confidence. With Nicholas she might soon feel like a normal woman, she thought with pleasure. But with the Headmaster –

Her mind veered away from the Headmaster. It was too confusing. Her erotic fantasies always featured strangers, men she glimpsed in the street or on television, and these she rendered even less threatening by imagining them as foreigners unable to speak English. Finding an actual person – someone she knew and would be compelled to deal with as long as she worked at Ashcombe – physically attractive, was utterly disconcerting. Time and again during her conversations with Ian she had been aware of him as a man: each time she blanked out the awareness.

"Can I join you, Miss Parker? Can I join you?" said Sophie.

"For a little while. I'm reading," said Charlotte. She was lying in the most secluded spot she could find, on the top deck well away from the canvas-rigged swimming pool where the hordes of sixth formers were conducting their daytime courting rituals, drinking fizzy sugar water, chewing gum and throwing each other into the pool.

Some yards away a group of Turkish students played poker; beyond them two cheerful English typists stretched their black limbs to the unexpected North Sea sun. Charlotte was wearing a decorous swimsuit, designed for swimming. She surveyed herself discontentedly. Her skin was smooth, unmarked by use of any kind. No feeling, no experience, no bodies pressed against it in anger or desire, no children.

She imagined herself in a bikini like the taller black girl, three scraps of red cotton material.

"Is it still fashionable to wear gold chains around your waist? If you're wearing a bikini?" she asked.

Sophie, bulging out of an orange sun dress which flattened the tops of her matronly breasts, was not an obvious choice as fashion guide, but Charlotte had taught for long enough to know that outsiders like Sophie, even dowdy ones, were usually acutely observant of the customs of their peers.

"Those very thin ones?" Sophie reflected. "I haven't seen any, this year. Miranda is wearing chains round her ankle, so that must be in. Miranda's got off with that tall Wimborne boy. The one who thinks he's so cool."

Charlotte looked at her ankles. They were slender enough for gold chains, her toes well-shaped enough for sandals. She could paint her toenails.

"Only tarts paint their toenails. Like your mother," said

her father's voice, as clear as a parrot perched on her shoulder.

"Rubbish," replied Charlotte.

"What?" Sophie was confused.

"It's all right, Sophie. I wasn't talking to you."

"There's nobody else here."

"I was talking to myself."

"I do that, sometimes," said Sophie. "I hear voices inside my head, saying things like, pull yourself together you slob, don't eat that piece of cake, you'll regret it. My waking hours are spent in a struggle with food. Hey, Miss Parker, there's a disco after dinner. The ship's group are going to play. What d'you reckon?"

"Should be good," said Charlotte.

"Might be a giggle."

Nora Bridge cornered Charlotte after lunch, beside the ship's shop which was perpetually closed. It also appeared to have little merchandise; a row of forlorn dolls designed to be fitted inside each other for some inscrutable purpose, several clumsily painted wooden boxes and some small pots of caviare of awesome antiquity. "Let's have a chat, shall we?" said Nora, gripping Charlotte's arm supportively as if she were a car crash victim about to succumb to shock. "Here's a cosy nook. Would you like a coffee? No, perhaps you're right. Just a word about the new HM and the Humanities Department."

"What Humanities Department?" stalled Charlotte.

Nora rolled her eyes and smiled intimately. "Our plan," she said. "Our plan that we discussed last term. To amalgamate the History, Geography and English Departments. Thoroughly in line with current educational thinking, encouraging a free exchange and fruitful cross-germination of ideas."

"More in line with Sixties' and Seventies' educational thinking, surely," parried Charlotte.

"But well tried. Well tested." Nora sighed, looking disappointed. "I had hoped you were receptive to new ideas, Charlotte."

"I am," said Charlotte. "I'm just not sure that a Humanities Department is exactly what we need at Ashcombe. And besides, Paula Madders won't like it." Paula Madders was in her early forties, a brilliant historian but utterly traditional in her approach. She made no attempt to hide her contempt for Nora's machinations and ran her History Department uncontaminated by educational theory of any kind. Her one comment on Nora's proposal to an open staff meeting had been "Humanities is BUNK".

"Well," said Nora, "it upsets me to hear you allying yourself with the forces of reaction."

"I didn't ally myself with anything," said Charlotte, a trifle dazzled by this leap of paranoid reasoning. "I just said Paula won't like it."

"Ah. What Paula likes or doesn't like isn't nearly as important as what the HM likes."

"You surprise me. My impression was that Mr Craig Stewart was extremely right-wing. Didn't he contribute to one of those Black Paper publications in the Seventies?" It was usually easy to outflank Nora where extra-Ashcombe information was concerned. She was too busy whispering to people in corners to keep up with the outside world, and the only newspaper she read from cover to cover was the *Ashcombe Gazette*. She had total recall, however, so if you wanted details of a local vicar's peccadilloes in Cheltenham public lavatories or wanted to know how much the house on Court Road was selling for this time, she was your woman.

"Right-wing? He didn't give me that impression at all. He listened most sympathetically."

"Perhaps he's one of those people who listens sympathetically to everything."

"Two-faced, you mean?" Nora's face worked in confusion; shadows of deception and persecution chased each other across her features.

"Let's not think about it now," said Charlotte. "This is a holiday, after all."

"Not for us," said Nora. "We are still working, looking after the girls."

"But we needn't discuss administration."

Nora gave a characteristic sound, halfway between a gasp of dismay and the sharp grunt of discovery. "Ah. So you're not entirely the dedicated teacher we all admire."

"I don't agree that a Humanities Department would be useful, and I don't want to talk about it now," said Charlotte as pleasantly as she could manage. She knew as she spoke that Nora would never forget the rebuff, and wondered at the feminist vision of a superior political system run by women. It seemed to her that women and men were equally prone to power struggles; women's were simply confined by accident of circumstance to less globally significant matters.

"I was Miss Dairy Products 1962," said Wendy Craig Stewart. "I thought it would be the start of a modelling career. Then, of course, I met Ian and he swept me off my feet."

There was silence while all the staff, clustered round the bar, tanking up for the disco shortly to start, produced their own mental pictures of this event. The Headmaster's face tightened with impatience. "I didn't sweep you off your feet in 1962," he said, and, turning to Charlotte, "Tell me, who is that girl in the red sweater?"

All six Ashcombe escorts stared at the girl he pointed out. She was tall, slender, with very short blonde hair fluffed up with gel, very bright red lipstick to match the thigh-length sweater, and bare legs. She was the centre of a noisy group.

"That's Miranda Chalker," said Charlotte. "She's one of the school notabilities."

"Well, it was soon after 1962," said Wendy. "Not long after. I'd only been modelling about a year."

"Really?" said Heather Noakes. "Did you enjoy modelling?"

"Why is she a notability?" said the Headmaster. Charlotte hesitated, but he seemed determined to ignore his wife. "She's the Deputy Head Girl; she's a very talented musician – she reached the Finals of Young Musician of the Year. She plays the violin – she's clever as well, and very popular."

"I wasn't hard enough for it," said Wendy. "You have to be hard, for modelling. You have to push and make the best of yourself and you must be prepared to trample on other people's feelings."

"And you put on weight," said the Headmaster.

His wife brightened childishly when he spoke to her, even in such dismissive terms. "Of course I did put on weight," she agreed. "That was because the competition was too much for me. I felt lonely and so I ate too much. That's always been my downfall."

"I read in a magazine that seventy-five per cent of females over the age of thirteen feel themselves to be overweight," said Charlotte.

"But of course some of them are," said the Headmaster, with such a sharp edge to his tone that the company was momentarily silenced.

From the large saloon came the first scrapings and twangings of the ship's disco band. Their first number was initially unrecognisable and jaw-numbingly loud. Charlotte was relieved that this stopped conversation. Quite apart from her own reaction to him, she found the relationship between the Headmaster and his wife unnerving. She was sure that there was much more going on below the surface than she could see, but the indifference to other people's feelings on the Headmaster's part augured badly for his ability to pick his way through the minefield of school politics. Wendy Craig Stewart was certainly irritating: self-pitying, self-indulgent, vain, foolish; the worst possible version of what Sophie might turn into if life went badly for her. That made it no less unpleasant when her husband snapped at her.

"Come and dance, Miss Parker," said the Headmaster and led her into the large saloon. It was in darkness with some attempt at strobe lighting which lurched and juddered across the ill-assorted dancers. It took her a second to realise that he had taken her hand: when she did, she checked her impulse to snatch it away. Girls were watching. She didn't want to draw attention to herself. She disengaged her fingers gently, then wiped them on her dress. The music thumped close by: five grimly smiling, bulky Russians wrestling with a Beatles number.

The Headmaster began to dance, moving up and down on the spot and waving his arms in a purposeful manner. They were surrounded by a circle of girls, their attention riveted by their new Headmaster. Charlotte began to perform a mild version of the dance the girls were doing. At first nervous, she began to find the movement invigorating and forgot that she was being watched. When the dance ended she was immediately snapped back into tension; the rhythm of the band changed to a slow number and though she tried to leave the floor the Headmaster grasped her wrist and pulled her into his arms. His hold was decisive and efficient: her skin crawled under it. She would have bolted but there was too much to lose and nowhere to go. The panic was back in nauseating waves. To vomit on the floor, a distinct possibility, would get her out of the situation – but it would be physically humiliating.

After a tormenting five minutes the music stopped and she could step away.

"Why did you pull away from me just then?" said the Headmaster. He spoke in a possessive and intimate tone, appropriate to the opening stages of a flirtation. Charlotte had never been spoken to in that tone before and it made her shiver.

"I'm sorry?" said Charlotte.

"You heard me," said the Headmaster.

"I don't know what you mean."

"Never mind. If you don't want to talk about it."

This easy acceptance was provoking, and meant to be.

"Excuse me, Headmaster. I'm rather tired."

"I'm on duty tonight," said Heather Noakes. Charlotte was lying on her bunk. She had retreated out of the Headmaster's reach to the stuffy cabin. She was reading a Wilbur Smith novel about girls who faced gunfire unflinchingly and flew helicopters and swum sixty feet down in icy water into undersea caverns. They would certainly know what to do with the Headmaster.

"Any tips from last night? Any difficulties?"

"Miranda and Emma were out late. Tip the wink to their cabin mates and they should rake them in for you."

"Hmmm," said Heather, and she stood by the bunk, undecided. Her face was just on a level with Charlotte's and, so close, her indecision was wide screen and impossible to ignore. It was probably about the Headmaster, thought Charlotte. But Heather's loyalty would preclude gossip or comment, certainly at this early stage. "It's a pity you had to go to bed early," she said. "Were you feeling ill?"

"Just a little uncomfortable," said Charlotte.

"Understandably, if I may say so." Heather cleared her throat. "I have the highest admiration for you, Miss Parker."

Charlotte gulped. Heather continued. "You have a sense of propriety. You have standards." Charlotte felt hypocritical, to be praised for something which was mostly fear. She was amazed that Heather would even get as near as this to criticising her Headmaster. Perhaps it was something to do with being on the ship. She had felt ever since they stepped on board that there was something disturbing and liberating about being in such an enclosed, detached environment. The girls were taking on separate identities of their own; not just because they could dress and make up and behave more or less as they pleased instead of being under the strict regulations of school, but also because the teachers themselves were thinking of themselves less as teachers than as people. Nora was more openly power-seeking, Heather less restrained, Charlotte breaking the taboos of years. And possibly the Headmaster was more snappish to his wife because of the unreal atmosphere. Perhaps, too, his wife was more clinging because of the strangeness of her surroundings.

Heather was still standing heavily beside her. She looked very tired and, for once, hopeless. She was facing a bleak two years to retirement if Ian Craig Stewart was as he appeared to be, impatient, self-seeking and (possibly) with an eye for the ladies; a contrast indeed to the last Headmistress, Heather's ideal, who had reigned over Ashcombe for fifteen years. Several times during Heather's career tentative offers had been made by other private schools, suggestions that she should apply for headships – but she had always refused. Her loyalty was to the school and to the Headmistress; or to the school through the Headmistress. They were indissolubly intertwined. Now she had to see the possible ramifications of the appointment of the new Head and she was rocked to the foundations by them.

"The Headmaster seems very able," said Charlotte. Certainly, judging both by his qualifications and his performance so far, his intelligence was the best thing about him.

"Pheeew! It's hot!" said Wendy Craig Stewart, throwing open the cabin door and hitting Heather a sharp blow on the ankle. The door then rebounded, hitting the Headmaster's wife in the face. Charlotte rose on her elbow and made incoherent noises of encouragement and regret.

"Sorry," said Heather. "Are you all right, Mrs Craig Stewart?"

"Do I look all right? My nose is bleeding," said Mrs Craig Stewart. "I hate this cabin, there's no room in it! Four grown people, I ask you! Is it reasonable?"

"Have a tissue," said Heather briskly. "Come and sit down."

"Sit down! Where? If I sit on my bunk I hit my head on the upper bunk. There isn't even a chair in this stupid little black hole in the bowels of the ship." She cast a glance of malice at Charlotte who turned away, guiltily conscious that she was half-enjoying the Headmaster's attentions, that she felt flattered and excited by them, that she wished she had not been too frightened to experience anything except panic when they danced.

"It's all very well for the young ones," said Wendy.

She moved up to the far end of the cabin and Nora, who had been waiting behind her throughout the incident, winked at Charlotte and lifted her elbow meaningly. Charlotte inhaled the stuffy air of the cabin, now swamped by Wendy's rich flower scent and the smell of brandy, and regretted the fact that she had already changed into a nightdress. It seemed there was no escape, so she turned her head to the wall and earnestly began to read.

The Oslo fjord was spectacular. Mile upon mile of pine-covered, low-level country; near the waterline, rocks as smooth as if they had been rubbed by a thousand fingers, and occasionally bays with fleets of little boats bobbing at anchor and tiny patches of sand. It was an overcast day with a slight chill in the air but still everyone was on deck. Charlotte, keeping well away from the Headmaster, was standing alone when the two black typists joined her. "Not a lot of talent on this boat," said one of the black girls.

"Talent?" said Charlotte.

"You know," said the taller girl. She had a gorgeous smile which revealed not only a finely white though irregular set of teeth but a panoramic view of her throat, which was a healthy pink. "Men. Unless you like foreigners, that is." She gurgled with laughter. "Turks and Russians, eh? Not very romantic. Still an' all – it's cheap. For a cruise. What d'you think Norwegian men are like?"

"Thin and blond?" suggested Charlotte.

"You'd know, I suppose. Bein' a teacher. What's your name? Mine's Jubilee and this is Babs."

"Charlotte," said Charlotte, and they shook hands.

"You workin' today, then? Goin' round with the girls, 'n all?"

"The whole party is going on a guided tour."

"Great. We're goin' too. See the sights," said Babs. She was much quieter than her friend but her smile was as broad.

"What made you choose this holiday?" she asked.

"Price," said Jubilee. "Makes a change, as well. We were fed up with Benidorm."

"Spanish waiters are cheeky. They think English girls are easy," added Babs. "No culture, in Benidorm. All beer 'n chips. I mean, Leningrad and Moscow. That's a bit different. There's boys enough at home, come to think. Without chasing after them on holiday."

"It'd be nice, though," said Jubilee. "Just one or two to dream about."

"That head teacher of yours is all right," said Babs. "I like an older man, they've got somethin' extra."

"He's too short for me," said Jubilee. "That's the trouble with bein' my height."

The ship was slipping between thickly wooded islands. Charlotte could see the little holiday houses near the shore, each with its bright paint, green, blue, pink like sugar cakes, and steeply sloped wooden roofs. They seemed self-contained, well-organised. Like I seem, thought Charlotte, amused by the comparison. Perhaps inside these little houses is the same muddle, the same sense of a powerful undertow pulling this way and that. Perhaps their jaunty self-possessed air is as much of a façade as mine. Perhaps they long, as I do, to be a Gothic castle or a multi-storey car park or a beach house in Santa Barbara.

"Excuse me," said Nora pointedly, standing behind the black girls. They smiled at her, puzzled. "I would like to talk to my colleague, please." Charlotte considered introducing the typists but decided against it. They were already moving away. They would hardly find Nora an entertaining companion, and she might be disastrously rude.

Nora was muttering. "Sorry, can't hear," said Charlotte.

"We have a slight difficulty," said Nora, just at the threshold of audibility.

"What difficulty?" said Charlotte. She was much more interested in the scenery and the approaching city. Oslo was a flat town with mountains rising steeply pine-coated behind it. The docks were clean, tidy, unused; several Swedish ships with yellow markings were moored in front of a half-ruined castle. The city buildings were painted variations on a theme of brown, red ochre, yellow, and all shades between. The churches had Russian-style turrets and the town had a medieval air.

On the quayside, some of the best-looking men Charlotte had ever seen were securing the ship and standing round in official uniforms waiting to come on board. The black girls, further along the rail, were leaning over enthusiastically.

"Disgusting," muttered Nora. "Blatant. Overt."

"I think the men are rather handsome," said Charlotte.

"I meant those girls you were talking to. Those – foreign girls. Look at them. Flaunting. Anything in trousers."

Charlotte was taken aback. Nora had never spoken about sex before, to her recollection. The subject had not come up. It was evident, however, that it was one of the many topics for which Nora had laid down strong guidelines, and smiling happily at dockhands fell outside these.

"Tell me about the difficulty," said Charlotte.

Nora looked at her blankly. She was absorbed in her condemnation; it had strong emotional force for her; she didn't want to think about her original pretext for engaging Charlotte in conversation.

"Difficulty? Aah – yes. It's a difficulty of protocol, really. We've only got one guide for our whole party so all of us will be needed to marshal the girls along. You know how they tend to struggle and dart off in odd directions. But so far the HM and Mrs HM have been spared escort duty – on the grounds that they don't know the girls yet."

"So what's the difficulty?"

"Should I get Heather to ask HM?"

"Why not?" said Charlotte, hardly hiding her impatience. Nora liked creating little problems, little eddies of disturbance in the smooth running of life. While other people's lives ran smoothly they paid scant attention to Nora.

"So you think that's the right thing to do?" fretted Nora.

"Or you could ask him yourself," said Charlotte.

"Or you could," said Nora meaningly. "He likes you, doesn't he?"

"Whatever you think," said Charlotte.

"He only talks to you."

"He gets on all right with Nicholas."

"Oh, Mr *Embrey*!" said Nora with a wealth of scorn in her voice. "He's only part-time. He doesn't matter."

With a lurch of the heart Charlotte saw the Headmaster step out onto the deck, notice her, move purposefully in her direction, closely followed by his wife. She was clad in another Gauguin tent (possibly a job lot from the Tate Gallery Shop, thought Charlotte giddily) and spindly high-heeled shoes.

Behind her came Heather: behind Heather, a troop of self-conscious girls. Heather had inaugurated a policy of introducing girls to the Headmaster on a rotating basis. He appeared indifferent to this and to them. It was left to his wife to make the running, which she did with her usual combination of goodwill and ineptitude, calling them "pretty young girlies" and referring to incidents in her own youth which merely bewildered them.

Nora moved to intercept the Headmaster and spoke to him. She stood directly in his path so he had to pause. He looked over her shoulder at Charlotte watching him and widened his eyes in a knowing stare.

"He doesn't appreciate you," said Nicholas, appearing at Charlotte's side abruptly and making her jump. "He doesn't even realise how beautiful you are."

Charlotte was taken aback. "I'm not beautiful," she said.

"You would be if you abandoned the flour-sack house of couture and stopped parting your hair so neatly and brushing it behind your ears like a novice nun. Don't be taken in by Craig Stewart. Lingering glances across a crowded deck, I ask you. Show-off."

"Was it as noticeable as that?"

"More noticeable than that. It was worse at breakfast. Wink, nod, nudge, 'could I have the butter please Miss Parker so that I can brush your fingers with mine'. I reckon he's getting his own back on his wife."

"Thanks," said Charlotte, hurt.

"Not to mention fancying you rotten."

"Oh, do you think he does?" The idea held an enduring fascination for Charlotte. She couldn't hear it said too often.

Nora got her way. The HM and Mrs HM agreed to escort and Mrs HM attempted to do her duty in a way that was both irritating and touching. She moved so slowly on her tottery heels that she usually held the party back as they rambled around trim and houseproud Oslo.

Sophie didn't like walking. She stayed with Charlotte who stayed with Mrs Craig Stewart. Between them Charlotte felt like a Weight Watchers' lecturer. Sophie seldom stopped talking. "Coke costs an amazing amount, Miss Parker. More than a pound. I didn't know Ibsen was Norwegian, did you? Gosh, look at those sweaters. That was an amazing ski-jump. I do think they're brave, those ski-jumpers."

"We are now in Frogner Park," said the guide. "Here we see the fine art of Gustav Vigeland. The city of Oslo came to his assistance and paid him a salary to produce his fine art work, examples of which you see around you." She was a small grey-haired woman in her fifties, a lighter and more rat-like version of Heather Noakes.

"They wouldn't do that in England," said Wendy, determined to enjoy herself. "I think it's lovely, supporting a sculptor like that."

The school party was standing, footsore and largely disconsolate, amid a large expanse of representative statuary. Some of the figures delineated were old, others young. There was a giant totem pole with countless writhing human forms incorporated in its relentless design. "Can you imagine a local authority in England doing something like that?"

"Just the kind of damn fool thing the GLC would do," said Ian. "No wonder the government wants to abolish it." He looked round at the figures. "I don't like them," he said.

"Very, very famous," said the guide firmly. "These sculptures are renowned throughout Norway and beyond. We are very proud of Vigeland."

"Most striking," said Wendy, patting her sweating face with a small embroidered handkerchief. "Do you suppose these each represented someone out of his life? People he knew?"

"I hope not, for his sake," said the Headmaster, gazing scornfully at a stylised rendering of male old age.

"What a captivating idea," said Heather Noakes.

"Imagine being able to people a park with the characters from your life. Most intriguing. What fun, working out who to include."

"It would be difficult for me to decide," said Wendy. "I've led a very full life. In Kenya, then that splendid time we spent in the West Indies – such loyal servants in the West Indies. They really love their employers. But I suppose one wouldn't include servants, would one?"

"Please stop saying 'one'," snapped her husband. "It ill befits 'one' who started life in Balham."

"And what's wrong with Balham, may I ask?" Wendy began, but Ian walked impatiently away.

"What do you think of the statues, Nicholas?" asked Charlotte. Nicholas had just wandered up looking decidedly pleased with himself; he had previously been sketching a naked Norwegian child splashing hardily in a fountain which was already abounding in stone children.

"Plenty of them, anyway," said Nicholas. "I admire a hard worker."

"Just so," said the guide. She waved her hands to indicate the girls from Ashcombe who had started to lie down in groups on the grass. "It is beautiful statuary. All visitors feel it. They wish to enjoy it. They drink in the loveliness of the surroundings and their spirits are at peace."

Wendy was quietly weeping into her handkerchief.

Charlotte moved tactfully away and sat down. So far on the trip it was as if she had been taking part in a game of Blind Man's Buff; as if she had been blindfolded and whirled round several times. She was disorientated. No points of reference, it seemed, remained from her Ashcombe self. Every now and then she was peaceful, usually in Nicholas's company. At other times she was elated, terrified, lustful, possessed by visions of herself and the Headmaster, possessed also by intermittent flashes of her past. Every now and then she was back in time, a child, remembering all the scenes she usually blocked out, remembering her father.

At first, she had believed she was with her father because he wanted her. He must have, she reasoned, otherwise she could have gone with her mother. That was the usual solution in divorces. Then one day she had been having tea with the aunts in their club in Bayswater. Henrietta had left the room to hurry up the tea; Ivy had been taken queer with emotion and gone upstairs to lie on her bed till she felt better; Victoria had confided in her. "A TERRIBLE CHOICE," she said. "That's what poor Tessy had to make. A TERRIBLE CHOICE." Her breath smelt of orange, which also meant gin.

"What choice, Aunt?" said Charlotte. She felt uneasy. Victoria's face was even more flushed than usual. She looked like the other aunts: wide face, cheeks with broken veins, small curranty eyes. From physical appearance alone you would not have expected Henrietta to be the only married aunt. She was just as plain as the other two. If anything, Victoria was the best looking. Her eyes were marginally larger — sultana size — and her neck was reasonably long. She had good hands, pale and slender. She often wore white cotton gloves to protect them. She was wearing gloves now and swaying her head on its long neck from side to side, cobra-fashion.

"A TERRIBLE CHOICE," she said again. "What kind of man would make conditions like that? For a woman who was being honest with him? A woman who'd tried and tried again to get on with him, to no avail."

"I don't understand, Aunt," said Charlotte.

"Poor doaty," said Victoria and gushingly hugged Charlotte to her mothballed bosom. "Your father made your mother choose."

"Choose?" Charlotte was being deliberately slow. She resisted understanding as long as she could, though her nimble and intuitive mind could easily have worked out the problem by now.

"Between you and your brother. Between you and Liam. Your mother had to choose between her own children."

"Oh," said Charlotte. It was at the same time blindingly clear to her and very painful. She knew Liam was her mother's favourite: she herself was supposed to be Daddy's girl, back in the days when they had been that good-looking

Parker family. Looking back she wondered how much she had believed that she was Daddy's girl. He had always been cool, ironic, preoccupied, brushing away the mess of childhood. He was devoted to his wife (besotted, the great-aunts said) but he warmed to Charlotte only when, dressed up for a special occasion, she looked like her mother.

But Liam was certainly Mummy's boy. Tessy Parker preferred males to females in general, and Liam to Charlotte in particular.

"What are you telling the child, Victoria?" said Henrietta chidingly. She staggered in under the weight of a huge old fashioned tea tray. "Bit of trouble in the kitchen," she said. There was always trouble in the kitchen of the Reduced Gentlefolk's Club, mostly because the club employed gentlefolk reduced not only in circumstances but in competence. The work was too much for them.

"I'll help, Aunt," said Charlotte, neat and dutiful in her father-approved pinafore dress, white socks and submissive manners. Perhaps, she thought as she helped unload the tray with its dribbling tea pot, concrete scones and nasty pink and yellow cupcakes, her father had always wanted Liam. Perhaps if he had had Liam, he wouldn't have treated her so cruelly.

Looking back, cruel was the word she used. Her father was cruel to her. Not physically. He never hit her. He never touched her. Before the family split up she used to kiss him good night – a brush on the cheek. The first night when they were alone together in the Oxford house after the afternoon flight from Ireland, the house cold, comfortless and dark without Tessy to light and warm it, she had offered her usual good-night kiss but he had drawn away so sharply she had never tried again.

"You look very thoughtful," said Wendy. She had subsided onto a stone balustrade near Charlotte. "A penny for them."

"They're very dull," said Charlotte. "I was thinking about my childhood."

"Oh, my dear," said Wendy, "I often think of mine. I

used to go to dancing classes. I won medals. I tell my children about it. They're very patient and they listen."

"How old are your children?" said Charlotte. There was something anomalous about the mental picture of a cross between Wendy and Ian; he so small, so precise, so like a John Buchan hero, she so expansive and foolish. Her mind also resisted the idea of them copulating.

"Matthew's sixteen, Carina's fourteen," said Wendy. "I do miss them on this trip. They'd have loved every minute of it. They're very intellectual children, you know, they take after Mr Craig Stewart."

"I bet they're good-looking, like you," said Charlotte. Wendy seemed to her to need liberal applications of straightforward flattery simply to survive. She simpered and smiled, obviously delighted.

"Do you like the sculptures, Miss Parker?" Sophie joined them, squatting down awkwardly beside Charlotte. "I think Henry Moore is better, what d'you think?"

"We should now be moving, to meet the bus at the backside of the park," said the guide. Sophie giggled and so did Wendy; the Headmaster shot her an impatient glance. He was leaning against the balustrade some yards away. He was wearing pale blue linen trousers, a darker blue linen shirt, and a Panama hat. He looked self-confident and natty. Charlotte wondered what it would be like to be married to him. Were the public tongue-lashings he gave his wife part of his idea of the married state? Or were they symptoms of some much deeper irritation that she didn't know about?

"Have you ever been married, my dear?" said Wendy, as Sophie moved away without waiting for Charlotte's reply, ushered with the rest of the girls by the chivvying of the guide, assisted by Heather, Nora and the Headmaster, who took authority naturally, Charlotte was glad to see.

"No," said Charlotte.

"It's not always as easy as it looks."

"No," said Charlotte. She was trying to stop Wendy, but the woman either had no discretion or was under too much emotional pressure to exercise any.

"Some people said I should have let him go. His friends, mostly. And her friends, of course," said Wendy, "but I don't believe in divorce. I don't approve of it. Why should I let him go and leave me and the children?"

"Mrs Craig Stewart —" interrupted Charlotte, but she was in full flood.

"I know what you're going to say. I shouldn't be telling you this. But I'm so unhappy, I must talk to someone, and I don't trust the others. You're a good, loyal girl, I can see." The blatancy of this appeal was a sign of Wendy's desperation, especially as she was certainly jealous of her husband's attentions to Charlotte, slight as they had been. Or was she warning her off? "Would you have let him go? What would you have done?"

"I don't know," said Charlotte. "I really must go and hurry up the stragglers."

"Don't be so silly, girl, we are the stragglers," said Wendy. "This is just between you and me." She was making as much speed as she could on her tiny heels and Charlotte offered an arm to steady her. "He said it would ruin his career. He missed the professorship, you see. He was doing so well in education. So many developing countries called on his expertise. When he returned to the Department of Education at Oxford it was on the clear understanding that when the Chair fell vacant, he'd get it. On the clear understanding. But he didn't. Some left-winger got it, who didn't even believe in reading and writing. Ian said it was my fault, that I made him look a fool. That can't be right, can it, Miss Parker? They wouldn't stop someone being a professor just because his wife made him look a fool. But then Ian said that being a headmaster was the only thing he could do. It was too humiliating to stay at the Department when another man had been promoted over his head. But he said he couldn't be a headmaster if there was a contested divorce. I wouldn't agree to a divorce. And once he started at your school with one wife he couldn't trade her in for another. That's what he said. So now I've got him for good and all."

Chapter Three

"There's altogether too much fuss made about sex," said Heather Noakes. She and Charlotte, coincidentally clad in almost identical dressing-gowns – Heather's cherry red, Charlotte's ice-blue to match her eyes – were brushing their teeth at adjoining basins. Brush, brush, spit, the gurgle of the water down the plug.

"Sorry?" said Charlotte.

"Too much fuss is made about sex," repeated Heather firmly. Charlotte looked anxiously round the washroom but there was no one else there. All ten lavatory doors were open, the cubicles empty. It was seven in the morning and most of the girls were still asleep after their day in Oslo. It had been a late bedtime; at ten, just before the *Tallin* sailed, a Norwegian and Miranda's Wimborne boy had come to blows on the dock side. Discussion of the fight, its causes and aftermath had kept everyone up late.

The ship groaned and creaked, particularly in the washroom. Charlotte had been awake since five o'clock.

"That poor boy," said Heather. "The Wimborne boy. He was quite upset. Fancy Miranda going off to dinner with a Norwegian she had only just met. Without even being introduced properly. And then kissing him goodnight. On the quay. Where the other poor boy could see. Really, it makes you wonder."

"What about?"

"How she made such a good Deputy Head Girl. It's a responsible position."

"But not one in which she encountered many Norwegians," said Charlotte. She was disconcerted by the enforced intimacy with the Deputy Head. First Wendy Craig Stewart's revelations; now Heather on the subject of sex.

"Young women can be very cruel," said Heather. "But they have feelings, too, I suppose."

"I don't know if Miranda has feelings," said Charlotte. The girl always seemed to her too perfect, too talented, too polite. Perhaps the alchemy of the boat was also releasing her true nature. Or perhaps she was simply too lucky and Charlotte was jealous.

Charlotte looked at Heather in the unremitting light of the washroom. She looked resilient. Late fifties, still hale and capable of tireless exertion; even the long day in Oslo hadn't taken its toll of her.

Funny to think that the aunts had only been in their fifties when Charlotte's parents had divorced. To Charlotte then the aunts were an indistinguishable age, grey-haired and past it, but also resourceful and mobile, not old. Now Ivy was dead. She had died three years ago, leaving Charlotte her small insurance policy. Victoria was more erratic and unreliable than ever – hard to tell how much she drank, but it was certainly too much.

Sometimes Charlotte wondered what it would be like when the remaining aunts were dead. Would she be swamped with guilt about them? She had deliberately excluded them from her life at Ashcombe. She visited them in Ireland every summer, but she had never once asked them to her house in Ashcombe. She couldn't, not if she were to succeed in building a new Charlotte. But Henrietta, she knew, felt the slight bitterly, even though she at least partly understood Charlotte's motives.

"I try to understand," said Heather soaping her face in a remorseless manner. "I try to keep up with changing times, with educational theory, with social conventions. I know that things have changed. I read books, modern novels, and there is more and more sex in them. Have you read the Booker short list for this year?"

"Yes."

"Did you read the one about the one-legged black transvestite who had an affair with a priest? In Canada?"

"Yes," said Charlotte.

"What did you think of it? As Head of English?"

"It's notoriously difficult to judge contemporary works," said Charlotte.

Heather looked admiringly at her. "I like it when you talk like that. Authoritatively. You went to Oxford, didn't you?"

"Yes," said Charlotte. She wanted to go to the lavatory but felt unable to with Heather listening.

"I always wanted to go to Oxford. But the money wouldn't stretch. It had to go to my brothers, you see. They were men. They needed the money to prepare them for careers. One was a doctor, one a solicitor. They've done very well. I went to teacher training college. My father always encouraged me, you know. He said I was very good at physics. And of course I did get a degree eventually. Open University. But I felt that Oxford would have been a marvellous experience. My mother was absolutely opposed to it. She believed that women should be feminine. Then there was the money question. But I imagined Oxford. A society of learned women, discussing everything under the sun. Cocoa evenings, like in the Dorothy Sayers books. Did you ever read Dorothy Sayers? At least the sex in those was treated tastefully."

That day, entirely spent at sea, settled down into tranquillity. The previous night's fight was still the talk of the ship. Miranda's friends rallied to her defence saying she had just been normally nice to both young men and it had got out of hand. The leader of the Wimborne party came and apologised formally to Nora Bridge. Nora whispered her regrets for any contribution Miranda had made to the unfortunate misunderstanding.

Charlotte arrived at lunch to find only Nora at the staff table, fresh from a conversation with the Headmaster. "Isn't it pleasant to have a man about the place," said Nora. She was fluttery and pink.

Charlotte felt disobliging. "I'm glad you like Nicholas Embrey," she said.

"Nicholas Embrey! Pah!" said Nora. "I meant the Headmaster. The best kind of man. They're easier to deal with, somehow. Less emotional."

"Oh," said Charlotte. "You mean less emotional than Miss Noakes, for instance?"

"Dear Miss Noakes," twinkled Nora in a conspiratorial mode that Charlotte particularly disliked. "I'm sure we're second to none in our admiration for her. But you could hardly call her *feminine*."

It would be futile to argue over this seasoned battle ground, thought Charlotte, especially since she wasn't even certain where she stood. Are women weaker than men, or merely conditioned to be? She knew that she was emotional and insecure. She knew that she was a woman. Whether the one was the consequence of the other, she didn't know. Certainly the aunts thought that her father was to blame for the unsuccessful adult Charlotte, but Charlotte herself wasn't sure. Looking back over the eight years that she sat numbly allowing her father to blight every moment of her waking life, and often haunt her dreams as well, she wondered why she hadn't stood up to him, or simply left. Perhaps it was because her mother had asked her to stay; the sense that she was useful to her mother by providing a hostage for her father. Another feminine characteristic, the desire to be useful.

"It'll be good to have a man's hand on the helm," said Nora. "Unfortunately – ummm – his wife isn't – quite –"

"One advantage of men is that they tend to gossip less," said Charlotte. Nora tossed her head and looked away.

The dining-room was filling up. The rest of the staff joined them but Charlotte was aware only of Ian Craig Stewart, though careful not to meet his eye.

"Has Miranda come in yet?" said Heather. "I had a word with her earlier. She was very apologetic and very upset."

Miranda was sitting two tables away, hardly eating, looking crestfallen. Charlotte wasn't convinced.

"Girls will be girls and boys will be boys," said the Headmaster. "I don't think any bones are broken over this one, do you?" The Wimborne boy was at the next table, just out of earshot. His friends were working hard to enliven his spirits. He looked downcast and hurt; his black eye was ripening nicely.

"I think it's all quiet now," said Nora. "I have some small experience in these matters."

Nicholas Embrey, sitting next to Charlotte, sensed her irritation with Nora. "I think the girl's a heartless flirt," he said. "Needs beating like a drum."

"Inexperienced, surely," said the Headmaster. "Doesn't know how to handle herself yet." He looked at Charlotte as he spoke. She chose to take the comment as addressed to her. It certainly applied. "I'll have a word with her after lunch. Could you bring her to me in the forward lounge, please, Miss Parker?"

When she delivered Miranda (the girl could perfectly well have gone unescorted) the Headmaster asked Charlotte to stay. She sat down at a table a little apart from them and half-listened to his cool and certain voice, so sure of its rights and facts, admonishing penitent Miranda who was wearing a most impenitently tiny pair of white shorts and a strapless red suntop. Charlotte was aware of Ian's hands, squat and muscular; his forearms with blond hair on them, glinting in the sun, reflecting the light as if they had a life of their own. He had a smell, too, of skin and aftershave. Charlotte dragged the smell into her lungs and held it there until a wave of panic and revulsion hit her.

"Yes, Mr Craig Stewart," said Miranda with her demure expression. Charlotte made an effort to be rational, to control her fear. She was intensely curious. What would it be like to enjoy physical contact without tension or guilt?

She forced herself to concentrate on Miranda. What was she thinking? Probably it wouldn't be pleasant to know.

She was an arrogant girl under the yielding charm, in Charlotte's estimation, but the arrogance had never yet been evoked by adverse circumstance.

"I'll remember that, Mr Craig Stewart. Thank you."

"Off you go, then," and Miranda went, with a sliding glance at Charlotte.

"Looking forward to Stockholm?" He came and stood beside her and she immediately rose to her feet, ready to leave, self-deprecating. Was this what other women felt?

Was this what Miranda had felt for her Norwegian, for her Wimborne boy, for both?

"Moderately," said Charlotte. Ian laughed.

"That's the first time I've ever heard you speak normally. Unguarded. You're a very reserved girl, Miss Parker."

The forward lounge was surrounded with glass. It was empty except for the two of them, but outside on the deck casual strollers, some strangers, some girls, kept glancing in at them.

"Do you think so?" said Charlotte. It was very hard not to be drawn into the game he was offering. He was very good at it.

"I do," he said, balancing lightly on his feet as if he were limbering up for a hundred yard dash.

"Not with everyone," said Charlotte. "I find your wife very pleasant and easy to get on with, and she's very kind."

"Kind?" he said consideringly. "That's possible. But does it matter? Is it a useful virtue?"

"Should virtues be useful? Surely moral qualities need not be utilitarian."

"Do good for the sake of good? You're probably right. But kindness is not a virtue, surely. I spoke carelessly. Kindness is a social attribute." He was ruffled. He was annoyed at being argued with. Possibly, thought Charlotte, he had left Oxford not just because he had missed the professorship but because he thought that, as Headmaster, fewer people would argue with him. Possibly also, turning forty, he wanted to peacock among young impressionable girls. Earlier that morning he had been spotted on the top deck in a track suit doing press-ups and the word had quickly gone round. He could still do hand-clap press-ups. Sophie had faithfully reported to Charlotte Miranda's observation, "Hand-clap press-ups are all very well. So long as he knows when to stop clapping."

"Now, Sophie," Charlotte had said automatically, but she could say little more. Miranda hadn't made the remark to a member of staff. It was Sophie who shouldn't have repeated it. The thought was disturbing, though. Miranda as human mat and the Headmaster as athlete. Miranda could, thought Charlotte. She felt sick. She was jealous, she realised.

"Tell me about yourself," said the Headmaster.

"I went to school in Oxford," said Charlotte.

"And university? Or was it training college?"

"University," said Charlotte. She was sure he was an education snob and would be impressed by her having been to Oxford. She was irritated by that. She hadn't wanted to go to Oxford, she had wanted to get away from her father. In the end she had been too feeble to resist. She still wished she had had the courage to stick up for her own choice. She'd wanted to go to university in America.

"Which university?"

He'll ask which college next, thought Charlotte, and then we'll start the "did you know" game. Sometimes educated England was a tiresome place. The smallness of it and the snobbery, the ranking and the exclusivity and the squabbling over pecking order in a dilapidated off-shore museum of cultural history.

"I went to Oxford," she said.

"Really?" he said, his voice warming in the way she had expected. "So did I. Which college?"

"St Bartholomew's," said Charlotte, knowing that would set him off again. St Bart's was one of the top colleges. She had been a top scholar in a top college, all because she could deal with words. An accident of birth, a talent with little subsequent application. Unless you want to teach other people how to deal with words, of course.

"Oh," he said. "I was at Magdalen." Magdalen was a marginally better college. Depending on the subject he read.

"Weren't you glad to leave?" said Charlotte, a little maliciously.

"No," he said, affronted. "I enjoyed my time there. It was a golden time."

"Like *Brideshead Revisited*," said Charlotte. She remembered Sophie's comparison of him to Anthony Andrews. She saw him with a teddy bear lolling in a punt; but her mental picture had a hot air balloon floating above it in a jungle print and an amiable expression.

"Not exactly," he said, and gave a very heterosexual laugh.

"What do you think Stockholm will be like?" Wendy asked brightly, joining them. Charlotte wondered if she had heard the laugh. Or perhaps it was a laugh he frequently gave.

"I think it'll be Swedish," said Ian. He said it facetiously and, Charlotte thought, not intending to give offence.

"I know that," snapped Wendy. "I'm not stupid."

"Excuse me," said Charlotte looking preoccupied, "I must just . . ." She slipped away to leave them to it.

The Stockholm tour occupied a whole morning. After lunch, the girls were set free to wander on their own. The staff stood uncertainly in a big square of modern buildings, between an outdoor café which was doing good business in the sun, and a giant chessboard. "That's quaint," said Wendy. "Imagine playing chess in the open air. With chessmen that size. They're bigger than I am."

"Hardly," said her husband. She ignored him.

"And open-air table tennis. That's really original."

Charlotte drew a little apart and closed her eyes, lifting her face to the sun. She loved sun, her body soaked it up and turned a delicate honey colour marked here and there by freckles. Soon, she promised herself, she would buy a bikini. She ran her fingers through her hair, feathering it upwards. That morning she had borrowed styling mousse from Miranda and worked on her hair for twenty minutes. She was pleased with the result.

"I want to go back to the Stockholm Town Hall," said Heather Noakes. "We had a very brief and superficial tour, I thought."

"Long enough for me," said Wendy. "I liked the look of some of those dress shops. Who'll come with me?"

Charlotte was ready to volunteer but Nora Bridge forestalled her, presumably with an ulterior motive, however obscure. "I would like to," she said. "The clothes shops were remarkable."

"What a pity that the city is so Americanised," said Heather. "Not nearly as picturesque as Oslo."

Charlotte moved away to a table overlooking the chess game and began writing postcards home to the aunts.

"Lovely weather today," she wrote. "Hope it's the same with you. No disasters so far." Then she looked at what she had written. What a view of the world it revealed, "no disasters so far".

It was Saturday. The Swedes were in their best clothes. Charlotte looked round with appreciative curiosity. She felt like an eighteen-year-old. Stockholm, the hottest day of the year so far, her skin was warm and her painted toenails sparkling and bare in the sandals she had intended to keep for evening.

"Those aren't very sensible shoes," said Nora Bridge pointedly. Sometimes she seemed to read people's minds.

"They haven't hurt my feet," said Charlotte. "Aren't you going to shop with Mrs Craig Stewart?"

"Just off. Mrs HM wanted a word with HM before we go."

Charlotte watched Ian standing some yards away in earnest consultation with his wife. His head was bent. She could see the white skin below the weatherbeaten red of his neck. She wondered if men's skin was as soft as women's. The softness of her mother's skin had been almost magical. She wondered if a man would be absolutely different.

"Mind if I join you?" said Heather, and sat down before Charlotte could answer. "I am disappointed by Stockholm. It's so commercial and Americanised."

"What do you have against America?" said Charlotte. She could never understand the British contempt for America. Dislike would be at least comprehensible; contempt, from Britain especially, seemed irrational arrogance.

"I'd just like Sweden to be more Swedish," said Heather. "When you go abroad, you expect it to be foreign."

"Like an amusement park. The countries should stay primitive and diverse for our entertainment."

"Not necessarily," said Heather, surprised by Charlotte's astringent tone. She looked sideways at her, saw the liveliness of her expression, the specially chosen dress, the sandals. "Who are you writing to?"

"My aunts," said Charlotte.

"Ah," said Heather, looking worried. Charlotte saw her worry but ignored it. "Would you like to come with me to the Town Hall?"

The Headmaster and Nicholas Embrey were walking towards them. "We want to see the seventeenth-century ship," said Nicholas. "Would you care to join us, ladies?"

"Yes," said Charlotte.

Heather looked disapproving. "I'm going to the Town Hall," she said. Her desire to protect Charlotte had warred with her stubbornness, and lost.

"Ah well," said Charlotte, rejoining Nicholas in the bar. They were once again on bedtime duty. The rest of the staff and most of the other passengers had already retired. At past midnight the only other occupants of the bar were a group of Turks, playing a card game.

"Next stop Leningrad," said Nicholas.

Charlotte settled herself comfortably in the ugly pitch-pine and plastic chair. "Are you glad you came?"

"Yes. Board and lodging free, plenty of your company."

Charlotte was disconcerted, looked at him, looked away, started to bite her nails, checked herself, shifted in the chair, swallowed, cleared her throat. Nicholas watched her. He was a tall, lanky man and his movements were spiderlike. In repose his limbs seemed over-long.

"Didn't your mother teach you how to respond to a compliment?" he teased. Charlotte took him seriously; she was too anxious to do otherwise.

"I haven't seen my mother since I was ten," she said.

"What did she die of?"

"She didn't die, she left. My father didn't want me to see her until I was eighteen."

"You obeyed your father?"

"It was part of the divorce. Part of the agreement. That

was how my mother wanted it. She wrote to me."

It had been two weeks after Charlotte and her father returned to the Oxford house. Charlotte came down to make her own breakfast. No sound. Charlotte came into the dark, poky kitchen (Tessy spent as little time as possible in the kitchen, so it hadn't had much money spent on it; it was as primitive as it could be and still be serviceable) to make herself coffee and toast. The coffee always came out too strong but she couldn't work out why; already she was learning to accept without making any attempt to change the things around her. So she drank the too strong coffee and went to fetch the post. Several letters for her father, one for her. With a London postmark and her mother's handwriting.

She took it into the conservatory. The conservatory was her mother's favourite room and somehow typical of her, with its Edwardian extravagance and its suggestion of pampered and idle charm.

"Dearest little Charlotte,
I can hardly bear to write this, but I have promised your father that I will. Your father and I are going to be divorced, and we have agreed that you will stay with him and that Liam will be with me. We both think that this is for the best. Your father is particularly anxious that I do not see you until you are eighteen."

Charlotte stopped reading to calculate. That would be seven years, three months and two days. Too long to make an end of term chart and cross off the days, and an end of term chart with blocks for years would be disheartening. She felt quite hopeless. The house was too big and she and her father together were too small. The silence filled corners and rooms and Charlotte couldn't banish it. Sometimes she tried, when she and her father were alone together, eating lunch in the dining-room while the daily woman hovered. She made conversation from her limited social resources, telling anecdotes about her day's activities playing tennis with a school friend. Her father listened with an expression of mild discomfort on his face which darkened to active irritation. "Have you a book you're reading?" he snapped at last.

"*My First Gymkhana*," said Charlotte, happy to be asked a question she could competently answer.

"Bring it to lunch tomorrow," said her father.

"I'll have finished it by then." She was a very quick reader. She didn't expect her father to know that but she took pride in telling him.

"Reading that kind of rubbish, I'm not surprised. Bring *My Second Gymkhana*, then. We'll read at table from now on."

Charlotte was relieved, and hurt. She sat in the conservatory with the letter on her lap and tried to imagine seven years of meals reading her way from pony books to the kind of books that her father read: *Aspects of Anglo-Saxon Verse*, things like that. She took refuge in the letter.

"Your father is particularly anxious that I do not see you until you're eighteen. He also wishes you not to see Liam."

Not see Liam! Charlotte gave a stifled moan. She felt suffocated, like someone buried alive who hears the long screws biting into the coffin-lid.

"Charlotte, try to understand. It is very important that you do not get in touch with me. Your father doesn't wish it. It is *very important* that you do what your father wants."

Charlotte put the letter down and held it in her lap. This was something she could do for her mother, a helpful act she could perform. She was still not inured to failure; still eager to please, hopeful to be of use.

Looking back, she couldn't estimate how honest she had been. Perhaps she had half-known that whatever she did, she couldn't retrieve the love or even the attention of either parent; half-known that it was a pretence to bolster her own importance and give a meaning to meaningless endurance. But she had been so young, so unaware of the limits of human goodwill, that perhaps she had meant it seriously.

"Remember, dear little Charlotte, that I love you very much.
Mummy."

Love. I love you very much. Charlotte said the words over and over to herself, then and for many days afterwards; but she could feel belief in them slipping away from her.

She began to elaborate fantasies. It would be time to go back to school soon and who would prepare her school clothes? The daily woman couldn't do it, she had never been asked to do that kind of thing and she certainly couldn't sew on name-tags. Tessy always organised Charlotte's clothes. Tessy would have to come back and do it, perhaps when Charlotte's father was out. The house would be warm again, she'd play records loudly and open all the windows and tell Charlotte what she and Liam had been doing and where they were going to live . . .

The fantasy always stopped there.

"Hey," said Nicholas. "Have a drink, come on, don't look so stricken. Explain to me. What exactly did your father do that upset you so much?"

"He didn't love me," said Charlotte. "He didn't even like me. He almost never spoke to me, and when he did he went on and on about women and how corrupt they were and how sex was disgusting."

"Your mother left him for another man, is that right?" asked Nicholas. Charlotte nodded. "So your father was jealous, his pride was hurt, he took it out on you. What a small-minded bastard."

"I didn't see any of that," said Charlotte, surprised by how simple and unimportant it sounded. "I thought of him as an omnipotent monster, I suppose. Latterly I couldn't wait to get away from him."

"So what happened when you did get away from him?"

"Nothing. I hated them all, by then. My father, my mother, Liam. Especially Liam."

The last night on board ship, four of the Ashcombe escorts were invited to dine at the Captain's table. Nora called an impromptu staff meeting after lunch. She announced the invitation, then said: "I have decided on our envoys. The Headmaster and Mrs Craig Stewart, of course. Mr Embrey and Miss Parker, will you make up the four? My place is with the girls of my party, and Miss Noakes has been good enough to volunteer to stay with me. Guests assemble in the forward lounge at seven this evening. Any questions?"

"Oh good," said Wendy. "This will be fun, quite the highlight of the trip so far. I always like captains, I think it's the uniform. A uniform does something for a man. Do you think I'll sit next to the Captain?"

Ten minutes into the Captain's dinner, Charlotte was enjoying herself. She was looking attractive, she knew because Nicholas had told her so, and he commented on her appearance with a seriousness and attention to detail which she found convincing. The Headmaster frequently glanced at her and widened his eyes in his flirtatious gesture which, for once, Wendy Craig Stewart was too happy to notice. Wendy was sitting next to the Captain, a polite and taciturn man whose grasp of English was poor but who listened to Wendy with flattering attention. His eyes were fixed on the plunge and billow of her neckline.

There were eight at the Captain's table. Four from Ashcombe; the Captain and the Purser; two Poles, one male, one female, members of a computer delegation to Leningrad. Charlotte sat between the multilingual and courteous Purser and the male Pole. He was about thirty, with straight, thick brown hair, a face like a Botticelli angel, and lozenge-shaped green eyes. He was swaying slightly. It was evident to everyone except Wendy that he was extremely drunk.

"We have a toast," said the Purser. "Our Captain will give us a toast."

"To peace," said the Captain.

"Peace, to peace," said everyone except the female Pole who spoke only Polish and muttered something in that language.

"'Sall righ'," said the male Pole, licking his thumb and punching it forward into the air over his head as if he were inserting a thumb-tack into a noticeboard.

"I beg your pardon?" said Wendy.

"'Sall righ'," said the Pole again. His erratic attention fastened on Charlotte. "This my swee'hear'," he said.

Charlotte smiled. He was good-looking, he was a stranger she would never see again, he spoke very little English. He was in all respects an embodiment of her erotic fantasies.

"I would so like a souvenir of this evening," said Wendy producing a small camera from her tapestry evening bag. Her husband groaned quietly. "I'd be honoured, Captain, if I could have a photograph of me sitting next to you. I suppose it's no use asking you, Ian. Spoil sport. I know! The Polish gentleman!"

She pressed the camera into his hands and he examined it closely, tilting it this way and that, like a bomb disposal expert assessing the best way in.

"I don't think . . ." began Ian.

"'Sall righ'," said the Pole. "Japanese camera, no pro'lem." He repeated his thumb-licking gesture.

Wendy moved closer to the Captain. The Pole attempted to point the camera in their direction, but he lurched and swerved. Wendy and the Captain lurched and swerved after him in a vain attempt to make his task easier.

"Kee' still," he complained. "Japanese camera, no pro'lem, kee' still." He snapped the shutter several times at random, then handed the camera back to Wendy with a formal bow that dipped a lock of his hair in the borsch.

He turned to Charlotte with a charming smile. "You my swee'hear'," he repeated, and placed one hand on her breast.

Charlotte registered the astonished, shocked, anxious faces round her with a small part of her mind. The rest of her was absorbed in the new and delightful sensation of the Pole's hand on her breast. Dutifully, reluctantly, she pushed his hand away and readdressed herself to the borsch.

The aspect of party leadership which Nora Bridge most evidently enjoyed was holding briefings. She assembled girls and staff, and harangued them in her loud and monotonous teaching voice. She had held a briefing before Oslo, a briefing before Stockholm, and after breakfast on the last day of the voyage, as the coast of Russia hove in sight, she held a briefing.

Her rhetorical style was repetitive and smug: she said the obvious, in detail, twice. After thirty minutes of this her audience was usually swift to seize an opportunity to depart. "That's all, girls," she said, and the forward lounge emptied like a punctured balloon. Charlotte found herself gripped by Heather Noakes.

"I want to say a word to you, my dear," said Heather. "It's about the Headmaster."

Charlotte felt only a little guilty. She thought she was behaving well in relation to Ian; keeping him at arm's length, avoiding *tête-à-têtes*, keeping well clear in dark corridors. In fact, she was getting as close to him as he would allow. Her experience was too limited, her need to feel loved overwhelmingly too great, for her to resist a close physical relationship with the first attractive man she was not entirely afraid of.

If she had had even a little more experience she would have recognised the type; a man who chooses the most attractive girl in any group and flatters her to evoke a flattering response. The extent of his ambition is usually a kiss in a dim corner at a party, perhaps a squeeze of the arm, a murmur of desire. He was not a wolf. He didn't want the passion or even the pleasure of a brief affair. He was a peacock; what he liked was strutting.

This was clear to Heather though she had seldom been the object of such a man's attentions. She tried to convey the information to Charlotte in a subtle manner. Heather was naturally as subtle as a hog in ski-boots; even Charlotte, dazed and inebriated by her unaccustomed feelings, totally absorbed in herself and Ian, counting over the glances, the compliments, was forced to pay attention.

"Men are different from us," said Heather. "Even men in responsible positions – even married men – they don't have the same scruples. They're not serious, as we are."

"Yes, Miss Noakes," said Charlotte. She remembered the brush of Ian's fingers on her arm when he helped her on with a shawl.

"I am speaking about the Headmaster," said Heather.

This open acknowledgement of possible error in her superior must have been painful for Heather. It brought home to Charlotte Heather's views of the seriousness of the matter. It became school business. For what would happen to her carefully nurtured career, her meticulous lesson plans, her detailed and punctilious mark book, if she caused even a mild scandal? And what Heather found scandalous, others would also.

"Miss Noakes, I haven't – in the least –"

"Of course, of course," said Heather hurriedly, blushing. "My dear, I'm sure you have the highest standards. It's just that I don't want you to be hurt. Now we'll say no more about it, shall we? Just between us. Not a word," and she patted Charlotte's shoulder in a most uncharacteristic gesture. A good hearty thump of encouragement was more her style, thought Charlotte as she watched Heather's retreating figure.

As soon as the ship docked, the atmosphere changed. An air of tension and repressiveness came over the ship's company; they began to bustle about officiously, giving peremptory orders about visa control and customs and where everybody should wait.

Leningrad was obviously a working port. The *Tallin* moved up-river between hulks and polished modern ships, tankers and passenger vessels and tugs, many with names written in Cyrillic script. There were many Cuban ships and one or two from England. The familiar place names,

Liverpool and Southampton, looked attractive and welcome, like friends in a strange assembly.

Even the girls began to feel subdued. It was a dull overcast day again, humid and with little fresh air. There was horseplay and joking as they queued up as requested for the visa inspection in four sections by first initial of the surname. Charlotte Parker found herself next to Sophie Preston who was shivering. "Don't you feel it?" she whispered as they filed towards the drab khaki-uniformed officials, their broad features expressionless. "The sinister atmosphere?" Soldiers stood everywhere, some with machine-guns slung across their backs. Charlotte gazed at them, interested. She wondered what they thought this party of schoolchildren were likely to get up to that soldiers with machine-guns were needed to guard them.

"They've got guns, Miss Parker."

"I can see that, Sophie."

"Why, do you suppose?"

"Probably the custom of the country."

Miranda, standing nonchalantly behind Sophie, leaned forward, widened her black-rimmed eyes and said, "I expect they plan to shoot you, Sophie. Seeing as you represent such a threat to the Union of Soviet Socialist Republics."

Sophie was taken aback, then realised it was a joke and smiled weakly.

"Isn't it a pity that your name doesn't begin with a C, Miss Parker," said Miranda. "Otherwise you could have had a nice chat with the Headmaster while you're waiting."

Sophie opened and shut her mouth. She didn't understand why Miranda was being so daring – or perhaps malicious – as to approach Charlotte in this way when so many of the other girls could hear. Charlotte and Miranda had never been specially close and it was an unwarrantable piece of cheek. So, at least, Charlotte thought. "Better get back to your proper place, in alphabetical order," she said. Miranda grinned and left.

The quayside was scattered with people; family groups,

often with old women clutching bunches of red flowers, and the casually strolling soldiers. Charlotte watched the Headmaster move towards her, his wife in tow, Heather and Nora skirmishing around on the outside like tugs. Miranda, hitherto concentrating on the clumps of Wimborne boys standing not much further along the rail, edged back towards the Headmaster as soon as she noticed his arrival. Sophie sniffled anxiously.

"Where's your handkerchief, Sophie?" said Heather sharply. "Really, you are disorganised! What's the matter?"

Sophie blushed, looked sulky and shuffled from foot to foot. Then she sniffed again. Heather's body tautened with irritation. She was still wearing her golfing cap, but she had lost weight in the last few days; she looked gaunt.

"What is it that worries you, Sophie?" prompted Charlotte gently.

"It's all so grey and ugly and *big*, and the people wear shapeless hideous clothes, and there are soldiers with guns everywhere."

"Have a piece of chocolate," urged Wendy Craig Stewart. "Cheer up, my dear. The city'll be better. Docklands are never much fun."

"Remember the museums and art galleries," said Miranda. "Remember the rich historical associations." This paraphrase of part of Nora's briefing was offered seriously but Heather and Charlotte looked suspiciously at innocent Miranda, who continued, "And think of the opportunity to observe another culture at close quarters; the food, the accommodation, the people, all different from us yet sharing in our common humanity." By now Nora was also looking suspicious.

"I wish I hadn't come," said Sophie miserably.

"Have some more chocolate," said Wendy.

Chapter Four

"With pleasure I inform you that you are to be accommodated in the Hotel Astoria," announced their Intourist guide through the bus's intermittent loudspeaker system. She was a thirtyish woman with black-rooted yellow hair, eyes like steamed gooseberries and the air of one who has stood in a queue too long. "The Hotel Astoria was built in 1911 and designed by the architect Lidval. It is situated in the very heart of the city, overlooking St Isaac's Cathedral. The hotel has three hundred and eighty comfortable rooms." She switched off the loudspeaker and conferred with Nora over the allocation of rooms. Nora was once again clutching her plastic wallet of documents as if the KGB wished to wrest it from her.

Charlotte was sitting next to Nicholas. He was groaning faintly with his eyes closed against the light. He had been drinking with the Chief Officer on the previous night and he was now attempting to drum up sympathy for his hangover. "Look, Nicholas," said Charlotte, "the Winter Palace! I'm sure that's the Winter Palace!"

One of the girls tapped her on the shoulder. "Miss Parker –"

She turned round. "Yes, Emma?"

"Do you know what hotel the Wimborne party are staying at?"

"No," said Charlotte. "You can ask the guide later, she might know. Look at that view!" Across the river a fantasy cathedral of shimmering pale stone seemed to float on the water.

"Will you ask the guide, Miss Parker?" Emma was entirely uninterested in the view.

"Come on, Emma, you're quite capable of doing that yourself. And for heaven's sake, make the most of this holiday. You can meet boys in England whenever you like."

Emma subsided into her seat and looked glum.

"Quite so, Miss Parker. You can meet headmasters in England whenever you like," murmured Nicholas without opening his eyes.

Charlotte didn't need the reminder. She was aware how adolescent she was being in her response to the Headmaster; aware that what she chiefly enjoyed was mulling over and cherishing the small indicators of his interest in her, and allowing her imagination free rein in dreaming about them together, what he would say, what she would reply. She half-wished she could keep the secret better, was half-proud that she had an emotional secret to share – and could be teased about it by a man.

"This morning, you will settle in your rooms. After lunch, we will go for a tour of this beautiful city, with its many breathtaking ensembles," said the guide, with the lilting intonation of the learner by rote.

The Hotel Astoria was a massive building in the style of an Edwardian office block. The cavernous public rooms were skimpily furnished; upright armchairs upholstered in brocade and impractically low tables. There was a recognisable reception desk, a souvenir shop, and familiar signs. Bar. Pepsi-Cola. American Express. Restaurant. The girls milled around waiting for their rooms to be allotted, visibly relieved. After all, it was not so different.

"To travel this distance and find oneself in a Midlands station hotel," said Nicholas. "The pity of it."

"Better than finding yourself in a jerry-built concrete monster at the back of beyond," said Heather. "That's what we were warned to expect."

"Good news! We can have a room each," said Nora, pink with power. "Mr and Mrs Craig Stewart have a double room; the rest of us are alone."

"Please, Miss Parker," said Sophie, tugging at Charlotte's sleeve, "which floor are you on?"

"I don't know yet, Sophie."

"Because it's double rooms for us and Sally Wong and me are going to share, and we'd like to be near you. Just in case. Well, I would. Sally isn't bothered but I still find this country spooky."

"Shhh," said Charlotte. "I don't know what floor I'm on, yet. Miss Bridge is just about to tell us."

"What luck, you're next door," said Nora Bridge. She stood just outside, clutching her tour wallet. Since she had allocated the rooms her surprise seemed overdone. Presumably she had some reason both for the allocation and the surprise, thought Charlotte opening the second of two heavy doors to her room and standing back to let Nora come in.

"I just wanted a word," she said confidentially, prowling round the room and peering interestedly into the open wardrobe. "You do seem to like blue," she observed. "A very safe colour, of course. I wear a lot of blue, you've probably noticed. My goodness, aren't we fortunate in our rooms? Ample space. Generous accommodation. An impressive edifice."

"Built before the Revolution, of course," said Charlotte, politely nudging the conversation along.

Nora started to mouth silent words.

"What?" said Charlotte.

Nora mouthed more emphatically. She appeared quite agitated. Charlotte could make no sense of her lip movements. "Remember the briefing!" Nora was eventually driven to outright speech.

This was very difficult. It was of the nature of Nora's briefings that the mind of the listener mercifully erased all memory of them as soon as they were over. Charlotte groped for Nora's admonitions. Not selling jeans; carrying an umbrella at all times; keeping together in groups of three, one to have an accident, one to go for help, one to stay with the afflicted; not photographing docks, railway stations, airports – none of this was relevant.

"I wanted to talk to you about the Humanities Department," said Nora eventually, winking.

"Do sit down," said Charlotte, removing a pile of T-shirts from an angular pitch-pine chair. Her room was on the fourth floor; the furniture was basic and varnished a virulent yellow colour. "I thought we'd agreed not to talk shop on this trip."

Nora sat down graciously, as if she was doing the chair a favour. "I thought you'd like to know. The Headmaster and I have discussed the Humanities Department further. He agrees with me that there is much to be gained by cooperation between the English, Geography and History Departments. He wishes to discuss it further with you."

"Then I expect he will," said Charlotte. The remark sounded jaunty; even insolent. She was slightly shocked at herself. She was losing moderation and occasionally she saw herself from an outsider's point of view, behaving, if not badly, at least without decorum. She felt startled, as though she had missed a step coming down stairs; then she reimmersed herself in her memories of the Headmaster. His remarks were like a tape loop, running in her head. "You're a very reserved girl, Miss Parker." "Why did you pull away from me, just then?" "Lucky fellow, that Pole."

"So tell me why you never saw your mother again," said Nicholas.

Charlotte and Nicholas were sitting in the only remaining lighted area of the ground floor of the hotel. Near them was a window that overlooked the square. Behind them was the reception desk, manned by a clerk who either could not or would not speak English. The bar had closed half an hour before. Charlotte was still waiting for the Headmaster to talk to her about the Humanities Department; she had been waiting for this all day, since Nora spoke to her. She had changed her clothes twice, once for the sight-seeing tour, once for dinner. Dinner had been inedible and at six-thirty, in a brightly lighted half-empty cavern of a room. She had been sitting three places away from the Headmaster. He had smiled at her on four separate occasions, and once he had winked. She was reluctant to admit that, as it was past midnight, he was unlikely to raise the Humanities question now. He had gone upstairs with his wife, presumably to bed, more than an hour ago.

Charlotte had lapsed into a trance.

"Tell me about your mother," prompted Nicholas. "I understand you wanting to get away from your father, but what about your mother?"

"I told you," said Charlotte. "I hated her — because she had left me, because she took Liam, because she sounded happy. It was all mixed up. She sent me an invitation to stay. With my eighteenth birthday card. Just an invitation. 'Darling Charlotte, it would be so lovely if you could come to stay.' She didn't even telephone. Liam phoned, but I was out. My father told me. 'That brother of yours rang this morning. I didn't speak to him. While you're in my house, I'd prefer you not to speak to him either.' I didn't ring Liam. Not because of what my father said: because of what I felt. So then Liam wrote."

Charlotte paused. She could remember the letter exactly.

"Dearest Carly,
Can't wait to see you. Ring me IMMEDIATELY at the London number above, I'm there till end of week. Reverse charges if you're as skint as usual. News when we meet. Please ring. Liam."

"I tore the letters up," she said.

"Very neatly, I suppose," said Nicholas. "Into little squares."

"Um," said Charlotte, not listening. "I wrote back, to both of them. 'Thank you for your letter. Please don't get in touch with me again.' I was afraid to see them. I knew how odd I appeared — how gauche, how stiff, how nervous of men. And I didn't know how to wear clothes. My mother wouldn't have liked that. She valued appearances so much. She always used to say that, in the old days. 'How lucky we're such a handsome family.' And she used to laugh at people for being plain and awkward. I didn't want to be a disappointment. Isn't that odd, considering how I hated her?"

"Not really," said Nicholas. "You're proud, stubborn and slightly obsessional, and you'd want to meet your mother in triumph, not supplication."

"That's rubbish," said Charlotte. She was irritated by such a clinical description of herself. "Since you're so clever about relationships, tell me what went wrong with your life."

"Nothing," said Nicholas.

"You mean it's been perfect?"

"I don't mean anything of the kind. I mean things don't go right or wrong with lives, one just lives them."

"Do you mean you've never done anything you regret?"

He said nothing, twirled his wine glass about on the varnished wooden table, his face in lines that made him look an old man. "Things have happened that I would have wished otherwise. But I'm not haunted by them."

For a few minutes they sat in silence, gazing at St Isaac's Cathedral, which loomed over them with its floodlit golden cupola.

"That thing's like a giant golden ball," said Nicholas.

"It's one of the greatest constructions with cupola in the world," said Charlotte, in the guide's lilt. "It is a beautiful specimen of the architecture of late classicism. Each of the forty-eight columns of the portico is seventeen metres high and weighs one hundred and fourteen tons."

"Like our revered Headmaster's wife," said Nicholas. Both laughed weakly. They were extremely tired and full of wine.

Outside, the streets were all but deserted. "We could go to see if they're raising the bridges on the Neva," suggested Nicholas.

"No, I'm too tired."

"You don't want to miss the Headmaster, you mean," said Nicholas. "Just in case. What would you do if he asked you to walk through the streets of Leningrad?"

Charlotte didn't answer. She enjoyed all talk of Ian. She enjoyed the picture Nicholas conjured up. She enjoyed the fact that Nicholas was a man, that she was sitting so easily with him. She felt omnipotent. She could hardly remember her past self. Why had she been frightened of men? Her father seemed a pathetic figure, spending so much time brooding over his failed marriage, and the loneliness and misery he had made her suffer seemed merely absurd. She could have escaped from it at any time, made friends, gone to parties. The world had been there ready for her to enjoy.

The first taste of sexual power had gone to her head.

"You look very pretty," said Nicholas. "Every day you look prettier."

"Thank you," said Charlotte. She felt it was no more than she deserved. The image that faced her from mirrors – and she looked in them much more – was daily more attractive. She wondered what the aunts would think when they saw her. She wondered what her mother and Liam would think. At this time of night, she could allow herself to imagine seeing them again.

"The bar's closed," said Nicholas. "Sure you don't want to go for a walk?"

"Positive. I think I'll go to bed."

"What would you say if I asked to come too?"

Charlotte blushed at the thought, ducked her head. "Nicholas! Why did you say that? You know about me and men –"

"Not any longer, surely? You're no longer frightened in the same way. You're flirting with Ian, you're telling me your almost innermost secrets and you weren't even particularly upset when the Pole groped you yesterday."

Charlotte began to laugh again at the memory.

"See what I mean? Five days ago you'd have thrown sixty purple fits."

"You're not serious, are you? About coming to bed with me?" She was embarrassed. Nicholas wouldn't have attracted her physically even if he had not been eclipsed by Ian. He was old, he was thin. He was gossipy, intuitive and good company – not masculine enough in her view. Real men – like Ian – were aloof and condescending, not to be easily won, not to be understood.

"No," said Nicholas. "I'm not serious. I'd be honoured and all that, of course, but I'm not serious."

"I'm going to bed."

Nicholas nodded without expression and he didn't get up when she left.

The lift was old and creaky. It had a will of its own. Charlotte pressed the button for the fourth floor but it went straight up to the sixth floor and stopped, its hydraulic components hissing ruminatively like a mechanical cow. Charlotte pressed the button once again and this time the lift went down with irregular lurches to the ground floor.

Its behaviour disturbed Charlotte and she felt her confidence slipping away. She pressed the fourth floor button again. The lift refused to budge. She pressed every button. The lift hissed louder and Charlotte decided to walk. She closed the lift doors quietly, trying not to attract Nicholas's attention. He was still sitting staring out of the window framed against the cathedral of St Isaac. He looked very old. She felt her euphoria ebb still further. Perhaps she'd encouraged him too much.

The fourth floor was dimly lit and quiet. The desk woman, large, pasty-faced, unsmiling, nodded to Charlotte and slammed her room key down on the counter. A kettle of hot water simmered at her side. Charlotte walked away to her room feeling the woman's eyes on her back. Nora said that the floor women worked for the KGB and, for once, Charlotte was inclined to believe her. Nora also said that their rooms were bugged. She had explained to Charlotte during the afternoon's tour that she had been trying to remind Charlotte of a possible bug in her room when they had been discussing the hotel. That accounted for the faces she had made. Charlotte, trying to make the key turn in her warped door, reflected how appropriate a place the Soviet Union was to confirm Nora's view of the world; drab, pernickety, paranoid.

As the key finally turned, Sophie popped up beside her. "Miss Parker, Miss Parker. I can't sleep. Sally went to sleep ages ago and I've been lying awake all this time. Please can I come in and talk to you a minute?"

Charlotte longed for bed. Taking her clothes off, washing, soaking her sandal-battered feet; lying down between the much-darned linen sheets; she closed her eyes briefly and imagined. But Sophie looked desolate. She followed Charlotte into the room. She was wearing an expensive silk dressing-gown and her fine, shapeless hair, just washed, crackled loose around her head. She looked pathetically unloved: her eyes sought Charlotte's, watching, hoping for a response. She reminded Charlotte of Wendy Craig Stewart.

"Do you suppose the woman at the desk really does work for the KGB? Do you suppose she has a gun? Why do you suppose I can't sleep?"

"Your first night in a strange country," said Charlotte.

"I feel sick as well."

"Probably all that chocolate."

"Mrs Craig Stewart was very kind. She gave me masses of chocolate, all day." Sophie was proud of this. Charlotte kept quiet. "I do feel sick, though."

"I'll give you an Alka-Seltzer, then you can go back to bed. I'm shattered and I expect you are too."

"I'm worried about my O-levels," said Sophie. "The results will come in exactly six weeks' time. I'm afraid I've failed most of them, Miss Parker. Did you fail any of yours?"

"No."

"I expect you're the clever type. I'm not. My father wants me to go to university, stay on at school and get my A-levels first, of course. But if I fail lots of my O-levels I'll have to leave and my parents will be furious. I wish I was clever, like you. I wish I was thin. I wish I was you, Miss Parker."

"Come on, Sophie. You don't wish you were me. You probably did better in the exams than you think."

Never in the career of dutiful Miss Parker had Charlotte felt less like being civil. She wanted to get rid of Sophie as quickly as possible, but could not bring herself to be unkind. She knew that spending time and energy on Sophie was futile because it could never be enough, but the vulnerable, suffering-animal quality of the girl compelled attention.

Charlotte swallowed her yawns and allowed Sophie to moan at her for a few minutes, then gently edged her out. Sophie as she left seemed resentful at having been dismissed so summarily; Charlotte shut the door behind her with an irritated click.

It was past two o'clock when Charlotte went to sleep. She dreamt she was following the Headmaster along institutional corridors, never reaching him. She was desperate to reach him but she couldn't hurry because Sophie and Nora were dragging at her arms. She woke sweating, dry-mouthed and with the beginning of a hangover.

The long-awaited interview with the Headmaster was a disappointment, as long-awaited interviews are apt to be. It took place during an outing to Petrodvorets, the summer palace of the tsars. It was a hot afternoon, the first sunny day the party had had in Russia. Most of the bulky yellow palace was being restored so no visitors were allowed inside. "We will drink in the majestic surrounding of the gardens, admiring the work executed by famous Russian masters in restoring the imposing façade after the damage inflicted by the fascist army during the Great Patriotic War," said the guide.

"I didn't catch that," panted Nora, rejoining the party.

"They had to rebuild it after the German occupation," said Nicholas.

"Once a place of extravagance and luxury, now a holiday resort to be enjoyed by the workers," continued the guide, leading them amid the formal gardens and geometrically planted trees. The place had, for Charlotte, a forlorn air. It was built in imitation of the French style but overgrown and distorted, like Versailles's plainer sister. Fountains were everywhere, some large, some larger. "We now approach the tricky fountains," said the guide. "These fountains have caused much amusement. Prepare your cameras, please."

The Ashcombe party straggled to a halt and looked, perplexed, at the paved courtyard she was pointing out. "If some of you would like to walk?"

"I will," said Sophie, plunging forward onto the stones.

Halfway across a jet of water sprang up, then another, then another. She dodged between them, laughing. Other girls joined her and ran across squealing with pleasure as their light, bright cotton clothes were sprinkled with water-drops.

The sun, the fountains, the rest from fine art, all put the girls in a good humour. When they encountered the Wimborne party their pleasure was complete, and soon both parties had indissolubly mingled, much to the irritation of the guides who liked things clear-cut and organised. Miranda was apparently reconciled with her Wimborne boy. He had lost his black eye and looked most impressive in blazer, white trousers and Panama hat; he and Miranda walked up and down near the Headmaster several times, Miranda demure and apparently absorbed in her escort but displaying her tanned and slender limbs to the best advantage.

"She's got her eye on our boss," said Nicholas quietly to Charlotte.

"Vain little so-and-so," said Charlotte as lightly as she could manage. Ian was watching Miranda appreciatively. Charlotte had spent an hour in her room before setting out on this trip, doing her hair, lining her eyes, trying on different clothes. Not that she had many to try. She was pleased with her appearance. Several of the girls had commented on it. She felt that she was every bit as good-looking as Miranda: but she lacked, she knew she lacked, the glow of youth and the confidence.

They were in a forest glade, surrounded by the shade and scent of overhanging trees. Nicholas sat down on a bench and began to sketch. The other staff disposed themselves on seats nearby.

"Are you sketching Miranda?" asked Heather, looking over Nicholas's shoulder at his drawing-pad. Heather was much impressed by Miranda's beauty, by beautiful young girls in general. Nora Bridge had nodded darkly about this. "Something wrong there," she had whispered to Charlotte on a previous occasion when Heather had praised a girl's looks.

"I'm sketching Sophie Preston," said Nicholas.

Sophie was sitting on the grass a little way away, her head bowed, her dress clinging lumpishly to the figure beneath. She seemed to have put on weight since the holiday began. She was tearing up the grass in chunks, with violent yanking jerks.

"What on earth for?" said Heather. "There is so much beauty around us, why choose Sophie?"

"Mr Embrey is an artist," said Nora Bridge acidly. "They see the world differently from normal people."

"Have you exhibited much?" asked the Headmaster.

"Here and there," said Nicholas.

"Mr Embrey is very distinguished," said Heather. "Several major galleries have bought his work."

"Isn't that nice," said Wendy. "Imagine being an artist and having a creative talent. I do admire people with creative talent."

"So do I," said Heather. Her disapproval for the man did not interfere with her admiration for his work.

"I've never seen any of your work," said Nora. She made this sound a strategic move on her part.

"We're friends of the Royal Academy, you know," said Wendy, fanning herself and crossing her ham-like legs at their dainty ankles.

"With friends like us, who needs enemies?" said the Headmaster, not quietly enough. "Miss Parker, Miss Bridge tells me that you have views on the reorganisation of the History, Geography and English Departments. Perhaps this would be a good time to discuss them – if you don't mind thinking about work for a moment."

He stood up and moved away. Charlotte stood up too. Under the scrutiny of the others they walked to another bench, out of earshot though well in view. This was not at all how she had imagined the discussion taking place. Presumably it was actually business he meant to discuss. If so, she would pay attention. She had invested five years of hard and intelligent work in reaching the position of Head of English. She had just concluded her first year in the job, she had plans for the Department and she was not going to let inattention on her part give Nora an opportunity to wreck everything.

Carefully and clearly, she outlined her theoretical and practical objections to the amalgamation plan. The Headmaster's arm was stretched along the bench behind her and his short fingers tapped an increasingly irritable rhythm as she spoke. Eventually he interrupted:

"Yes, yes, that's as may be. But we don't have to talk about it now, do we?"

"But I thought . . ."

"Just a pretext. Every now and then I like to get away from your worthy colleagues Miss Noakes and Miss Bridge. Good ladies, but of a certain age, and too earnest and keen for me."

"Miss Bridge is in her thirties," said Charlotte. His contempt was disconcerting. She felt disloyal to Heather, accepting his slighting reference in silence. She felt mortified at her own vanity in looking forward to a *tête-à-tête* with Ian. At the same time, she wished she had the courage to lean back against his arm. She felt her heart beating faster, her breath quickening, and she suspected from his expression of amusement and self-satisfaction that he knew all about her excitement.

In the boat back to the centre of Leningrad, Charlotte avoided the staff and the girls, and was sitting by herself in the stern. She had reached the stage of a party expedition where she knew the others much too well. Nora's habit of stirring the food into patterns on the plate and then spooning it in with a fork while muttering with her mouth open, Heather's throat-clearing, Nicholas's contrariness, were all irritating her intensely. She wanted no more of Wendy's stories and she never wanted to hear the guide's voice again.

"You wish to be alone?" said the guide. She was standing yards away, hesitant.

"Do you want to sit here?" asked Charlotte.

"Outside, where there is cool wind, yes, please." Charlotte moved along the seat to make her welcome and turned her head into the wind to avoid the strong smell of unwashed hair. The guide wedged her shopping-bag against the side of the boat.

"That looks heavy," said Charlotte.

"Excuse me?"

"Your bag. Looks as if it weighs a lot."

She opened the bag to display roll upon roll of lavatory paper. "There has been shortage. The toilet paper is very difficult to find, so I am lucky. Did you find much of interest at Petrodvorets?"

"Oh yes. It is very beautiful."

"The people of Leningrad voluntarily worked to restore it. Over three hundred thousand man-hours of free labour. Without charge. I have question to ask you, please. Have you met Elton John?"

"Elton John?" Charlotte could not believe that she had heard correctly.

"Elton John is English singer, excuse me?"

"Yes, he is."

The guide was scrabbling deep in her shopping-bag, under the rolls of paper. She produced an old and crumpled magazine photograph of Elton John, lovingly encased in a home-made frame of cardboard and cellophane. "Elton John came to the USSR and gave many concerts, very successful. He is exciting modern musician. So I expect the young in England go to his concerts also. That is why I ask you, because you are the youngest teacher and you would know."

"I'm afraid I've never had the chance to meet Elton John."

"It is possible you will meet him?"

"Oh yes."

"Then, please, you will tell him. He has a fan (that is right idiom?) in Leningrad. Nadia Nikolayevna."

"Yes," said Charlotte. "If I ever meet him, I'll remember."

"What were you talking to the guide about?" murmured Nora at dinner. The soup plates had been taken away and they were waiting, without any sense of urgency, for the meat course.

"Nothing," said Charlotte.

"You must have been talking about something," said Nora. She had dragged her hair more tightly still back in the ponytail and there was a white border of skin, untanned because previously hidden, around her scalp. The style emphasised her eyes and the expanse of whites that the opaque blue irises bobbed about in.

"Probably the Humanities Department," said Nicholas. Nora ignored him and concentrated on crumbling black bread into tiny pellets.

"Are we looking forward to Moscow?" said Heather.

"Not to the train-journey," said Wendy. "We'll all be cramped together in a tiny compartment again. I hated it on the boat."

"You'll just have to grin and bear it," said the Headmaster. "The train from Moscow to East Berlin will be worse. That'll be thirty hours in a tiny compartment."

He widened his eyes at Charlotte. "Of course, in certain circumstances that could be enjoyable."

She shivered, imagining being alone with him in a tiny dark compartment, shut away, secure, with his hands moving over her as the drunken Pole's had done.

Heather tapped her knuckles impatiently on the table. Her annoyance was directed partly at Charlotte, who turned away, refusing to acknowledge it. Her feeling for the Headmaster was irrational, ill-regulated, ill-conducted. She knew that, but she didn't mind. It was instinctive and undeniable. There it was. The only emotion that rivalled its intensity was her phobic fear, and that recurred less and less frequently: Nicholas could dispel it by his presence.

Charlotte couldn't sleep on the train to Moscow. The four female escorts were once again in snoring proximity, the narrow bunk was hard and the sheet too narrow to protect her from the sticky plastic. Charlotte escaped into the corridor. At one end, on a small tip-up seat, sat a sleeping attendant, a middle-aged woman in uniform. Beside her the kettle bubbled.

The train rattled and jolted. They were passing through featureless landscapes; no light picked out the darkness. By train through Russia! It sounded romantic. Her aunt Victoria would certainly think it so; Anna Karenina was her heroine and she had seen the Garbo film at least twenty times. Victoria had artistic longings. She had wanted, when young, to be an actress, a singer, a dancer, anything which would give her an opportunity to perform and be watched by large numbers of people.

She retained past her youth a belief in her own creativity. One outlet became designing clothes for Charlotte. Victoria couldn't sew: Ivy made the clothes her sister designed, secure in the belief that Victoria was the talented one of the family, unquestioning. Charlette went through agonies of embarrassment as a teenager, tormented by these clothes, designed by Victoria with an eye for lurid colour, and made up by Ivy, whose sight was going and who would not admit it, with drunken stitching and uneven hems.

Before Charlotte was left with her father, the aunts had proudly made clothes for Charlotte and Tessy made Charlotte thank them prettily and put the clothes away. She only had to wear them for the aunts and Tessy made them look passable. A tuck here, a belt there, quick tacking of the hems and suddenly a dress would look normal under Tessy's blossoming touch. But Charlotte alone didn't have the confidence to do that and the oddity of the clothes came to reflect her own oddity, her feeling of peculiarity.

Charlotte's ordinary clothes, bought under her father's instructions, were designed to obscure her femininity, and the aunts' clothes made her look ridiculous. This didn't matter so much when she only had to wear them for the aunts' benefit: it mattered much more when they started trying to introduce her to boys.

The enterprise was not a promising one. The Reduced Gentlefolk's Club was hardly propitious for romantic meetings and the aunts were so obvious in their purposes that the poor young men produced for sixteen- and seventeen-year-old Charlotte withered in the dusty air of the place: their manhood shrivelled. Also the aunts' social net did not trawl wide; large, determined and self-assured fish easily escaped their clutches. Only the bullyable or the desperate, Charlotte thought, would consent to meet a perfectly strange girl under the auspices of such perfectly strange people.

Ten years later Charlotte could hardly remember them apart, but they were all subdued by the club and the battle-worn teacakes, Henrietta's brusqueness and Victoria's gush. Ivy had been fading even then, prone to sitting weakly in chairs and smiling apologetically for her weakness.

The boy with red hair was the most memorable one.

Charlotte had been wearing one of Victoria's more fanciful creations, much trimmed with ribbons. The boy had been eighteen. He was intelligent and funny; not good-looking, not bad-looking, still unused to his height and the size of his hands. He was composed and Charlotte had begun to forget that she didn't get on with boys. Then Victoria had got carried away by the apparent success of the introduction and she had started talking. She drew up a large chair which looked as if it had been stuffed with material as lumpy as the club custard. "You don't know what this poor girl has had to put up with," she confided. "There's a SADNESS in her life."

The boy had just been explaining his plans to go to Cambridge. Charlotte made a face at her aunt trying to quieten her, though she should have known it was hopeless. She did in fact know but she tried anyway. Her heart had lifted at the simple achievement of talking to a boy for half an hour without doing something to show him that she was peculiar. She always knew the moment when she said or did something to put people off, and looking back she could see what she had said, but she couldn't predict it or prevent it. Like some mystic's idea of hell — repeating your mistakes. This time, however, it was Victoria who was scuppering her, and that was somehow worse. She often felt embarrassed for the aunts. They were very embarrassing people, eccentric and increasingly so as the Anglo-Irish world in which they would have been normal vanished round them. In England they frequently appeared ludicrous.

Charlotte caught Henrietta's eye, willing her to interrupt. She tried.

"I went to Pontings today," she said. "For elastic by the yard. But they'd closed it down. Such a pity."

"Elastic by the yard," mourned Ivy. "Fancy that. No more elastic by the yard."

"No, no, Ivy. It's Pontings that's closed, that's what disappointed me. I dare say elastic is on sale by the yard elsewhere. It's the principle of the thing. All the shops I knew, closing down. And what do you suppose happened to the woman on the haberdashery? She was getting on."

"Getting on," echoed Victoria, who was sipping a cup of tea with gin through it.

"She was certainly getting on. Older than us," said Ivy.

"Not old at all," muttered the boy, confusedly polite.

"Oh, did you know her?"

"No, no. I meant you weren't old, Miss Gascoigne."

"Well, she was," said Ivy. "Poor old thing. She was deaf and her arithmetic went peculiar. Decimalisation, you know. It was the last straw."

"That wasn't Pontings. That was Gorringes," said Victoria.

"No it wasn't," said Ivy.

"This isn't entertaining our guest," said Henrietta reprovingly.

"Yes it is," said the red-haired boy. "I like old-fashioned shops. There's a grocer in the village near us in Wiltshire that sells things out of sacks and elastic by the yard. I like it in there."

Charlotte took to him. He was polite and kind. He was trying to be pleasant, to adapt himself to his surroundings. She was mortally tired of her own serpentine attempts to adapt to a father who didn't want her there: she was grateful for a male who made concessions.

A year later he had written to invite her to a May Ball.

It was only a matter of weeks before she left school; she had decided to leave her father at the same time. She could have gone to the ball. She had plenty of money, from her mother's birthday and Christmas presents, to buy herself a dress. She knew her father would disapprove, but knew also that he couldn't stop her. Several times she started to write an acceptance, but the prospect frightened her. Where would she stay? Would there be other people in the party? How could she manage to talk to them? And what if one of the other boys, one of the strangers, asked her to dance? Eventually she wrote, thanked him for the invitation, said she would be in between A-level exams and needed to revise, so couldn't come. It was a chilly little note.

Chapter Five

"Leningrad was breathtaking. Two more days in Moscow, then home. See you soon," wrote Charlotte.

"Writing to your aunts again," said Nicholas, sitting down beside Charlotte in the front seat of the Ashcombe party's Intourist bus. It was a bleak day, the sky obscured by muddy grey clouds, the temperature kept in the mid-sixties by a stiff breeze from the north-east. The rest of the party was standing beside the buses, looking across the Moskva at the Kremlin. The guide was intoning her catalogue of facts. It was imperative to listen to her, the party had discovered. She was the only source of treats such as a visit to the ballet; she was also powerful over simple matters of comfort such as meals. The day she had taken them round the Hermitage and the group listening to her had dwindled from sixty-odd to three, dinner had not been provided for them at the hotel. "What a misfortune," she had said. "Now we must wait. Perhaps the cooks will find some cold food for you."

After that, Nora had instituted strict rules, exhaustively expounded at an emergency briefing. Nobody was to walk away while the guide was talking. Everyone was to look interested.

"Two thousand, two hundred and fifty metres of crenellated wall surround the Kremlin," said the guide. The girls were unmoved. A Chinese mathematician, placed in the front row by common consent because her delicate blush ivory features never displayed boredom, looked interested. "Standing on a steep elevation overlooking the Moskva river . . ."

"Ian was talking about you last night," said Nicholas.

"Um?" said Charlotte. She knew that Nicholas disapproved of her flirtation with Ian, of Ian's behaviour to

Wendy. She also knew that Nicholas thought Ian vain, selfish, humourless and dull.

"Asking about your background, your boyfriends."

"What did you say?"

"Told him you were nearly engaged to a weight-lifting psychopath."

"Seriously, what did you say?"

"Oh Miss Parker, you have a bad case of infatuation."

"Come *on*, Nicholas," Charlotte snapped.

"I refused to talk about it and went to sleep."

"Did he say anything else?"

Nicholas closed his eyes, pretended to snore. Charlotte watched Ian, who had moved away from the group round the guide and was taking photographs of the Kremlin, making much play with light-meters and focus adjustment. He was wearing jeans again, a slightly more faded pair. His shoulders were very square. Charlotte fluffed up her hair.

"Remind me why you hated your mother," said Nicholas.

"Because she left me."

"And she shouldn't have done," said Nicholas.

Charlotte was taken aback. "Well – of course not. She was my *mother*. She was married to my father. She should have stayed married."

"Even if she was in love with someone else?"

"In love, in love – it's easy to say," said Charlotte impatiently. "She should have stayed with me, it was her duty."

"I think you're confused, Miss Parker."

"Stop calling me that. I don't know what you're getting at. Are you saying my mother was right to go?"

"I'm not the one who labels things. This is right, this is wrong. I'm just wondering about your parents, that's all."

"What were you wondering?"

"If they were well matched."

"I'm never going to forgive them," said Charlotte, determined to deny the childishness she could hear in her voice.

"Now you have ten minutes to take pictures," said the guide. "Next we go to the hotel for dinner."

It was their last night in the huge concrete skyscraper set in a suburban wasteland, the Hotel Sevastopol. It was only a few years old – built for the Olympics – but already cracking, its window frames buckled and jammed, lavatories out of service. The showers were only hot or only cold, the rooms tiny boxes, the restaurant a hundred-yard walk away to another building, the bar hidden in the basement and smelling strongly of sewage. The girls preferred the Moscow hotel to the Leningrad one because they were sharing it with the Wimborne boys.

Charlotte and Nora were in room 1214. There were fewer cockroaches on the higher floors but then again the lifts seldom worked. By midnight Charlotte was washed, undressed, ready to go to sleep. Nora had performed her usual bedtime rituals: first she checked and read through the contents of her blue plastic wallet and put it under the pillow; then she prayed, little-girl fashion, kneeling by her bed, hands clasped, head bowed, the yellowed soles of her feet upturned, for fifteen minutes.

She rose from her knees, pulled back the bedclothes.

"Good night," said Charlotte.

"I cannot keep silent! I must speak!" said Nora. "Charlotte, you know I am a devout Christian?"

"Um," said Charlotte. She knew Nora was a curate hopper, tempting them with her doubts, pursuing each for a month or two then fixing on another. She veered between high and low Church like an English weather forecast.

"You have been much in my prayers. Now I am moved to speak to you. About the sacred bonds of matrimony."

"I don't think . . ." began Charlotte.

Nora swept on. "I have been much with dear Wendy lately. Seeing as her husband isn't. I have heard the sad story of her marital difficulties, from her point of view, though I dare say you have other sources of information. She is so distressed, Charlotte. So distressed. And I do want this to be a happy group. No! Don't attempt to reply. That is all I have to say."

She lay down and pretended to sleep. Charlotte lay

awake, irritated, knowing it would be futile to argue. Nora's opinion was of no consequence to her, but she was annoyed that the other woman was in a position to reproach her with even a glimmer of right on her side. She was also annoyed at Nicholas, though she couldn't pinpoint why. What had he been getting at, about her parents being well matched? And what had that to do with Ian? Emotion clouded her thought processes. The only version of her childhood that she would accept was that it was all her parents' fault.

She willed herself to sleep. Nora was snoring. Water gurgled and whined in the pipes. She tried to fantasise about Ian but, for once, couldn't. She squirmed round in the bed, trying to find a comfortable position. It began to dawn on her that even if she was overcoming her fear of men, she would still not be happy or at peace. There was too much anger in her, too much resentment, too many unexplored memories.

All she knew about her parents' meeting and marriage, the aunts had told her. According to them Tessy was spoilt: her mother (the only pretty sister in the aunts' family) had died when she was young, her father was rich and spoilt her. He had kept a nanny, later a governess, ignoring all the aunts' offers of a home and hints that they should come and live with their brother-in-law and help with the child.

"She never took to us," said Ivy. "Even though she was motherless. I think we were too dowdy for her." Ivy was the most charitable of the aunts but even so there was a touch of astringency in her tone. The aunts never criticised Tessy to Charlotte but gradually, over the years, she deduced how little they had liked her.

"She never took to us," lamented Ivy once. Charlotte, aged fourteen, was playing Patience at a glass-topped table with a crack in the glass. She was near the window. Outside the traffic rushed past with a vibration that rattled the windowpanes and beyond the traffic was Hyde Park. It was that day it had occurred to Charlotte that the aunts were spending much more time in London at the Reduced Gentlefolk's than before her parents' divorce. They now came for at least a week at Christmas, a week at Easter and two weeks in the summer. It must have cost them more than they could afford, but Geoffrey, her father, was adamant about his refusal to let Charlotte go to Ireland. She hoped that, now she was married to a much richer man, Tessy would help the aunts.

Little as they liked Tessy, they liked Geoffrey even less. "Of course he was brilliant when she met him," Henrietta admitted grudgingly. "A Fellow. Everyone said he'd be a Professor. He wrote for the newspapers, he spoke on the radio. And a handsome man. Not quite quite, I'm afraid. His father was a dentist in Solihull, but good-hearted." Charlotte had never met her father's parents. He never visited them. They sent cards at Christmas and birthdays, brightly coloured with her age printed in gold on the front. "Now you are FIVE." "Best love to an EIGHT year old." "What can they think?" Tessy said once, prodding an offending card with her long nails. "Do they suppose you don't know what age you are?"

What went wrong between her parents? Charlotte didn't know. Her mother had seemed so delightful. She was pretty, amusing, extremely well dressed – everyone had said so – and she enjoyed life. Even the day before they parted, Charlotte remembered her mother teasing her father into laughter, and her father's look of pride as he hugged his wife.

But for the last year at least before the parting, Tessy must have been preparing to bolt, cementing her relationship with her soon-to-be second husband. Charlotte was not surprised that she had managed this; she could remember her mother's skill at disguising her feelings, raging one minute at a minor annoyance like a laddered stocking while only Charlotte was there to see, then all buoyancy and laughter when a man appeared, or when she needed to impress.

Nora coughed and turned over. Charlotte kicked irritably at her bedclothes. Memories of her parents troubled and annoyed her. She had decided what she thought of them: as little as possible, and all critical. She could see, however, that Nicholas was nudging her towards thinking of them as people. I won't, she said to herself. I won't, I won't. I'll think about Ian instead.

They arrived at the hotel in Berlin just after midnight. Girls and staff were exhausted. The hotel was just off the Kurfurstendamm; after the shabby respectability of public places in Eastern Europe, the strutting German prostitutes were like animated symbols of the tawdry West. The Kurfurstendamm girls and the Ashcombe girls eyed each other as the school party left the bus. "Are they really prostitutes?" said Sophie. "Miranda says they're prostitutes, but they can't be, can they? They're so young, younger than me, some of them. And they're so pretty – and they have such nice clothes –"

"Miss Parker, allocate rooms, please," said Nora thrusting the blue wallet into Charlotte's hand and disappearing into a lavatory. She had eaten one of the hard-boiled eggs in the Russian packed lunch and had spent most of the train journey occupying one of the carriage's two washrooms.

"The Headmaster and Mrs Craig Stewart – room 204. Miss Noakes, Miss Bridge, Mr Embrey – 304, 305, 306. I'll take 403."

"I'll see to Miss Bridge," said Heather, taking both keys. "I'll leave you in charge here, Miss Parker." She hesitated, glanced at the Headmaster, decided he was paying no attention and needn't be considered.

"Right, girls," said Charlotte. "One group of three, the rest in fours, one from each group come to get the key." Exhausted but still obedient, the girls stumbled up for their keys.

Sophie was left by herself. "Single room, Sophie," said Charlotte. "Aren't you lucky?"

"Oh no, Miss Parker, I can't," she wailed. "I'm afraid. By myself. Look at the number, I'm on a floor all by myself."

"I'll come and check that you're all right," said Charlotte. "When I've had a shower."

Charlotte's room looked out over the Kurfurstendamm.

Fastened to the outside wall just beside the window was a large neon sign advertising the neighbouring strip club. GIRLS GIRLS GIRLS, it said. She didn't turn the room lights on, she could see well enough and was in a hurry to undress and shower. She began to unpack her night bag then, most uncharacteristically, tipped it up over the bed-side table and let the contents stay where they landed, some on the table, some on the floor. She locked the door, removed her clothes, dropping them on the floor also, and stood under the shower, turning this way and that, tilting her face upwards to the water, shampooing her hair again and again and washing away dust, sweat, and thirty hours in the train. Then she wrapped herself in the fluffy capitalist towels and stood by the window so that the breeze could reach her damp face and body. Lavishly stocked, brightly lit shops lined the wide road as far as she could see. Her mind was empty, her body relaxed.

Eventually, she put on a cotton smock and sandals and slipped along the corridor to Sophie's room. The hotel was a vast shadowy rabbit warren, several houses joined together at different levels. When she got to Sophie's the girl was half-asleep and had forgotten her fear.

On the way back, she could hear footsteps behind her. She stopped outside her door, expecting it to be Nicholas.

It was the Headmaster.

He took the key from her hand, opened the door, urged her inside and followed her. He was carrying a bottle of wine.

"Not tired, are you?" he said, darting into the bathroom in search of glasses. Charlotte scuttled to gather up her discarded bra and pants, and thrust them under the pillow.

"Here's to us," said the Headmaster.

"What if somebody comes?" said Charlotte.

"Wendy's asleep and Miss Noakes is nursing Our Leader."

Charlotte took the toothglass half full of wine and clasped it so tightly she expected it to shatter. She was embarrassed by the contents of her night bag, spare underclothes and a roll-on deodorant with an unmistakably phallic outline in plain view on the bedside table. She was also excited.

He sat down on the bed and patted the space beside him. His hair was still damp and he was in clean jeans and a knitted cotton sweater. Charlotte remembered she had nothing on under her smock.

"Come on, sit down," he said impatiently. She couldn't move. She longed to touch him but didn't want to appear awkward and had no idea what to do.

He took her hand and tugged sharply, pulling her down beside him. The contact was much less frightening than when he had first touched her, at the disco on board ship. She trembled with the strangeness of the sensation. He kissed her hand, then her bare arm, then brushed his lips against her cheek.

The telephone rang with single sharp brrrs.

"Bloody hell," said the Headmaster.

"Hello?" said Charlotte.

"This is Nicholas. Just to let you know, Heather is looking for Craig Stewart."

"Thanks," said Charlotte and rang off. She relayed the information to Ian.

"Bloody hell," he said again. "Sorry, I'll have to go. Wouldn't do to be found here. Bad for both of us. Good night."

"Good night, Headmaster."

When he had gone, Charlotte rang Nicholas back. "Why did you think Ian was here?"

"Wasn't he?"

"That's not what I asked you."

"I thought Ian was there because there was where I would have been had I been Ian," said Nicholas.

"How did you know Heather was looking for him?"

"She came here first. She's worried about Nora: what we do if she isn't well enough to travel. I told her we all burst into song and leave her behind, but Heather wouldn't wear it. Very serious girl, Heather. Did I interrupt something vital?"

"Not at all," said Charlotte stiffly. "The Headmaster and I were having a quiet drink."

"As opposed to a noisy drink where you gargle and spit?"

"Don't be so silly," snapped Charlotte.

"All right, teacher."

"Three cheers for Miss Bridge," said Miranda. "Hip hip . . ."

"HOORAY!" shouted the carriage-full of Ashcombe girls. They were so elated at being back in England that they would have cheered anyone.

"Hip hip . . ."

"HOORAY!"

"Oh, they do sound happy," said Wendy, fanning herself. "I must say it's good to be back."

"Hip hip . . ."

"HOORAY!"

All six escorts looked happy too. Even Nora was smiling. The fields of Kent, British Rail, light drizzle, the suburbs of London – they were home.

The train stopped. The girls piled out. Nora consulted her blue plastic wallet for the last time, to check lists of girls being met at Victoria and girls going on the coach to Ashcombe. Charlotte scanned the platform for Suki, with whom she was going to stay.

"Goodbye, all!" said Wendy. "See you in September!" She was eager to get away but she smiled at Charlotte, almost in apology. The Headmaster shook hands with Nora and Heather, nodded to Charlotte and Nicholas, and walked unsmiling away towards the taxis, a few steps behind his wife. Before he was out of Charlotte's sight, he turned and waved once.

Nora and Heather, occupied with the girls, didn't see. Nicholas did: and so did Suki, who was waiting beside them for Charlotte to notice her. Eventually she spoke, and Charlotte jumped. She had been absorbed in thoughts of Ian.

"Sorry, Suki. I didn't see you."

Suki was a tall, buxom woman, with a mass of frizzy red hair. She wore dungarees and hand-made Swedish boots and she looked as if she might be Australian. She hugged Charlotte enthusiastically and greeted Nicholas with goodwill admixed with surprise.

"Nicholas Embrey is a friend," said Charlotte, smug.

"Ah," said Suki. "Do you want to stay the night at my flat, friend?"

"I'm sorry your tall chap didn't come," said Suki. "He looked good value. Do you want to eat in front of the telly?"

"Will it be on?" said Charlotte.

"There's a documentary about the Third World I don't want to miss."

Charlotte settled herself on the heavily cushioned sofa with her plate and a glass of wine. "What is this, Suki?"

"Paella. Risotto. Rice with odd bits in. Come on, Charlotte, don't faff on about food. Tell me all about Russia, tell me how come you have a man friend. Your hair's good like that. Was it the Headmaster who waved at you?"

"How do you know about the Headmaster?"

"He had a starring role in your postcards."

My postcards, thought Charlotte. She could remember writing them, in Oslo, Stockholm, Leningrad, Moscow, light-years away from Suki's flat. It was a large, shabby, crowded flat near a railway line between the Finchley Road and Kilburn High Street. It was the ground floor flat so she had the back garden as well, a riot of untended weeds and vegetation. The main room was thirty feet by twelve: the middle wall that separated the two original rooms had been removed long since in the process of gentrification. The remaining walls were hung with Oriental rugs brought back by her husband from various excursions into the Middle East. Oliver was in the Gulf now and Hector, Suki's baby, away at his grandparents'. The flat was quiet.

"Come on, Charlotte, talk. Move your mouth, get the larynx going."

"I don't know where to start," said Charlotte.

Suki was impressed, delighted, and finally shocked. "Charlotte, he's *married*," she said. "Don't you care that he's *married*?"

"No," said Charlotte. "He's got a perfectly useless wife. She's fat and snobbish and stupid and she drives him mad. He was in love with someone else and his wife wouldn't divorce him. It serves her right."

"He could have gone ahead without her agreement."

"A messy divorce would have ruined his chances as a headmaster."

"Being a headmaster isn't the only job there is. Have you gone soft in the head, Charlotte? Don't you hear what you're saying?"

"I don't care," said Charlotte simply.

Two days later, she went to tea with her aunts. They were hovering in the hall of the club. Even now, four years after Ivy's death, Charlotte still expected her to make up the auntly trinity.

"You're here! Safe!" said Victoria. "I had a premonition." She was prone to dark prognostications – this plane will crash, that guest will be late, this company will go bankrupt. She reminded her listeners when she was right and forgot ten minutes later when she wasn't.

"Have you had lunch?" said Henrietta. She was keen on regular meals and believed that terrible things happened to your blood-sugar levels if you didn't eat them.

"Yes," said Charlotte. "But not much. I've saved space for tea."

"Good," said Henrietta. "Since the renovations, even the rock-cakes have improved."

The Reduced Gentlefolk's, in an unusually bold and effective stroke, had converted the top floors of the ponderous Bayswater building into six flats, and spent some of the profit on redecoration. They didn't need so much space: the membership was dwindling. The Club Newsletter, once quarterly, then biannual, now annual, had become a dismal list of those who had moved into nursing homes, those who had died, after a long illness bravely borne.

Victoria was depressed by the changes. She relied on the

drabness and predictability of the Reduced Gentlefolk's as a foil to what she saw as her creative originality. She was sitting slumped in a fresh chintz armchair, eyes watery and red-veined, hair uncombed. Henrietta looked youthful by contrast. "The curtains were such a wise choice. You can't go wrong with a flower print."

"Yes you can," said Victoria. She looked as if she would like to.

"And there are kettles in every bedroom."

"With those dreadful triangles of milk that squirt in your eye," said Victoria. "Not to mention the tea-bags filled entirely with dust."

"Such a joy to see you, Charlotte," said Henrietta. "You must visit the lavatory."

"I don't want to, thanks."

"You should. They've been thoroughly renovated. The basins are in shades of apricot and peach. There are also hot air hand dryers – so much more hygienic."

"The draught from those things would give you the death of cold."

"Don't you look well!" said Henrietta. "So pretty, just like – so pretty. Doesn't she, Victoria?"

But Victoria was sullen. "Don't like those clothes," she said. "Dull. Need a splash of colour to liven them up. Pity poor Ivy kicked the bucket – we could have knocked together a bright cotton frock." She looked even more dishevelled than usual. She was recently out of hospital after a gall bladder operation.

"It's aged me," said Victoria. "It took its toll."

"The operation?" asked Charlotte.

"No. The humiliation. O'Flaherty's, that's sold drink to our family man and boy. Supplies cut off at source."

"I had to," said Henrietta. "I had no choice. You were making yourself ill."

"The drink had nothing to do with my gall bladder. It's natural in a woman at my time of life." Victoria crossed and uncrossed her puffy ankles. She was wearing pink slippers with pom-poms, Charlotte noticed, disconcerted.

"Anything special the matter with Victoria?" asked

Charlotte, when Victoria had shuffled off to the peach or apricot lavatory.

"Partly the little difficulty with the horse."

"What little difficulty?"

"The brute had a bad case of the slows. Victoria put our money on it."

"What money?"

"Our allowances for the quarter. From Tessy and Liam."

"Don't worry," said Charlotte. "If it's only money, I've got some. Tell me how much you need."

"I wouldn't take your money, Charlotte. Ivy wanted you to have her insurance, and you work for your salary. Your life has been hard enough already. Poor dear Charlotte! If the worst comes to the worst, I'll ask Liam. It's not the money I worry about as much as the dishonesty. Victoria's spending money we haven't got, then we have to beg for more. But don't let's talk about us. Let's talk about you. I was so glad that you went on this trip to Russia. Such an important step out into the world. And it's not too late, not by any means. You're a good-looking girl with a charming figure. Somewhere you'll find the right man. Tell me about Nicholas Embrey."

"What about him?"

"He isn't married, is he?"

"No."

"And he isn't – ah –" Her voice trailed away delicately.

"No, Aunt, he isn't queer. But he is about fifty."

"An older man," said Henrietta hopefully, her robin eyes twinkling. "Guidance."

"I don't need guidance."

"Stability."

"I'm stable."

"Not without a man," said Henrietta gently. "Poor dear Charlotte. I can't begin to tell you what you're missing." Then she thought of the implications of her remark and blushed. "Men are different," she stumbled on. "They know what to do."

"About what?"

"Everything. Bank managers. Betting. Relations.

Maxwell would have known what to do about Victoria. He would have sorted it out."

"Maxwell was very special," said Charlotte. She had no means of knowing this as he had died in a ditch in France long before she was born. She thought he was special to have married Henrietta and made such a deep impression on her. Henrietta was not readily impressionable.

"Nowadays marriage isn't always a good bet," said Charlotte. "And I don't want a man."

"You may not want a man but you certainly need one. Take you out of yourself. It's just that judging by your face I thought perhaps you had. The little line between your brows has smoothed out."

Charlotte was silenced by this perception. Henrietta was sometimes disconcertingly commonsensical. She was now looking at her, worried.

"And you didn't meet anyone else? No men on the staff of the boys' school that you got to know?"

"Not really," said Charlotte.

"Well, all I can say is that I'd have sworn you met a man. Or got religion, one or the other. Not been listening to Billy Graham, have you, or joined the Moonies?"

"Definitely not."

"Then it's that Headmaster," said Henrietta. "I thought as much from the reference you kept making to him in your postcards. Didn't think I'd noticed, probably. Thought I'm past it. Well, in lots of ways I am, but I've seen as much as you've seen, my girl, and don't you forget it."

"But won't life be difficult at school if you're mooning about after a married headmaster?" Suki returned to the attack. She and Charlotte were kneeling on the polished wood floor of Suki's drawing-room, sorting out leaflets for Suki's latest crusades. She was currently saving the whale, fund-raising for the Greenham women and collecting signatures for a petition on proportional representation. The floor was both slippery and hard.

"You're inconsistent. For ten years you nag me to find

a man. Now I've found one, you nag me to give him up," said Charlotte reasonably. "Where does this brochure on Nicaragua belong?"

"Don't try to distract me," said Suki taking the brochure. "Nicaragua isn't mine any longer, the woman in the flat upstairs took it over. I'm talking about your Headmaster. Won't it make life difficult?"

"Not if nobody notices."

"In a *school*?"

"We may be lucky."

"And I may join the National Front. You know what strikes me about this, Charlotte? Not only have you gone stark raving mad over the most unsuitable man in the western hemisphere, but you've also picked a man exactly like your father."

Charlotte laughed. "That's absurd. He's too young, for a start."

"He's cold, selfish, half-successful, irresponsible, vain."

"That's not how I see him."

"You don't see him at all. You're submerged in a bath of infatuation. Like I was when we were both sixteen, remember? For that youth who looked like John Lennon."

"He had terrible spots."

"But as far as I know he didn't have a leprous soul like your Ian. He might very well wreck your career. Take a pull at yourself, Charlotte, do."

Charlotte sat back on her heels, remembering the hotel room in Berlin, wondering what would have happened without Nicholas's interruption. Suki's remarks hardly touched her. She felt as if a thick glass screen separated her from the rest of the world: whatever was said or done only came to her faintly unless it was Ian who said or did them.

"He's still in the house at Oxford," she said.

"Your father?"

"No. He, Ian. They have a house in North Oxford. They're moving in the middle of August, to a house quite near mine in Ashcombe."

That night, Suki went out to dinner with her father.

Charlotte was invited but she claimed already to have arranged a visit to the theatre with the aunts. She avoided Suki's father because he always reminded her of one of the worst days of her adolescence.

Suki's family lived two streets away from the house in Norham Gardens which Tessy had abandoned to Charlotte and her father. There were five other children, all large, blotchy-freckled and cheerful as Suki. Their father was a professor.

One day Charlotte decided to accept an invitation to tea with Suki. Before her parents split up she and Suki had been in and out of each other's houses without thought of an invitation, but since then her father took such detailed interest in her social life, cross-examining her as to whom she had seen and what she had done to provide fuel for one of his diatribes about women in general and Tessy in particular, that Charlotte hadn't taken the risk of a visit.

She asked her father's permission. He agreed to let her go, then told her what he knew about Suki's father, mostly critical and dismissive, his characteristic tone. Later on when she was at Oxford herself Charlotte got an inkling of one of the causes of her father's bitterness. He had been a very young professor and never quite fulfilled his early promise. His publications were regular but peripheral. Charlotte thought privately that any publication on Anglo-Saxon literature must be too little, too late, but in the field some work was known as central, significant, seminal, while other work was peripheral and that was what Geoffrey did. Charlotte found it hard to make up her mind whether he had been a promising scholar whose obsession with the break-up of his marriage distracted him, or a shallow and superficial thinker glad to seize an excuse for lacking to develop. She didn't actually care. All scholarship bored her. She couldn't see why, if she enjoyed a work, it mattered who wrote it influenced by whom, under what circumstances and with what intention.

After school the two girls walked back together. It was winter and bitterly cold. The sky was dark and heavy with promised snow and Suki was complaining about her chilblains. From the end of the road you could recognise her house by the light that poured out from it. They never seemed to draw their curtains and there always seemed to be people in every room, like an over-equipped doll's house.

Suki quickened her pace as she got nearer and Charlotte wondered what it would be like to hurry home. Inside, the wave of heat was almost overpowering. Suki's mother was Australian and she had never accustomed herself to the English climate. She took in typing to pay the heating bills. Suki talked incessantly about every detail of her family life; at first Charlotte had found it threatening and made constant comparisons with her own, but gradually she had come to treat these accounts as reassuring, friendly fiction like a scaled-down Barsetshire or Jalna.

The living-room was warm and full of people and noise. Charlotte liked that: she would obviously be a minor part of the entertainment. Everyone greeted her but then carried on talking. At the time Charlotte had thought it a fortunate chance; looking back she suspected Suki had briefed them about her self-conscious friend. Suki ran straight to her father, large and red-haired and blotchy as she was, and jumped into his lap. He was talking to another of his daughters and clutching a tea-cup. When Suki arrived he hugged her with delight and went right on talking over her head, holding the tea-cup at arm's length so as not to spill the tea.

Charlotte almost never cried: when she did it was ostensibly for a sad book or film. Now, however, she could feel her throat thicken and the beginning of tears behind her eyes. "Excuse me," she muttered, and backed into the hall, closing the door behind her. In design, the house was like her own and she went straight to the downstairs lavatory and locked herself in. Even here she was pursued by the contrast between her life and Suki's. Where she was accustomed to seeing her school coat and hat, her father's Burberry, two pairs of Wellington boots, there was instead a jumble of coats, boots, croquet mallets, tennis rackets, a jam-jar full of maggots, several drawings executed by an enthusiastic child, newspaper clippings chosen for their absurdity: the accoutrements of a populous and lively household.

She sat on the lavatory seat, crossed her arms as if hugging herself, and bowed her head to her knees. The cloth of the school skirt was rough against her forehead. Scraps from the past floated into her mind like the detritus of a submarine explosion. Liam's face that morning. Her mother's high heels on the stone flags. The pony and trap moving away down the avenue, always receding, never vanishing. She almost welcomed the memories to blot out the picture of Suki in her father's arms.

She had no idea how long she sat in the lavatory. Suki knocked on the door. "Charlotte? You okay in there? Charlotte? Are you ill?"

Charlotte wiped her face with a handkerchief. Nothing could disguise the blotches, the swollen lids. She hesitated, then opened the door.

"Come and have some tea, you'll feel better. Do." Suki was talking brightly, not showing that she noticed anything unusual.

"No, thank you. I'm not feeling well, actually. I think I'd better go home straight away. Should I say goodbye to your parents?"

"Sure you want to go?"

"Certain sure."

"Okay. Don't worry about the parents, I'll deal with them."

Charlotte sidled towards the door, back to the wall in helpless dismay. "Thank you. Goodbye." She pulled the door to behind herself and made for the street with the ears-back mindlessness of a bolting horse.

Halfway home she noticed her missing satchel. "I can't go back, I can't," she said to herself out loud, tugging at her plait in agitation. "I can't go back, I can't, I can't."

As usual, what she couldn't bear to do was what had to be done. Otherwise Suki or her parents might bring the satchel round and her father would start to ask questions to which no answers would be possible. She marched back to Suki's, swinging her arms to keep her spirits up, concentrating on putting one foot in front of the other and not stepping on cracks in the pavement.

Her marching faltered at the gate and she sidled rather than walked up to the front door. She lifted the letter box and peered through, hoping to catch someone's attention without ringing the bell and making a public arrival. She could just see the back view of Suki's father, at the foot of the stairs, calling up.

". . . won't be long."

"Why'd she leave?" called back a woman's voice from the landing.

"Upset, poor little thing," said Suki's father. "Bloody Parker, bloody useless. I wish he'd grow up. You'd think no woman ever left her husband before. Back soon," and he opened the front door.

Charlotte was holding the letter box in a catatonic clutch and she was pulled forward with the door. She disentangled her hand and straightened up. Appalled and silenced by the impossibility of disguising the rent in the social fabric, they looked at each other.

"I – I'm – I – didn't mean to eavesdrop," said Charlotte. The words came out thin and voiceless.

"Your satchel," said Suki's father. "I was bringing – your satchel."

"Thank you. That's what I came back for."

Again they stood in silence. Waves of heat were eddying out of the house.

"Shall I drive you back?"

"Oh no, thank you," said Charlotte. "I'm not well, you see. That's why I left. A sudden stomach upset. It'll do me good to walk."

"Not too cold?"

"Oh no, oh no. I like the cold. It suits me. My – my natural habitat, so to speak."

Suki's father smiled. "Come to tea another time. When your stomach upset's gone."

"Oh, I *will*," said Charlotte with the momentary sincerity of imminent escape.

She went back to her father's comfortless house where the Swedish au pair's Beatles records battled vainly against the seeping silence of emptiness. The light was on in her father's study. She carried her shoes through the hall and upstairs, past the au pair's room, without letting her know she was back. The au pair found her heavy going. The foreign girls changed every six months. Charlotte's father didn't want them to stay long enough to make judgements about his behaviour.

In her room, Charlotte locked the door behind her and turned on the two table lamps, the standard lamp, the bedside light and the ceiling light. In the resulting blaze the posters on the wall, all famous American beauty spots, looked at home, sun-baked. The Grand Canyon, the Sierras, Salt Lake City: usually a comfort, Charlotte found. Not now, however; she was beyond that.

She sat at her desk in the window. It overlooked the University Parks: in the daytime she could see trees, games pitches, and, meandering in the distance, the river. Now the window was a shiny wall of black with the lights dancing in it. She was shaking with cold and shock. "Bloody Parker, bloody useless," she thought. A terrifying thought. If she had a useless father, what did that make her? And who would protect her, if her father was useless? Until then, she had tried not to criticise her father, not to herself, not to the aunts, not to anyone. She clung to the unexpressed fiction that her father was normal in an unusual way.

Suki's father's words, once heard, could not be forgotten. "You'd think no woman ever left her husband before." The idea was in Charlotte's mind: and like a drop of blood in a bowl of water, it spread and spread till it seemed to have vanished; but the composition of the water is nonetheless altered. Charlotte felt, without acknowledging it, from that day onwards that her father was choosing to be betrayed, that he wasn't as adult as he appeared, and that she was even more vulnerable than she had thought.

Suki remained her friend but she never went to tea at her house, never visited the house at all until Suki's wedding, ten years later. She avoided the reception line, talked to the women she knew, helped Suki to change and left, unobtrusively, before the bride. There was only so much contrast she could take. It had been a very happy wedding: Charlotte couldn't have wished it otherwise, but she still resented it. She could only cope with Suki's happiness in very small doses.

Charlotte lay in Suki's spare bed, remembering. The memories were not as painful as usual, she had found to her surprise. The episode seemed sad and embarrassing, but as if it had happened to a much younger, more vulnerable person. She had no longer had the sense of absolute identification with teenage Charlotte that had been such a disturbing feature of her excursions into the past. Perhaps now she would even be able to face Suki's father. The old wounds were healing. She drifted off to sleep thinking of Ian.

Chapter Six

"Entirely new curtains," said Nora Bridge. "Throughout the house."

Charlotte was absorbed in the range of supermarket yoghurts. Twenty-five different named flavours: all, in her experience, tasting the same. She wasn't expecting Nora. A week before the beginning of the autumn term, the supermarket should be Nora-free. The woman was usually well established in the staff-room at school by then, keeping a high profile as a diligent Head of Department preparing for whatever the term might bring while getting a flying start at the holiday gossip.

"Curtains," repeated Charlotte, bewildered.

Nora interpreted this. "Ah, so you've heard about them already? I wonder how? The decision's only just been taken. So a little bird not far from the inner sanctum told me."

"What inner sanctum?"

"The holy of holies. The Headmaster's office."

"You've been talking to the school secretary and she told you that they want new curtains for the Headmaster's house?" guessed Charlotte.

"Sh-sh-sh," said Nora, pressing her finger to her lips. "I was told in confidence, and I expect you were too."

"Yoghurts have ears," said Charlotte, choosing the three nearest her. "Would you believe me if I told you that I had no idea there were to be new curtains in the Headmaster's house?"

Nora pursed her mouth, eyes twinkling. "I think we both know better than *that*," she murmured.

Charlotte felt herself enmeshed in a sticky spider's web of intrigue and fantasy, spun from Nora's emotional entrails. "What a surprise, meeting you," she said, making as if to push her cart away. Nora peered in.

"Plenty of vegetables. Don't you eat meat? Oh, yes, a joint. Beef. Not many of us can afford beef any more, except for special occasions. A dinner party, I expect. Or perhaps you're having Nicholas Embrey to supper again. Less than a week, isn't it? Poor man, you're doing him a kindness. Takes so little care of himself. Hardly even shaves, in the holidays. Perhaps you could speak to him about it?"

"Are you entertaining?" counter-attacked Charlotte. Nora's cart was full of puffy packets: savoury concoctions of monosodium glutamate and permitted additives.

Nora nodded. "A few friends for drinks. To welcome the Headmaster and Mrs HM and their children to Ashcombe."

"What a kind thought," said Charlotte, heading for the Pet Corner. Nora was allergic to dogs, cats and birds so could not have any legitimate business there. But Nora followed her anyway.

"Have you bought a dog?"

"No," said Charlotte.

"A cat?"

"No."

"Are you shopping for a neighbour?"

"No. I made a mistake," said Charlotte. "I was looking for the way out."

Ashcombe College for Ladies was set in fifty acres of playing fields, gardens, and woodland. It had been purpose-built in the 1890s in a monastic style: it stretched along the north-south Cotswold ridge, constructed of yellow stone with Gothic windows and occasional whimsical outcrops of turret and tower.

Charlotte liked the school during the holidays. The long cloistral corridors smelt rich with polish, the desks stood in eager rows. The beginning of a school year is a hopeful time. The girls are generally relaxed and happy. The staff have forgotten the disillusionments and exhaustion of the end of the year and remember why they entered teaching, what they were working for: most teachers are idealists and enthusiasts. Charlotte certainly was. She hoped to make girls happy, to inform them, to encourage and strengthen them. She wanted to introduce them to English literature and to the emotions that poetry kindled in her, on the few occasions when she lowered her defences enough to allow any emotion to be kindled.

She was feeling intensely optimistic as she walked through the deserted afternoon school, up the ornately carved wooden staircase, down the Working Corridor to the English Room. This was her office and also the repository for most of the Department's books, housed in bulky wall-to-ceiling cupboards. The combination of functions was not a convenient arrangement; for some time now the Department had been agitating for a supplementary book-cupboard and Charlotte had an appointment with the Headmaster at four o'clock to discuss the matter.

It was not quite half-past three and she had plenty of small administrative tasks to complete: file the coaching requests, check the book orders against the boxes of books received, start work on the agenda for the first departmental meeting of term.

Then she sat at her tidy desk, Shakespeare's head paperweight aslant at one corner, and enjoyed being herself. That was a pleasure she had discovered during the holidays, a gift of the Russian trip, Nicholas Embrey, the passage of time: she was released from her suffocating emotional box, and this time without the constant expectation of having to return to it. Physically, too, she felt well. Her body was glowing all over from the sun: never previously allowed to reach more than her face, arms, legs from the knees down – but this summer welcomed everywhere except where the tiny bikini, bought on her return from Russia, precariously clung. She felt confident in her appearance and in her ability. She felt like an apprentice member of the human race.

Then there was the Headmaster. She kept glancing at her watch then at the view, the countryside washed in a faint sweeping drizzle lifted here and there by the breeze like a gossamer curtain. The hands of her watch edged round to four. The school gossip – mostly from Miss Garside, Chief Secretary – was that the HM was efficient, decisive, energetic. He must be, to want to clear up such a minor matter as extra cupboard space for the English Department. Charlotte had hoped it was a pretext to see her, but then learnt from Miss Garside that he was making an effort to clear his desk of all outstanding matters before term began.

Downstairs, Charlotte waited outside the Headmaster's office. Miss Garside fluttered up to her. In many day-to-day matters she ran the school and she was a woman whom Charlotte much respected for her acuity, good nature and common sense. She had the usual school secretary's prejudice against teachers, thinking them overpaid and underworked, but most of the time she masked it and she was unfailingly good-humoured. She had a pleasant, slightly puddingy face and bulging blue eyes. "I do like that dress. Not for me, mind you, unless I was two stone lighter and twenty years younger, but on you it's ever so pretty."

"HM ready for me?"

"Just about. Miss Noakes is in there – give her a minute. You're early."

Charlotte propped herself against a cold radiator and prepared for a chat. One of the many things she had latterly begun to enjoy was the small coinage of everyday life; the brief chats, exchanging the most commonplace of sentiments, merely reinforcing common humanity and common interests. Previously, she had hurried stiffly through as if her company would contaminate with awkwardness. She had felt her rigidity as contagious. Now she savoured the difference. "What's the state of play on the curtains?" she asked.

"Ah well." Miss Garside put her ringed hand on her frilled chest and breathed like a diva. "Thereby hangs a tale – the Governing Body must think highly of the Boss because they're going to pay for the whole lot! Every curtain! The Boss was delighted! In strict confidence, of course."

"Of course," said Charlotte, knowing well that Miss

Garside measured her disclosures carefully. She released only unclassified information.

Inside the secretaries' office, the telephone rang. Miss Garside rolled her eyes in jocular complaint and went to answer it.

Outside, Charlotte waited. She was thoroughly prepared for the meeting. She had notes on her previous conversations with the Headmistress about the English Department accommodation, copies of all memos exchanged, and plans of her suggested alterations.

She was less thoroughly prepared for her contact with the man. Three weeks in Ashcombe, seeing Nicholas, having time to ponder and reflect, could have been an ideal opportunity to come to terms with her infatuation. So Suki had hoped, so Nicholas hinted. But Charlotte's mind was still neatly split down the middle. Whereas once she had kept bulkheads between the past and the present, now she preserved her feelings for Ian quite separate from her perception of reality. She could give lip-service to the obvious: yes, she was being reckless; yes, she was being inconsiderate towards Wendy if not downright immoral; yes, she might find school intolerable if there was a scandal. But then again, yes, she loved Ian.

"Lust," said Nicholas.

"Love," said Charlotte.

She drove past Ian's house once he had moved in. She saw his car, a blue Volvo, the only one in Ashcombe. From then on her heart leapt when she saw a blue car.

So, standing outside the Headmaster's office, one half of her was resolved, thinking about her career, organised. The other half was choking with anticipated excitement and longing.

"Good afternoon, Miss Parker. Please come in."

He was wearing a dark suit. Heather, coming out and passing Charlotte, looked ruffled and merely nodded in acknowledgement of Charlotte's greeting.

The room had been entirely changed. New desk, new carpet, new furniture. The desk was large and solid, a modern but expensive reproduction with brass handles and inlaid leather. The Headmaster sat behind it and looked inaccessible, businesslike. Charlotte sat on the new leather armchair he pointed out and was very conscious of the leather against her bare calves and arms.

She had dressed and dressed again for this: finally decided on a white cotton sleeveless shift that made her look fragile and distinctive. It was not, now, entirely appropriate: rain was beating against the windowpane. But she knew – it was impossible not to – how charming she looked.

The Headmaster's eyes were strictly businesslike. He ran through the question of accommodation for the English Department as he understood it, Charlotte showed him the plans, he studied them briefly, asked her to explain a few points. He was certainly able enough, good on detail.

"Let's go up to the Working Corridor and have a look at the wall you want removed," he said. "Remember I'm still very much the new boy. It'll be easier if I have a clear idea what we're talking about."

Passing the secretary's office, the door only slightly ajar, Charlotte could hear the murmur of voices. Ian tapped sharply on the door and said, "Going to look round the teaching rooms, Miss Garside. Back in about twenty minutes."

The secretary fluttered out to reply. By this time the Headmaster was nearly out of sight with Charlotte in tow. He walked very fast and she almost had to run to keep up. Their feet clattered loudly up the wooden stairs.

"Who is likely to be in the building?" he inquired casually.

"The secretaries, possibly the caretaker or one of his men."

"No teachers?"

"Not usually in the afternoon," said Charlotte, "not with another week of the holidays."

"Um," said the Headmaster.

"The sewing-woman and the cleaners will probably have gone; the builders have finished their work for the holidays, so the Bursar told me . . . Any special reason for asking?"

"No," said the Headmaster as they stopped. "Is this the famous stationery cupboard?"

Charlotte pushed the door open, put on the light, a bare overhead bulb. The cupboard was actually a tiny room, about eight feet by five, lined floor to ceiling with shelves bearing stationery. Exercise books, file pads, file covers, reinforced washers, index cards, pens, pencils, in the lavish profusion of storage.

"And all this would be removed to . . .?" asked the Headmaster.

"The old Banda room down the passage. Mrs Jackson would have no objection – she looks after the stationery and supplies."

The cupboard was stuffy. There were no windows. Air vents, one on each side, opening onto classrooms, provided the only ventilation and they were very high up, just below the ceiling. Charlotte was unnerved by his silence. "It would make all the difference to the rest of the Department not to have to come into my office for books – and of course it would be better for me. Knock down the wall at the far end so we'd have access from the existing coaching room . . ."

The Headmaster closed the door behind them. Charlotte was in mid-flow: ". . . the groundsman told me it isn't a structural wall . . ."

The Headmaster took her hand. She felt the contact like a jolt of electricity where she hadn't even suspected a current. He held her hand trapped between both of his. She half pulled away: he was much stronger and held her. The rational part of her mind reflected that he would be stronger, being more heavily built and muscled. Her physical response registered it as male dominance. She shuddered and tried to back away, only stopping when wedged against boxes of felt-tip pens. Her nostrils were full of dust and his smell, the cloth of his suit and aftershave. She was wearing only the smallest of bikini pants under her dress. Presumably he would soon discover flesh under the cotton. And what about the accommodation for the English Department books?

"Do you remember the hotel in Berlin?" he murmured close to her ear. He nibbled her ear, blew into it. A shudder rippled through her body and into the boxes of felt-tip pens, which vibrated slightly. She was held motiveless by her desire to touch him, to be touched, to see what would happen.

"I had no time to tell you then – how desirable I found you." His hand was stroking her neck, light touches under her hair, around her ears. His other hand had slipped round behind her back and was pressing her towards him. She shuddered again and again; each shudder brushed her against his body. It was live to her like a powerful magnet.

He began to kiss her. His mouth opened like the door to a strange consuming country and her mouth sucked his, savouring, gulping at the sensation. All thought was momentarily lost in her immersion in her own reactions: it was not only physical, though the immediacy of that was delightful and the rhythm of his touch was hypnotic. It was also the emotional release. He was so sure in what he wanted, and what he wanted was to touch her. She did not even consider what she wanted, a question always so elusive and sometimes so painful. The simplicity of his intentions was deeply exciting and she moved to collaborate, easing her shoulders away from the shelves so he could reach her zip, shrugging the dress over her shoulders, stepping out of it. A very small part of her rational mind worried about the dress, now lying in a heap in the dust.

She was naked apart from her tiny pants. The Headmaster was wearing a three-piece suit. Though she longed to touch him, she could only reach cloth. But he touched her all over and she could see how absorbed he was, his eyes following the patterns of his fingers on her body.

She looked up, her eyes sweeping the shelves with their orderly load, reminders of work. She didn't see them. Her physical excitement was intense, but sterile; she knew there was to be no contact with his body, only his hands. She was being an object of pleasure for him, a valued and rare object. He was crooning, "So beautiful, so slender, so beautiful. Hold still, hold still. No no," he kept saying, pinning her hands with one of his, not letting her fingers undress him or touch his skin. He wanted to be the agent, the person acting. She was to be still and beautiful. It appealed to her. How tempting to be desired. Yet she resented it: she might as well not be there, he could be doing this to any body.

The dust of the room filled her nostrils, almost choking her. There was no air. She pushed him away and he accepted this more readily than she liked. He looked self-absorbed, alone with his desire. He was panting like a dog on a hot day. "Mmm," he said, "what's the matter?"

She picked up her dress, shook off the dust, and he sneezed twice, now thoroughly recovered, the glaze gone from his eyes. "Do you have to do that?" he said irritably.

"My dress was dirty," said Charlotte. She felt shaken but determined to stand up to him. Her excitement was also turning to irritation.

"I wish you hadn't done that," she said, hampered by the double knowledge that he was her employer and that she had encouraged him.

"You wanted it as much as I did," he said. "To coin a phrase."

"I wanted *something* very much. I didn't want to be undressed like a Sindy doll."

"You took your own dress off."

"I thought you would join me."

"And stand naked in a stationery cupboard?" He laughed in dismissal and derision.

Charlotte breathed deeply, trying not to feel sick, trying not to think about the part she had played in the scene. She couldn't wait to be away and scrambled into her dress.

"You've seen all you need to, as far as the stationery cupboard is concerned," said Charlotte, aiming for dignity, achieving absurdity.

The Headmaster laughed again. "I've seen quite enough, thank you."

"So may I take it that you approve the English Department's request? For the alterations and change of use?"

"Yes, yes," he said, brushing dust off his jacket, shooting his cuffs, opening the door. Charlotte hung back for a moment, wanting to be by herself. She felt as if a bucket of cold water had been dashed over her: shocked and left gasping by his absolute indifference and her foolishness. She couldn't learn, she didn't seem able to learn as far as the Headmaster was concerned.

"I've arrived," called Nicholas. "Do you want the wine in the fridge, or shall I open it?"

"Open it and bring out the glasses."

It was a warm evening and Charlotte was sitting at a table on the patio behind her house. Each side of the garden was protected by a high fence: at the end of the garden, the view. The ground fell away to fields; sheep grazed the hillsides and the wind blew straight from Wales. Charlotte loved sitting in her garden. She felt both secure and free there – the narrow fences each side reassuring, the view promising endless possibility.

"You're mounting my sketch," said Nicholas, peering over her shoulder amid the confusion of card, scissors, paste. She piled the work up neatly, took it inside. Nicholas poured the wine for both of them and settled their chairs in the best position for the late sun. They sat down together, as quiet as a long-married couple.

Eventually Nicholas spoke. "I like England," he said.

"I want to go to America," said Charlotte.

"Never been there?"

"Never. Always wanted to. Wanted to go to college in America. Was too feeble to stand up and insist. Also, probably, my father wouldn't have paid."

"Why didn't you go for a holiday since you started working?"

"Just couldn't bring myself to, somehow. It was a magic place; I wanted to keep it like that, as a refuge in case I ever needed it."

"What appealed to you?"

"The sun . . . the size . . . not knowing anyone there

. . . and the fact that my father hated it. A whole country with people who spoke in those marvellous accents. A country that was vast and sunbaked and unconfined."

"That's not a country you're describing," said Nicholas. "That's a state of mind. What's bothering you?"

"Two things. One I can tell you and one – I'd rather not."

"Okay," said Nicholas.

"I was in school today." She paused, remembered the stationery cupboard, blushed.

"And . . ." prompted Nicholas.

"I saw Heather Noakes." Charlotte was still blushing.

"Did she tell you a rude limerick?" inquired Nicholas. "To make you blush."

Charlotte laughed and her eyes lightened. "Of course not. She told me about Sophie Preston."

"Sophie . . . is that the fat girl who hung round you in Russia? The one you were telling me about last week, who failed all her O-levels?"

"That's right. Well, the plan was that she would repeat the year in the Upper Fifth, retake her O-levels and then go into the sixth form. She was too young for her year to start with, her parents kept pushing and pushing for her to be in a higher form. She failed mostly out of anxiety – she doesn't lack brains."

"I remember you telling me. But our new Headmaster wouldn't allow it, I suppose."

"How did you know? Who told you?"

"No one told me. He likes success. He didn't like Sophie. He wouldn't want his precious new school cluttered up with failures. If it had been Miranda now . . . 'girls will be girls' he'd have said and laughed indulgently."

"You're right, he won't let her stay. Heather did her best to persuade him, but he won't." As she said this she wondered. If she had known about Sophie, would she still have stayed in the cupboard with the Headmaster? She liked to think not. But her goodwill for the girl was a reasoned, liberal, acceptable emotion, utterly unlike and much less intense than her feeling for the Headmaster.

"What'll happen to Sophie, then?" said Nicholas.

"She's going to a crammer in London, apparently. She'll share a flat with some other girls."

Nicholas whistled. "At her age? What is she?"

"Fifteen. A lot too young."

"Have you tried talking to Craig Stewart about it?"

"He wouldn't listen to me. Besides, it's none of my business, officially." These were justifications. She was determined to keep away from the Headmaster, Sophie or no Sophie. She had herself to think of.

It was break on the second day of term and the staff-room was full. Two trolleys with coffee and buns stood in the middle of the room impeding everyone's progress. It was a well-proportioned, long room on the first floor with light green shiny walls – somewhat like a hospital – and the omnipresent Gothic windows and view. Charlotte sat in her usual windowseat, peering through the bodies, trying to see Nicholas.

Paula Madders swept up to her, pushed tousled hair back from an ink-streaked brow and groaned. "Isn't it murder being back with all that sunshine outside? What do you think of the Headmaster so far?"

Charlotte moved over to allow Paula to sit down. "I was on the Russian trip, remember, I've had plenty of time to get to know him."

"So what do you *think*? And about Sophie Preston? That was a bit harsh. He fancies himself in his gown, as well. How on *earth* did he marry that woman?"

"You don't want to know what I think," said Charlotte. "You just want to tell me what you think."

"Ah," said Paula, "you spotted it. His children look pleasant, though. Untidy and cheerful. Do you think he'll *do*, Charlotte?"

"Early days yet," said Charlotte.

"Stop being so proper and reasonable." Paula paused, hesitated, went on. "What's up with Nora Bridge?"

"How do you mean? I haven't noticed anything. I've hardly seen her since term began, I think she's avoiding me. Come to think of it, she isn't in her chair."

At one end of the staff-room, near the Gothic fireplace and the gas fire, the liberals clustered. At the other, under the unflattering Edwardian portrait of an early Head-mistress with an advanced case of goitre, sat the conservatives. It was the custom of the school to hang retiring Headmistresses' portraits in a room particularly associated with them and it was now popularly supposed that the lady with the goitre had spent much of her term of office listening at the staff-room door. The conservatives had the best chairs because they had, generally speaking, been in the school longer than the liberals and they included Heather Noakes in their number. The conservatives still said "jolly good" and "loyalty" and "chalk and talk". They called psychiatrists trick-cyclists and disapproved of jogging. The liberals thought they obstructed progress.

It wasn't always easy to tell what the liberals saw as progress. Some wanted the abolition of school uniform; others, the institution of study skills courses and an organ-ised system of pastoral care. Still others, among them Nora Bridge, wanted the present hierarchy replaced by themselves.

"She isn't in her chair, you're right," said Paula. "That's because she's moving among the staff fomenting disaffec-tion."

"So what's new about that?"

"I can't find out what she's fomenting disaffection about."

"Probably the Humanities Department. She was very keen on that idea all through the Russian trip."

"That could explain why she isn't talking to us."

"It could," said Charlotte. She wasn't interested. Nora was always muttering about something.

"She was doing it yesterday, too. So earlier this morning I asked Miss Garside," said Paula, then hesitated pointedly. At last Charlotte noticed the hesitation.

"Come on, Paula, what is it?"

"Miss Garside wouldn't say."

"Wouldn't say *what*?" Charlotte was irritated. Paula

didn't usually make herself important over trivialities, as she seemed to be doing now.

"Charlotte . . ." said Paula, stopped, pushed her hand through her hair again. "I'm worried. Miss Garside wouldn't say *anything at all*. I asked her what Nora was on about and she buttoned up. Not a word." Paula's mobile face had the incipient pouches and hollows of middle age, more so on the rare occasions when she was serious. She was ordinarily robust and level-headed, more interested in her subject and her husband and children than in school politics. If she was concerned, then . . . but what could be wrong?

"I've got to go," said Paula. "Upper Three, bless their little hearts, still so keen on drawing pictures of Roman legionaries in full uniform. Take care, Charlotte."

The staff-room was emptying. Charlotte was not teaching after break: she had an appointment with the Bursar to discuss the timing of the alterations to the stationery cupboard.

The Bursar's Office was fifty yards from Main School. Charlotte enjoyed the short walk. On the playing fields cut out in terraces below the path, girls were playing hockey, incongruous in the summer weather. She felt a surge of pleasure in her work. One day she would be Headmistress of a school like this, responsible for six hundred girls, able to help and protect them, to organise the school so it was orderly yet flexible. The Sophie Prestons would be safer under her regime, the Nora Bridges controlled and circumscribed.

"I'm afraid the Bursar won't be able to see you," said his assistant, a normally cheerful woman in her fifties. She spoke abruptly and wouldn't meet Charlotte's eyes.

"Oh," said Charlotte, nonplussed, beginning to feel the tick of anxiety that comes when all is not as usual and all is not well. The office was in a recently built, flat-roofed, over-windowed structure crammed with browning and dispirited plants. The Bursar's assistant, evidently embarrassed, began fussing with a plant mister around the cactus section.

"Do you mist cacti?" asked Charlotte.

"Of course not – I mean – things are difficult."

"When will the Bursar see me?"

"I'm not sure . . . it's the Extraordinary Governors' Meeting, you understand . . ." she began, then she looked horrified, checked herself, blurted, "Excuse me, Miss Parker, we'll be in touch with you," and bolted from the room. Charlotte was left alone with the plants.

She wandered back to the Main Building, no longer at peace. Little spurts of anxiety and ancient guilts snagged at her. Something was wrong, but it couldn't be anything to do with her, surely?

The cupboard; the cupboard beat inside her brain, the Headmaster and the cupboard. But it can't be. We were inside. Nobody could possibly have seen. I'm imagining things. An Extraordinary Governors' Meeting at this stage of term – that's serious. An expulsion, perhaps? Trouble with parents?

Once inside she went towards the secretaries' office, hovered outside in case any of them might be prepared for a chat, pretending to look in her pigeonhole for messages. None of them wanted a chat but there was a message.

16th September. 11.20 a.m.

To: Miss Parker
From: Heather Noakes, Deputy Headmistress
Kindly come to see me at your earliest convenience.

Chapter Seven

Heather couldn't express herself. She kept stumbling over her words. She was embarrassed and angry. It didn't really matter, because Charlotte, after the first horrific moments, couldn't bring herself to listen. One line was enough: "A complaint has been received by the Governors about improper behaviour on your part in the school building. The Headmaster is also involved." Although this was vague enough, Charlotte knew it must refer to the stationery cupboard incident.

Her attention kept drifting, refusing to be called back to Heather's small, cosy room, the mantelpiece covered with family photographs and golfing trophies.

"Do you belong to a union, Miss Parker?"

"Mmmm," said Charlotte.

"Which one?"

Charlotte didn't answer. She concentrated on the postcards stuck in the frame of the large mirror, views of Cornwall, Majorca, and a Paris traffic jam with the Arc de Triomphe in the background.

"Miss Parker? To which union do you belong? Is it AMMA?"

"Yes, AMMA." Charlotte wished Heather would stop calling her "Miss Parker". Heather was talking again but the words splintered, Charlotte couldn't reconstruct them to make sense.

"I want to go now. I want to go," said Charlotte.

"You must inform the Union and let them advise you. You have certain rights. Miss Parker? You realise this is a serious matter?" Heather was breathing heavily. She was evidently upset and Charlotte felt, from her drifting distance, sorry that she was so disappointed, so shocked. Considering the position impartially, the school was now in a most awkward situation. A complaint had been made so it must be investigated: a new Headmaster, a scandal. She absolutely refused to think about herself.

Heather went on talking. When she stopped Charlotte stood up. "Thank you, Miss Noakes, I understand."

"Don't be silly, girl, you've hardly listened to a word," said Heather impatiently. "What did I say?"

Charlotte groped for an answer. "That there's been a complaint of improper behaviour. That the Governors are meeting to discuss their action, that I may have to appear before them, that I should tell the Union."

Charlotte stood by the door, waiting to be allowed to go, but Heather went on talking. At last she stopped. "You look terrible, Charlotte," she said bluntly. Charlotte registered the use of her Christian name and tried to respond with a smile that seemed wan even to herself. Heather was worried by her pallor.

"Are you teaching next lesson?"

"Yes. Upper Sixth. They're a good group. I have high hopes for the results this year," began Charlotte, then remembered that this was not a normal discussion on school matters: remembered also that she probably would not still be there to see the A-level results.

"Is there anyone you can get in touch with? Anyone to come and stay with you? Family, perhaps?"

"I'm not bereaved," said Charlotte blankly.

"You're in a state of shock. Would you like some tea?"

"No, thank you."

She left the room, closing the door carefully behind her as if she were slightly drunk. The corridor outside was empty, quiet with mid-lesson order. She walked slowly along, pausing occasionally to lean against the wall. She passed the stationery cupboard, hardly gave it a glance. Her mind was empty. She felt burned out, like a video camera exposed to very bright light. She had never, as far as she could recall, put a step astray during her whole time at Ashcombe. Now she had: and it had been found out. She accepted immediately that it should be so. It was appropriate.

She had never understood, throughout her childhood,

what had caused the dreadful disruption of her family: as children do, she had supposed that it must have been her fault, but what act or thought or characteristic of hers was responsible remained a mystery. This stationery cupboard question was easier. She knew she had been at fault.

She collected her books from her office and walked along the rest of the corridor, up the stairs, waited outside the Upper Sixth classroom for the bell to ring. She was to teach a double lesson, then she would be free. It was her afternoon off. What would she do? Her mind was a blank, her eyes dry. She looked at her reflection in the glass door, saw old Charlotte, rigid and tense. Pre-Russia Charlotte. Oh well, oh well . . . she couldn't feel disappointment: she was cut off from hope.

Charlotte was sitting in her kitchen, doing nothing. A pile of papers, a mark-book lay ready. When at last she heard the doorbell she had no idea how long it had been ringing.

"About bloody time," said Nicholas, bursting in. Charlotte stood back to let him pass.

"Would you like some tea?" she said.

"It's nine o'clock at night, Charlotte. It's nearly dark. I brought some wine."

"Why?"

"Because Heather Noakes rang me. She told me what had happened, about the Governors."

"Why did she tell you?"

"Snap out of it. Stop talking like a zombie. Sit down and drink this."

Charlotte was conscious of vague irritation. She deserved sympathy, surely, not harassment? Nevertheless she began to drink the wine.

"Heather said somebody had complained to the Governors about you and the Headmaster behaving improperly on the school premises."

"The stationery cupboard," murmured Charlotte.

"They could sack you, Charlotte."

"I know. The moral turpitude clause."

Nicholas was looking at her steadily, his head on one

side, his expression sympathetic but impatient. "If you ask me, it could be an excellent thing."

"How can you say that!" Charlotte was stung into energy by this heartless dismissal of her career. "I've worked and worked – I wanted to be a headmistress – this is all I'm trained for – I'm ideally suited for it –"

"Garbage, garbage, garbage," said Nicholas.

"What do you mean, 'garbage'?"

"Rubbish, then. If you're so ideally suited to this work what on earth took you into the stationery cupboard with Ian?"

"We were discussing Department business," began Charlotte indignantly, then faltered as she heard her own absurdity. "He was being very formal and businesslike. I didn't expect him to grab me."

"He's grabbed you before, surely."

"Not like that. And not in school. He seemed so formal until we were inside the cupboard."

"Tell me about it," invited Nicholas, settling himself in a chair with his feet propped on the table. "What exactly did Heather say?"

"I didn't listen to most of it. Just about the complaint, and the Governors' Meeting."

"Who complained?"

"She didn't say. I can't imagine. There wasn't anybody about, how could anyone have seen? Unless Ian talked about it."

"Are there windows? In the cupboard?"

"Only air vents, that's why it's so stuffy." She paused, remembering the smell of the dust and her excitement.

"Where do the air vents lead to? Would it be possible to look in through them?"

"They lead into classrooms. You'd have to stand on a chair or something to look in. But who on earth would? And who would complain?"

"I can guess," said Nicholas.

"Nora?" Charlotte felt the queasiness that Nora often roused in her, the tendrils of hostility and sticky involvement. "I do hope not." The cupboard incident was distasteful enough in memory if it only involved herself and the Headmaster. With Nora as a shocked or gloating onlooker . . .

"I don't want to think about that," she said.

"Heather says you should get in touch with the Union. Apparently you can have someone with you at the hearing with the Governors. A lawyer."

"I don't want a lawyer. There's nothing much they can do anyway unless I'm prepared to make a fight of it, and I'm not. It's obvious I'll have to go. As soon as the story gets out my life won't be worth living, either with the staff or the girls. And the Headmaster has to stay. It would be very embarrassing for the school to dismiss him now. Much the easiest thing is for me to agree to go with whatever reference they'll give me, and the whole thing to be blamed on me."

"You're being a martyr."

"No I'm not. It's common sense. It could be the end of a school like this if I make a fuss; the papers would love it, can't you imagine the headlines?"

"Are you serious? What if Craig Stewart tries it on with the girls?"

"I don't think he would, and neither do you, realistically. He thought I was old enough to take care of myself, and he was right. I should have been."

Officially, there were nine Governors of Ashcombe College: the Bursar was ex-officio Secretary. In practice the Chairman, Guy Robinson, usually got his own way. This was partly because his judgement was sound and his manner persuasive, partly because three of the other Governors were his appointees, and partly because the Governing Body as a whole lacked reforming zeal. Robinson himself was not over-keen to interfere with the running of the school. He saw the Governors as a brake on the Head of the time, as a fund-raising and budgeting and enabling body.

When he opened Nora Bridge's letter he read it through several times.

"Dear Mr Robinson,

Painful as it is the truth must be known. I have pondered long and hard, I have prayed for guidance in the matter, and, I believe, have received an answer.

You will probably know who I am. I am Head of the Geography Department of Ashcombe College for Ladies. I have served the school to the best of my ability for twelve years and I look forward to serving the school, in whatever capacity the Headmaster may see fit, for many more. But there is a colleague of mine, though I blush to say it, whose lack of moral probity must prove dangerous if she is allowed to continue on the staff.

The Headmaster is too much of a gentleman, I am sure, to take any action in the matter. Perhaps he feels that the incident is an isolated aberration which will not be repeated. I, too, hope and pray that this is the case. But I also feel that you should know of it. You can advise the Headmaster as you see fit and I will not have the secret on my conscience.

The facts are these. (Thank God, facts at last, thought the Chairman.) Today I was in the Geography Room preparing it for the beginning of term. I was adorning the walls with relief maps of the United States of America, our set region for study in this year's Ordinary Level Examination. My eyes happened to glance through an air vent in the wall, an air vent which leads to the stationery cupboard. The cupboard was fully illuminated by an electric light. I saw Miss Charlotte Parker, Head of the English Department, making shameless advances to the Headmaster. She removed her dress and stood virtually unclothed, offering her body."

The Chairman paused and struggled to summon up some recollection of the Head of the English Department. He wondered, wistfully, if she looked at all like Charlotte Rampling. He cherished a passion for Charlotte Rampling and if she had offered her body to him in a cupboard he had no doubt what course of action he would have adopted.

Gripped, he returned to the letter to see what the Head-master had done.

"The Headmaster attempted, as far as I could make out, to soothe and restrain Miss Parker, before leaving the cupboard. Miss Parker seemed emotional, even angry, at this rebuff."

By now the Chairman had altered his mental picture of Charlotte, added twenty years, thickened her body, greyed her hair. Poor chap, he thought. Embarrassing.

"I do not wish to dictate any course of action; however, I cannot but feel that this incident falls well within the terms for dismissal set out in Paragraph 8 (sub-section c) of the contract in use for teaching staff at Ashcombe College for Ladies.

To the best of my knowledge, Miss Parker is not aware that she was observed on this occasion. I am sending a copy of this letter to the Headmaster, as I wish him to have no cause to doubt my loyalty to him or to the school.
Yours sincerely,
In sorrow,
Nora Bridge."

The Chairman whistled through his teeth. It took little imagination to see the scandal this could cause. Whatever the rights and wrongs of it – and he wouldn't make up his mind about the facts until he had spoken to all three people concerned – it must be kept under wraps, and dealt with quickly.

He was reluctant to occupy himself with Ashcombe. His daughter had attended the school years before: during her schooldays he had thought it important to be a Governor, subsequently he had held the Chairmanship almost as a hobby. The school was in a pleasant part of the country, the girls were pretty and well-mannered and often flirted with him, showing their appreciation for the new Art

Block or Computer Room. He was a very successful man, several things in the City, rich and self-reliant and shrewd. He was fifty-six, married for thirty years to a good-natured and kindly woman. He was a conscientious Chairman but his time was valuable and he had not expected to think about Ashcombe until the regular Governors' Meeting in two months.

He consulted the school solicitors: rang up the other influential Governor, a Brigadier, and between them they decided. An Extraordinary Governors' Meeting would have to be called. First, Guy Robinson would talk to the Headmaster and Heather Noakes would talk to Charlotte; then the Governors would interview each participant in the cupboard scene.

Traditionally, Governors' Meetings were held in the Colhoun Room, a panelled and dignified visitors' dining-room tucked away at the end of a corridor on the ground floor. The Bursar had prepared each place with notepad, specially sharpened pencils, a copy of The Letter and the career records of the Headmaster, Charlotte and Nora. There were only five present: one had just died; of the apologies for absence, one was too ill to attend, another was holidaying in the Himalayas, and the third was in Malaysia lecturing for the British Council.

"I'd like to open the meeting by thanking you all for coming here at such short notice. Obviously we are dealing with a most delicate and unfortunate matter. I have spoken to the Headmaster. He is naturally reluctant to discuss the incident at all, but his account substantially tallies with that of Miss Bridge."

"He's read her letter, of course," remarked the Brigadier, a small, slenderly built man with a deceptively visionary air.

"Of course."

"I didn't like the letter," said the Brigadier. There was a pause. His bluntness often perplexed the blander members of the Governing Body.

"It must have been a great grief to Miss Bridge – having

142

to write the letter, I mean," said the Bishop. He was a plump, good-looking man with the shock of white hair and sincere manner of a confidence trickster. This was unfortunate as he was not dishonest, merely gullible and tender-hearted. "She tells us – er – 'I have pondered long and hard, I have prayed for guidance in the matter.'"

"Since the incident took place shortly after four o'clock and the letter is postmarked the same evening, she must have a direct line to the Almighty," said the Brigadier. "If you'll excuse my saying so, Bishop."

The Bishop waved in an all-purpose gesture of acceptance and absolution.

"I wasn't mad on the letter myself," said the Parent Governor. He was, at thirty-six, the youngest member of the Governing Body by ten years, the owner of a large and rapidly expanding building company. He was an important voice on the Ways and Means Committee. "She sounded like a frustrated spinster to me."

There was an embarrassed pause while nobody looked at the remaining Governor, Miss Burke. She was seventy-five, a former Headmistress of Ashcombe reduced to genteel poverty by bad investments and her senile mother's long illness. Her mother was still alive in a private nursing home. The state would bear the cost of her upkeep only when her capital was exhausted, a time rapidly approaching. Meanwhile Miss Burke lived in rented rooms (her mother's house had been sold years before to pay the nursing home) on the pension provided by the Governors. She attended every Governors' Meeting assiduously and paid the greatest attention to the proceedings, though she found concentration difficult, because Guy Robinson padded her travel expenses and topped up her pension out of his own pocket. She suspected this and was embarrassingly deferential to him. Anxiety, illness and age had sapped her and the other Governors courteously discounted her as a poor old maid in the Chairman's pocket.

"As you see, the Brigadier is minuting this meeting," said Robinson. "It would make for awkwardness all round if we had the Bursar with us today."

"Quite so," said Miss Burke. "Hear, hear."

"I have here copies of Miss Noakes's report on her conversations with Miss Parker yesterday and this morning," continued the Chairman, passing them round. "As you see, Miss Parker does not deny that she was in the cupboard. She has given no explanation of the incident at all. She refuses to get in touch with her Union and has appointed Nicholas Embrey, part-time Art teacher, to accompany her on her appearance before us."

The Brigadier grunted. "That's not very satisfactory. Just an Art teacher chappie. What sort of protection will that give her? And how does it leave us, legally?"

"Legally we're all right. We're not yet instituting dismissal proceedings – just inquiring into a complaint, and she has quite explicitly waived her right to union representation."

"Is that Nicholas Embrey the water-colourist?" said the Parent Governor. "If it is, he's quite well known. I don't think part-time Art teacher exactly describes him."

"If there are no other observations you'd like to make on Miss Noakes's report . . ." said the Chairman. "Well, Brigadier, perhaps you'd care to . . ."

"Yes," said the Brigadier. "The Chairman asked me to do a recce of the terrain. Take a look at the famous cupboard – and the air vent. The cupboard is actually a very small windowless room, quite large enough to contain two people comfortably with the door shut. The air vent is six inches by eight of thick wire netting, placed twelve feet off the ground in the corner of the Geography Room."

He delivered this line without emphasis. The Parent Governor was the first to respond.

"Hell's teeth," he said. "It sounds as if we've got trouble."

"Trouble? Why?" said the Bishop, prepared to coat the trouble in well-intentioned platitude as soon as he understood its nature.

"I think that what our Parent Governor means is that twelve feet is a long way from the ground for Miss Bridge to be hanging her relief maps," said the Chairman.

"Of the United States of America," said Miss Burke, eager to display her grasp of detail.

"You fear she was taking a risk? Are the teachers not insured for hanging maps?" asked the Bishop.

"Just that if she was looking into an air vent twelve feet up it seems as if she might have been spying," said the Chairman.

"And if she was spying, then why?" said the Brigadier. "Did she suspect something was going on between the Headmaster and Miss Parker?"

There was a general murmur of disquiet.

"Perhaps it was not quite twelve feet," said the Bishop. "Eight feet – standing on a chair – that would be much more explicable."

"I measured," said the Brigadier.

Pause.

"Miss Parker's very young to be a Head of Department," said Miss Burke. "Judging from her records, she's an excellent teacher, but still, she's very young. She must be exceptionally dedicated."

Another pause. Miss Burke seldom initiated points, so she had a receptive audience, but they didn't follow her train of thought.

"And so . . ." prompted the Chairman.

"She's young, she's hardworking, her behaviour is exemplary in every respect. Why should she suddenly take her clothes off in the stationery cupboard? It doesn't make sense. There must have been something between them before that incident, it stands to reason."

Pause.

"Shall we ask Miss Bridge to come in?" said the Chairman. "Brigadier, would you be so kind."

The Brigadier opened the door and signalled to Heather Noakes who was waiting in the corridor. She went to fetch Nora Bridge.

All three participants were in different rooms: Nicholas, sitting with Charlotte in a small coaching room, listened to Nora's footsteps echoing on the tiled corridor outside. Charlotte was lost in her thoughts, didn't hear. The window was open and the breeze wafted practice noise from the music block.

"Charlotte . . ." he said gently. "Charlotte . . . I wish you'd tell me what actually happened. How can I help you if I don't know?"

"I was a fool," she said. "I made a gigantic massive awful fool of myself." She was dressed neatly, in a navy blue dress with a white collar and navy patent leather shoes. Her face was even paler than usual, her hair brushed straight back from her forehead and held by two combs.

"Everyone does from time to time. Some day I'll tell you about my worst moments."

She smiled abstractedly. "I don't want to talk about the Headmaster."

"In a few minutes, you'll have to. How long were you in the cupboard?"

"I don't know. Five minutes? Ten?"

"Did Craig Stewart kiss you?"

"Yes."

"Had you encouraged him, before he kissed you? Were you flirting?"

"No. I was talking about the new storage arrangements for the English Department books."

"So you were talking about books with no come-on signals and he kissed you?"

"Yes."

"Then what?"

"He stroked me."

"Did you stroke him back?"

"The parts I could reach. Then I took my dress off."

"Why?"

"I was enjoying it. I thought . . . we were going to . . ." She clasped her fingers between her knees. "He didn't even take off his jacket." She looked at him anxiously. "Are you laughing?"

Nicholas shook his head. "Far from it."

"So then I was angry because I realised what a fool I was being, and I put my dress on again. He went off in a temper. Nicholas, why was I so stupid?" She shook her head in disbelief. "Any teenager could have seen he was just . . . just . . ."

"The man's an oaf," said Nicholas.

Charlotte dabbed at her eyes with a handkerchief. Tears trickled down her face, meandering among the freckles. "That's not the worst," she said, looking less childlike. "Afterwards, when I heard about Sophie Preston, I thought of talking to the Headmaster, trying to persuade him to let her stay. But I didn't do anything, just because I was embarrassed to face him."

"That's understandable."

Footsteps outside, two women in one direction, one man returning. "The Headmaster's going in," said Nicholas. "All set to lie through his teeth."

"What do you think he'll say?"

"Probably that you threw yourself at him. It depends how much Nora Bridge saw and heard, of course. Or how much she has told the Governors."

"How do you mean?"

"She could decide to blame it all on you. That way she can, with a little judicious blackmail on the side, sweep through to the Headship of the Humanities Department."

"I still think the idea of a Humanities Department is fundamentally unsound," said Charlotte. "For one thing . . ."

"Don't go wandering off on educational theory. Not now."

"I suppose you're right," said Charlotte. "Ian will blame it on me. And it'll be partly true."

"Half-truths are the greatest lies."

"What on earth possessed Nora to spy on us?" said Charlotte. "When I spoke to Heather this morning she was very tight-lipped on the details. She wouldn't even have told me it was Nora who complained if I hadn't already guessed."

Nicholas shrugged.

"Nora Bridge doesn't need a reason to spy."

They were silent. The first eight bars of a Chopin *Etude* were played through and through and through again by a pianist with a light touch. The notes floated over the growlings of a tuba.

"I'm going to resign," said Charlotte.

"So you keep telling me. What will you do? Look for another teaching job?"

"Not for a while. I'll sell the house, go to London, see my mother and Liam, look about me."

"Why see your mother now?"

"It's the right time." She sounded absolutely certain of herself.

"You're much less shaky today," Nicholas observed.

"I didn't sleep much. I worked things out. I decided to make a break, go back to where I went wrong and start again. I shouldn't have escaped back into schools. I want to see the world."

The door opened. "They're ready for you, Miss Parker," said Heather Noakes.

The Chairman sat on one side of the dining table, flanked by the Governors, Charlotte at the other, facing the window. Nicholas sat a little behind her, arms folded, legs crossed. He was the most relaxed person in the room. The Governors had a ruffled air, as if they had been arguing. The Chairman's usually pleasant expression was now decidedly grim but he made an effort to smile, though not broadly, when he first addressed Charlotte.

"Good afternoon, Miss Parker," said Guy Robinson. He was struck by her slenderness and fragility. She was not unlike Charlotte Rampling but she moved him not to lust but to sympathy. "This is an unfortunate business."

Charlotte nodded.

"I believe Miss Noakes has already told you that we received a letter complaining about an incident in the stationery cupboard."

Charlotte nodded.

"We are inquiring into that incident."

Charlotte nodded again. She cleared her throat nervously. The simplicity of her earlier vision – I shall resign, leave Ashcombe, start a new life – was narrowed to the discomfort and guilt of facing these people who knew things about her she would never have wished anyone to know. Sexual desire now seemed shameful and inexplicable. She twisted her fingers together and looked at the row of faces. The Bishop, placid, well-meaning; disorganised Miss Burke; attentive Brigadier; impressive Robinson; finger-tapping Parent Governor.

"Have you anything you'd like to say?" the Chairman went on.

"No," said Charlotte, taking an envelope from her pocket and pushing it across the table to him. "I've brought my resignation with me."

The Governors stirred uneasily.

"Mr Chairman," said Miss Burke unexpectedly, "may I ask a few questions?"

"By all means."

"How old are you, Miss Parker?"

"I'm twenty-seven."

"The Headmistress thought very highly of you." She tapped the papers in front of her. "Your records are most creditable."

"Thank you," said Charlotte, relaxing a little. Miss Burke, old as she was, spoke in familiar tones.

"Why are you resigning?"

"Because I couldn't stay. Not after this. The whole school will know – it would be impossible for the Headmaster."

"Do you have the Headmaster's interests at heart, then?"

"Oh, no," said Charlotte. "The school's. And it would be embarrassing for me, naturally." Her voice sounded stilted and priggish in her own ears. She shifted in her upright chair and glanced at Nicholas. He smiled reassuringly. She noticed his clothes: he had made an effort for this occasion, and although he could never look other than angular and unhealthy, he had eliminated all traces of the shabby and down-at-heel.

"Have you thought about a reference?" asked Miss Burke.

"It doesn't matter. I'm not going on teaching."

There was a pause. Charlotte looked at the photographs

of teams and choirs ranked on the panelled walls, smelt the floor polish. Every inch a school room. Of all of them, only she and Miss Burke belonged there. The rest, Nicholas included, looked as if their real life was a strong current elsewhere and they had paused in a backwater for a short time to sort out the small fry's affairs.

"Don't make any rash decisions," said Miss Burke.

Nicholas stirred. "I'd like to make some points, Mr Chairman. Charlotte, why did you go into that cupboard?"

"To talk about the structural alterations necessary."

"And what happened?"

She blushed painfully, glanced at the Governors, shook her head.

"Answer, Charlotte."

"The Headmaster kissed me."

"Was the door shut?"

"Yes. The Headmaster shut it behind us."

"Was there anyone about?"

"Not as far as I knew. We hadn't heard anyone and the Working Corridor seemed deserted."

"So the Headmaster kissed you. What did you do?"

"I let him."

"Why?"

"I don't think this is relevant, Mr Chairman," protested Charlotte. Robinson raised one eyebrow at Nicholas.

"It's important for the Governors to understand, Charlotte," said Nicholas. "You may leave but the school will have to live with the Headmaster and Nora Bridge. The Governors need to know who they're dealing with. Why did you let the Headmaster kiss you?"

Charlotte twisted her fingers. "I was enjoying it," she said.

"Would you say you were very experienced with men?"

"Oh no. Not at all. But you know all this, Nicholas." She was agitated.

"And when this was happening, did you think anyone could see you? Girls, for instance?"

"Of course not. It was a week before the beginning of term."

"Staff, then?"

"No. I thought we were quite alone."

"You didn't imagine that anyone could see?" persisted Nicholas.

"No," said Charlotte. "The only way to see into the cupboard is through the air vents. They're right up against the ceiling. You couldn't even reach them if you stood on a chair. And who would want to?"

"What distance would you say the air vent was from the floor?"

"About double my height. Eleven feet, I'd say." Charlotte was relaxing more and more.

"Twelve feet," said the Brigadier.

"Twelve feet, two inches," said Nicholas. "I measured."

"I'm not sure I see your position on this, Mr – er – Embrey," said the Parent Governor.

"I wish I'd seen Miss Bridge's position at the air vent," said Nicholas.

"Miss Bridge was preparing a display of relief maps," said the Bishop. The other Governors looked away; the Brigadier smiled.

"Miss Parker, the Headmaster is married," said Nicholas. "Didn't it surprise you when he . . ."

"Not really," said Charlotte. "He didn't seem interested in his wife, and she told me that he had wanted to leave her before and she had blackmailed him into staying. Because of the job here."

"Did you get the impression that he was fond of his wife? Or that she was fond of him?"

"I really don't think –" began the Bishop, but the Chairman interrupted him.

"Let Miss Parker answer, Bishop."

"I didn't think they liked each other, or loved each other," said Charlotte. "When she talked about the other woman and keeping Ian with her, she was gloating as if she'd won a contest. He always treated her with contempt."

"Nevertheless," began the Bishop. "The family . . ."

The Chairman picked up several sheets of paper and tapped them into neatness on the table.

"Is there anything else?" he asked, collecting eyes. None of the Governors spoke.

"If we were to accept your resignation, Miss Parker, when would you be prepared to leave?"

"Straight away," said Charlotte. "Miss Noakes told me that my predecessor could take over for the rest of the term, to give the Headmaster time to advertise and appoint."

"Your predecessor?"

"Mrs Munroe. She left to have a baby. She knows the girls and the routine; she only lives up the road."

"Ah," said the Chairman, looking happier. "If you would leave us now, Miss Parker, Mr Embrey, we'll deliberate and let you know. Would you wait, please?"

The door closed behind them. The Brigadier whistled through his teeth. "Poor Miss Parker," he said.

"A charming girl," said the Bishop. "Pity she has to go."

"We're lucky she's resigned," said Miss Burke. "I'm not at all convinced the fault was on her side."

"If there was any justice we'd sack Miss Bridge," said the Brigadier. "Spying, hypocritical, self-dramatising —"

"She felt she was acting in the best interest of the school," said the Bishop.

"In a pig's eye," said the Parent Governor.

"Should we try to establish the facts?" said the Chairman. "We didn't ask Miss Parker exactly what happened in the cupboard. According to the Headmaster, she closed the door, kissed him, took off her dress, and assaulted him while he continued a disquisition on structural walls. Should we ask her for more details?"

"Surely not," said the Brigadier. "She's embarrassed, she feels her position here is untenable, she wants to resign. Why should we embarrass her further?"

"I'd like to know whether the Headmaster was telling the truth," said the Parent Governor. There was an awkward silence. The Chairman tapped his papers.

"We all have our views about that, surely, but is it a point we wish to pursue?"

"I don't think the girl should suffer more than she has

to," said Miss Burke. "What about salary? And a reference? What'll be the official story?"

"Salary till the end of term, the reference her service warrants, leaving for family reasons?" suggested the Chairman.

"Hear, hear," said Miss Burke.

"Seconded," said the Brigadier. The Parent Governor nodded and the Bishop gave his assenting wave.

"Thanks to Mr Embrey for his able assistance?"

More nods.

"I'll have a chat with the Headmaster," said the Chairman, more than a little grimly. "Make sure he doesn't do what he said he didn't do, again, and particularly not with the girls."

"No chance of that, in my view," said the Brigadier. "Too cautious for that."

"I hope you're right," said the Parent Governor.

"Convinced of it," said the Brigadier. "The chap's a show-off, Miss Parker misunderstood, Miss Bridge happened to be on a step-ladder . . ."

"Hanging relief maps," chorused the Parent Governor and the Chairman.

"Should we thank Miss Bridge?" asked the Chairman.

"For services to espionage?" said the Brigadier.

"Oh, come," said the Bishop. "You're being harsh. Who knows the motives that impel weak mortals? Which of us can honestly say . . ."

"I can honestly say that I've never squinted through an air vent to spy on two people who had every reason to believe that they were alone," said the Brigadier.

Late that evening, Charlotte was packing books into cardboard boxes. Nicholas lay on the sofa watching her and drinking wine. Her living-room already looked uninhabited: the ornaments and pictures were packed away, the desk cleared of paper and pens, the plants neatly assembled in a corner. She was flushed with excitement and wine, full of schemes, uncertain. She kept appealing to Nicholas for support or agreement. Most of the time, he just grunted.

"It was kind of them to pay me till the end of term. Considering."

"Considering you're doing the decent thing, it was the least they could do."

"And I got a reference. So if my other ideas don't work out, then I can always go back to teaching."

"What other ideas?"

"I've got enough money to live in London for six months, not counting any profit from the sale of the house. That should be long enough to find out what I want to do. What's the matter, Nicholas?"

Nicholas was grimacing, a hand over his eyes. "A babe in the woods," he said. "An innocent piece of cannon fodder for the big bad wolves."

"Come on, Nicholas, I'm not that naive."

"Yes, you are."

"I'm twenty-seven years old."

"No, you're not. You're twenty-seven take away the lost years with your father. That leaves you . . ."

"About nineteen."

"And you're nice with it. Take away four years for being nice. That makes you the same age as Sophie Preston and we agreed she was too young."

Charlotte perched on the sofa, pushing her legs to the back. "That's the only thing I regret, leaving the girls, especially the examination candidates. I do hope Sally Munroe reassures them enough. I'm sorry I disappointed Heather Noakes, as well."

"School's behind you now, Charlotte."

"So this is my leaving party." She lifted her glass in a toast. "To the future."

"Heaven protect all innocents," said Nicholas.

"I think I'd better stop drinking this," said Charlotte, unsteadily replacing her glass on the table. She leant against the back of the sofa, contact with Nicholas's long shins reassuring her. "Do you mind if I ask you a question?"

"Ask away."

"It's a little . . . embarrassing." She checked his face anxiously, but he remained amiable and encouraging. "I wondered . . . it occurred to me . . . Nicholas, do you desire me?"

His large, spatulate hands gripped hers. "Look at me, Charlotte." Slowly, she turned her head, afraid to meet his eyes. Their expression was unchanged. "You're beautiful."

"That means you don't want me. Why?"

"Imagine I made love to you. It would spoil us, wouldn't it?"

"What do you mean?"

"What would you feel for me? You trust me now. Would you then?"

Charlotte thought about it. "I feel close to you. I thought it might make us closer."

"If you have to think about it, sex wouldn't make us anything." He squeezed her hands. His touch was not exciting to her, but disturbing: threatening too. She was more afraid of his affection than of Ian's crass lust. "I'm nearly thirty years older than you are."

"That doesn't always . . ."

"Sh – sh," he said, putting his fingers to her lips. "Trust me."

"I do."

"Trust me not to make love to you."

"But . . ."

"Trust me."

The World

Chapter Eight

"It's all right, Suki. You can say 'I told you so'. You'd better, before you bite your tongue off."

Suki shifted nine-month-old Hector from one freckled breast to the other. "I wasn't thinking it," she said virtuously. "I'm sorry you lost your job, that's all. Ouch, Hector, that hurt."

"It's kind of you to have me."

"Stay as long as you like, I need the company."

They were sitting at the kitchen table drinking herb tea. "I thought Hector was weaned," said Charlotte.

"He likes the breast occasionally. In parts of France the women breast-feed children of three and four, did you know that?"

"I'm not sure I wanted to."

Charlotte had spent a week clearing out her house in Ashcombe and arranging for her furniture to go into storage. She stayed more or less indoors for most of the time. Various people rang her up but she didn't answer the telephone. Paula Madders and Heather sent her goodwill messages through Nicholas. "Paula says the staff-room's in an uproar," he reported one evening. "The general opinion seems to be that Nora has Gone Too Far. Oh, and Paula said to be sure to tell you that you've solved one problem, at least."

"What's that?"

"When the Headmaster retires, there'll be no doubt which room is particularly associated with him. To hang his portrait in."

Charlotte laughed unaffectedly at that. She felt quite free from the school, as if she had stepped out of a skin recently outgrown. Even when she packed her suitcases into the blue Golf and locked the front door of her house, possibly for the last time, she felt only relief. Nicholas was the one person she would miss, and Nicholas transcended Ashcombe.

"Can I use the phone?" said Charlotte, clearing their cups away, feeling slightly sick with apprehension.

"Of course. Anyone special?"

"Not Ian, if that's what you mean. I'm going to ring my mother."

At first Tessy had found the loss of Charlotte painful. She felt injured at a primitive level. For nearly a year she made plans to get her back, or at least to see her, but Roddy, Tessy's second husband, was at a crucial stage in his bid for a ministerial post and adverse publicity would have harmed him. In the event he didn't get the job anyway.

Over the years Tessy had stopped grieving for her daughter, had even stopped thinking about her. She made the right overtures when Charlotte was eighteen, mostly for Liam's sake (she wondered uneasily if he had ever forgiven her for what happened to Charlotte), but was almost relieved when the child wouldn't see her. She still thought of her as a child, even though the aunts tried to show her photographs of undergraduate Charlotte, teacher Charlotte, Head of Department Charlotte.

She was lying in the bath when Charlotte rang. She heard the telephone, the maid answering.

"A call for you, madam."

"Who is it?"

"Charlotte Parker," said the maid. She was new, she didn't even know Liam, otherwise the name "Parker" might have given her a clue. Tessy stopped tracing patterns in the scented bubbles on her breasts. Her heart beat unpleasantly faster. She heaved herself out of the sunken bath, wrapped herself in a vast, thick lilac towel, and brushed her way through the opulent carpet to the telephone in her bedroom. She felt guilt and the beginnings of irritation.

"Hello? Charlotte?" she said. There was silence: the line pinged and sighed.

"Tessy?" said Charlotte. She couldn't bring herself to say

"Mummy": "Mother" was too Victorian: "Mrs Lambert" was out of the question.

"Charlotte! Darling, darling, it's you!" said Tessy. "This is marvellous, imagine hearing your voice, I'm so glad! So, so glad! When are you coming to see me?"

Charlotte recognised the tone of voice. Just so had her mother spoken to unwelcome acquaintances and relatives. "I'm staying in London," she said, "near the Finchley Road. I'm staying with Suki."

"Suki?"

"The red-haired girl who lived near us in Norham Gardens. She's married now."

"Oh, how lovely," said Tessy at random. "But why are you in London, littlest? Surely it's not holiday time?"

"I got the sack," said Charlotte.

"Any particular reason?" said Tessy. In some ways she was still thoroughly Anglo-Irish, a true granddaughter of Mad Jack. She saw getting the sack as at least exciting, probably meritorious, and the gateway to a brighter future.

"I'll explain when we meet," said Charlotte.

"Come to lunch," said Tessy. "You must." She could do no less, though she already had a lunch date.

"Are you putting anyone off for me?"

"Only Liam's wife. Unless – would you like to meet her?"

"Not yet. I haven't seen Liam yet, I'd rather wait to get to know his wife. What's she like?"

"Pretty, pleasant, deadly dull. He seems to like her. They have two small children, did you know that?"

"Mmm."

"Roddy won't be here for lunch, but you must meet him soon."

"What's he like?" Charlotte remembered her mother as recklessly indiscreet and wanted to confirm that this was not just a childhood illusion.

"Very respectable, very kind. We have to be absolutely *sweet* to Roddy, he's put up with so much, poor lamb. What with me being so hopeless at housekeeping and spending so much on clothes."

Charlotte felt bewildered. Tessy was talking as if the long parting had not occurred, as if they were old friends. She herself was so moved at hearing her mother's voice that she could hardly keep the banalities in play.

"Come early. Come at twelve, then we can have a lovely talk." It was ten o'clock, Charlotte knew. Two hours to wait: too much to hope for that she could have gone straight away to see her mother. Perhaps it *was* too much to hope for. After all, she had waited nine years, had not wanted to see her mother for nine years. But before that . . . and after all, Roddy was only very respectable, very kind. Could her mother not have stuck it out with her father?

"I must dash, littlest, you caught me in the bath and I'm dripping all over the carpet."

"Till twelve, then."

As soon as she heard Charlotte replace the receiver after her telephone call to Tessy, Suki burst in. "You've spoken to her! At last! What was it like?"

"I don't know. I'm going to lunch with her at twelve. I feel – odd."

"Hardly surprising, is it? Here – take Hector a moment." Charlotte grasped the baby thrust into her arms. He was looking as puzzled as she felt, his mouth opening and closing in tiny puffing motions like a natural mud spring. Suki grabbed a pile of leaflets and rushed out of the house, after her next-door neighbour's retreating figure. "Thank goodness," she said returning, "it's a marvellous opportunity. Bronwen from next door promised she'd distribute the Save the Whale stickers. She's opening a fête in the country this weekend."

"Why is she opening the fête? Is she famous?"

"Semi-famous. She's on television, the detective's girl-friend in the new ITV cops and robbers. She'll always help out with animal causes, just doesn't like people."

She reclaimed Hector from Charlotte who was sorry to lose him. She liked his trusting innocence and the sudden lurches he made with his hands.

"Let's have some herb tea and you can tell me about

your mother," said Suki. "I'd like to hear every word. Unless you don't want to, of course."

Charlotte recounted what she could remember of the conversation. Suki looked troubled, said nothing. Probably thinks we were very cold to each other, thought Charlotte. Perhaps we were.

"Will you be seeing Liam, then?" asked Suki. "Because if so, ask him here. I always had a crush on him. Go on, ring him now, you might as well."

"No," said Charlotte. She was shaken enough by talking to her mother. Despite Suki's warmth, she longed for Nicholas, to laugh with her and put things into proportion. London was a vast, busy, preoccupied place. Soon she would leave Suki's: as yet she had nowhere to live, no job, and not even an idea as to what job she would like to do. It was just past eleven: at Ashcombe, she would have been drinking coffee, eating a currant bun and chatting to Paula Madders.

Tessy's flat was in Eaton Place. Charlotte pressed the intercom buzzer. "That must be you, darling! I saw you getting out of the taxi! Come up, come up! First floor, I can't wait!" squawked the intercom, and the heavy wrought-iron and glass door swung open.

The hall carpet was thick Wilton, the walls cream, the hall table a good quality reproduction. Charlotte started up the stairs. If she, not Liam, had gone with her mother, she would have spent part of her adolescence here. She couldn't imagine what it would have been like.

"Charlotte," said Tessy, opening the door. "My God, you've grown up, come in, let me see you." Charlotte let herself be kissed. She closed her eyes and reached back into memory for dreams of this moment, but they were elusive. Tessy smelt just the same. Her face was more set, more varnished: age or her hairdresser had tipped her hair with silver, but most of it was still as dark, as springy as Charlotte's. She was recognisably the same person, but unfamiliar.

The drawing-room of the flat was over thirty feet long,

thickly carpeted in a pale green one shade lighter than the walls. The curtains were pale cream, the pictures mostly eighteenth-century oils of horses and dogs, with over the mantelpiece a huge portrait of Mad Jack Hesketh, the aunts' father, Tessy's grandfather. He had inherited a fortune from an Australian aunt and bought Devlin's Castle with it. He later claimed to have won the house in a poker game, but he was a natural liar, one of those for whom truth is a tiresome interruption of the visions inside his head. He had been indifferent to his wife and three of his four daughters, but he loved Theodosia, Tessy's mother.

"Darling, sit down, have a drink. What would you like?"

Charlotte looked at the tray of decanters, bottles, glasses. "White wine, please," she said, and the association with Nicholas was comforting. Her mother was more strange than a stranger. It had been too long.

"I can't believe it. You must be quite twenty-four," said Tessy. "Are you coming to London for good? We must . . ."

"I'm twenty-seven."

"Oh surely not? As old as that?" trilled Tessy, pouring the largest gin Charlotte had ever seen with a hand that shook a little. "We must find you somewhere to live. Unless you'd like to come here? Roddy and I would love to have you."

"I wish you'd seen my house in Ashcombe," said Charlotte. "It only had two bedrooms but it had a spectacular view."

"Darling, how splendid, setting is so important for a house, Roddy and I are very lucky down in Wiltshire, you absolutely must come and stay –"

"I enjoyed working at the school. I did well, actually, to be Head of Department so young –"

"You are clever, you always were a clever girl and you did work so hard, all your reports said so –"

"Did you read my reports? I thought they were sent to my father."

"After I moved out they were – I didn't read them then – I meant when you were a little girl. And you must have been clever to go to Oxford, it's getting more and more difficult."

Even the vision, suddenly conjured up, of Tessy interested enough to read Charlotte's reports even though she was being lucky in Wiltshire with Roddy, flickered and died.

They went in to lunch, Tessy still chattering. Charlotte found it a struggle to maintain her composure. Under her acceptable answers surged all the things Tessy was refusing to hear.

"It's been so long, Charlotte. Have some salmon, real Blackwater salmon – the Pritchetts brought it over yesterday. I've missed you terribly, littlest. Salmon was your favourite, wasn't it?"

"It has been a long time." No, it was Liam who liked salmon. How could you leave me with my father? You knew him, what he was like, how bitter he would be, you must have known.

"Did you think of me? I thought of you, often, when you were a little girl."

Yes, I thought of you. All the time. Particularly when I was confused and miserable and my head ached so much that I couldn't read any more. I used to think about you then.

One of her most frequent fantasies started with a letter in her mother's handwriting. "Dear little Charlotte," said the letter, "I'm sorry to have to tell you that your father was killed very peacefully earlier today. I would like you to pack all the things you want to bring with you and get into the taxi that will be at the door in two hours' time. It will take you to the London train and Liam and I will meet you in Paddington."

Her favourite part of this fantasy was the train journey. She imagined herself combing her hair and replaiting it, taking her case down from the rack, leaning out as the train drew into Paddington and seeing her mother and Liam waiting. As the years passed they did not change. Even though she saw photographs and the aunts kept telling her how Liam had grown and what Tessy had done to her hair, the figures in her vision remained the same, until when she was sixteen she stopped wanting to see them.

"Did you think of me?"

"Oh yes, I did. No mayonnaise, thank you."

"Have you a young man in tow? No? Roddy knows masses of up-and-coming young Conservatives. Not all of them are as dull as that suggests. Thank you, Hilda" (to the maid), "that'll do. We'll look after ourselves now."

The door shut after the maid with a solid, moneyed click. The dining-room was dark, wood panelled and red velvet curtained. The mahogany table could have accommodated any amount of rising young Conservatives. Charlotte pushed flakes of salmon about her plate. Her mouth was dry. I hated him, she wanted to say. I hated my father, and between you I was nearly crippled. How dare you pretend it hasn't happened?

"Darling you are quite beautiful, have you ever tried growing your hair a little longer – you could tousle it up and look ethereal, less like a woman tennis player who lives under the shower . . . and perhaps less emphasis on the white huntress in your clothes . . . the tabs and buttons on that dress make me absolutely quake. Tell me how you got the sack."

"I was seen kissing the Headmaster in the stationery cupboard."

Tessy laughed. She had a charming laugh, spontaneous and surprisingly deep. "Was it fun?" she said. "What does he look like?"

Charlotte caught her eye. Against her will, against her determination to bring Tessy to a sense of her own iniquity, she began to laugh too. After all, it was absurd.

"And why the stationery cupboard?"

"Why not?"

"Why not indeed," admitted Tessy, a reminiscent gleam flitting across her face. "But, littlest, *can* they sack you for that? Roddy has a very clever lawyer, queer as a zooful of coots but sweet. Would you like him to look into it?"

At half-past three Tessy had to leave for a hair appointment.

"Best love, littlest. See you very, very soon," she said, and Charlotte closed the taxi door on her and watched the taxi pull away into the traffic. She had the beginning of a headache from all the white wine, and she was burdened with five carrier-bags of clothes Tessy had insisted on giving her. "Much too young for me – I've simply never worn them – we're *exactly* the same size, isn't that clever of us?"

"Is that really all she said?" Suki couldn't believe Charlotte's description of the reunion. "She didn't even mention taking Liam and leaving you?"

"Not a word."

Once again, Charlotte and Suki were sitting at the kitchen table. It was late evening and they were stringing beans.

"I don't understand your family, Charlotte."

Charlotte, on the whole, was beginning to think she did. Her parents were gradually coming into focus for her as if she was a camera pulling away from close-up. Tessy was frivolous and unintellectual and needed constant attention: Geoffrey was self-absorbed and cold and hadn't provided it. Tessy had found her security, emotionally and socially, and now wouldn't revisit long-forgotten and discreditable episodes.

Charlotte was surprised by her own lack of feeling. Her relationship with Tessy, she now saw, had died long ago, a year or two after Tessy left. After that, Charlotte had made a fantasy of her mother. She had waited for the return of her mother like the devotee of a cargo cult.

"She gave me some lovely clothes," she said. "And she is funny. She makes me laugh. She enjoys herself so much."

"She's not like a mother at all," said Suki.

"Not like your mother, certainly."

They peeled beans in disagreeing but companionable silence. Eventually Charlotte started to laugh.

"What is it?"

"Do you know what I think is the most exciting thing

167

– and probably the most important, as well – that's happened to me in the last two months?"

"The stationery cupboard drama?"

"Guess again."

"Getting the sack?"

"No."

"Making friends with Nicholas?"

"That's not what I was thinking about, but I see what you mean."

"I give up," said Suki.

"Being groped by that gorgeous Pole. You remember, the drunk on the ship."

"Why was that so important?"

"Because I enjoyed it so much."

"Charlotte? Charlotte?" shouted Henrietta into the telephone. "Is that you?"

"Yes," said Charlotte. "I can hear you, Henrietta."

"Oh, poor doaty, poor lamb!" shouted Henrietta.

"I can HEAR you," protested Charlotte. She was in the midst of a feminist anti-Cruise work party.

"Take the call in my bedroom," suggested Suki.

Charlotte did. She lay on the vast bed with its Early American patchwork cover. "It's me again, Henrietta, I'm alone now."

"God bless the innocent," shouted Victoria. "Imagine the bad luck of it, to be caught when you only loved him the once."

"I don't think . . ." began Charlotte, then stopped as she heard a scuffle on the other end of the line. A panting but triumphant Henrietta resumed the conversation.

"I wrote to Liam about you losing your job. And I gave him your telephone number. It's past time you saw Liam again. He's a man, he can help. He can find you a job, I'm sure. I know you'll think I'm interfering but it's all for the best."

"I saw Tessy for lunch today," said Charlotte. She could not resist the temptation to show Henrietta that she was making decisions for herself, that she would have got round to Liam on her own account.

There was no reply for several seconds. Then – "About time too," said Henrietta. "How is she?"

"Well. She looked very pretty," said Charlotte.

"Oh, yes," said Henrietta. "Looks Tessy has, though we'd better not ask what she's done to keep them. The surgeon's knife, you know."

"A face lift?"

"At least," said Henrietta darkly. "Victoria wants to speak to you now."

"Hello, hello poor Charlotte, hello."

"Hello, Victoria."

"I feel for you, poor lamb. Do you love him very much? Are you seeing him still? Does he look like Clark Gable?"

"Not at all like Clark Gable."

"Good," said Victoria. "A most unappetising man, I always thought. Is the Headmaster the love of your life, Charlotte?"

"Let's not discuss it on the telephone. Will I be seeing you soon?" She said this, thinking she knew the answer, as a palliative and a put-off. The aunts were generally Ireland-bound from September to Christmas. But Victoria replied, "We'll be at the Reduced Gentlefolk's next month. See you then. Meanwhile, Charlotte, remember that I understand. The heart has its secrets."

Next morning, Charlotte had time to think. Suki and Hector had gone to the Post Office with a bagful of letters: Charlotte was taking advantage of Suki's absence to clean the kitchen. She was wearing an old pair of shrunken running shorts and a torn sweatshirt. Her flesh was clearly visible in places beneath the shirt though her breasts were covered. She was listening to Terry Wogan on the radio and singing along to the records when she knew the words.

Her meeting with Tessy had left her aimless; so much feeling, so long familiar, had drained away. She scraped grease from under the cooker with unnecessary precision. Terry Wogan, still burbling on above her head, seemed all she had left of her previous life in Ashcombe. She had drunk her coffee, eaten her toast, to Terry's mellifluous and familiar Irish intonation before driving to school, parking in her usual corner, going up the stone stairs to her classroom and taking register.

She sat back on her heels, stared at the cooker without seeing it. Living with Suki would have its usual quota of inconveniences and adjustments: that wasn't the trouble. The trouble was the days stretching ahead with no point or purpose. Perhaps she had been foolish enough to believe that seeing her mother and Liam would be a step forward, a progression that would set her free to live her own life. If so, so far, no good. She shrunk altogether from a meeting with Liam. While she could look forward to that, at least . . .

With an effort she concentrated on the kitchen. An hour later the radio was leaving Wogan for Young. End of second lesson, thought Charlotte. Monday. Lower Sixth, *Hamlet*. She must do something constructive, and preferably before Suki came back, because otherwise she would be pressed into service for a fresh batch of envelopes.

She squeezed herself into the tiny spare room, dressed neatly in case the employment agency had a job she could apply for, made her bed (Suki disapproved of duvets – most uncharacteristic, thought Charlotte, struggling with sheets and blankets), and rang up Sophie Preston. She didn't expect an answer: the child should be at her tutorial college: but she could leave a message.

"Hello?" said a querulous, sleepy voice.

"Sophie. This is Miss Parker."

"Who?"

"Charlotte Parker. The teacher from Ashcombe."

"Oh! Right! Wow! Hello!"

"I'll take you for lunch, if you're free."

"Yes! Well, I mean, I should be at college really but I haven't got it together yet."

"I'll pick you up at one o'clock."

Sophie was a mess. Her hair was unwashed and only half-combed with a matted tangle at the back, her Indian cotton wraparound skirt only just met over her bulging stomach, and at first Charlotte was convinced she was pregnant. She touched on the topic when they had settled in their rustic-look chairs at the Italian restaurant round the corner from Sophie's flat.

"Gosh, no," said Sophie. "I'd like the lasagne please with a side salad. Salad is supposed to be slimming, isn't it? Well of course I'm not pregnant, Miss Parker, how could I be?"

"How's the tutorial college?"

"All right, I suppose. Most of the students are Arabs or Africans. I don't understand the teachers very well, they go so fast, and all the syllabuses are different. What I really want to do is lose weight. I worked it out, if I sleep until after lunch then I won't eat lunch, and that's bound to help."

"But then you miss your morning's lessons."

"Yes, well, I can always catch up."

"Where are your parents, Sophie?"

"They're back in Strasbourg, you know, Daddy's an MEP. They've been so generous, they're paying for the flat and I have masses of pocket money. Absolutely masses. I can buy plenty of food and drink for the other girls. They're really sweet. Two of them. They're older than me but they treat me just like one of themselves. Oh, and Miranda Chalker lives just round the corner. I asked her in for coffee one night but she didn't have time, she was meeting a friend. Maybe she thought it was a bit of cheek, me asking her, because after all I'm only Upper Five and she was Upper Six, except that she isn't now because she's at a college of music. Why are you here, Miss Parker? Are you ill?"

"No, Sophie, I had to leave Ashcombe. Family reasons."

"Oh, I'm sorry." Sophie tried to look adult and understanding. Then she brightened as the next thought struck her. "Are you living in London, then?"

"Yes, probably."

"Oh, good! Fantastic! Oh, I am pleased." She looked it. She stopped frowning, gnawing at her fingers. "Could you – I mean, it is a bit much to ask, but could you help me with the English? I know I should have passed both of them, I just know it. I learnt the lit. books backwards."

"Of course I'll help."

"And would you mind if I had some chocolate cake, after the lasagne? Cake's really good, here."

Next morning, Charlotte was once again cleaning the kitchen and listening to Terry Wogan, wearing the same pair of running shorts and an even more dilapidated sweat-shirt. She felt untrammelled and sexually powerful in those clothes, as if they expressed a physicality of which she was capable but no one had yet required from her.

The doorbell rang.

She opened the front door casually, expecting a visitor for Suki.

A man stood on the doorstep. She knew at once it was Liam. Jealousy seized her, and all the years of resentment; she wanted to slam the door in his face.

"Charlotte. You're just the same."

"Hardly," she said, and stepped back to let him in.

They stood and surveyed each other. Charlotte tried to trace familiarities. He still had the wide-spaced eyes, the well assembled features, his hair still curled crisply round his head: but a tan had overlaid the pale skin and the freckles and he looked, above all, successful, as if he had prematurely reached a middle age of money and suits and working breakfasts and conferences with his legal advisers. He was nearly six feet, slender as ever: Charlotte remembered his wiry strength.

He picked her up, hugged her, carried her inside. "I can come in, I hope? Are you alone? Are you busy?" he said, to fill the silence.

"I'm cleaning the kitchen."

"Why? Don't answer that," chattered Liam, "you're the sort of person who cleans kitchens – you always used to do my packing and whiten my tennis shoes. Charlotte, I've missed you."

Charlotte led him into the living-room where they stood about awkwardly. Charlotte struggled with the rush of emotions that threatened to swamp her. Liam was so much older, so much older. He could have been a different person from the thin-armed boy she had loved so devotedly, hated so much. Nothing could have more clearly marked the passage of time. She could see the lost years slipping past her, incarnated in Liam.

"You went," she said. "You left me, you pig."

"I know," said Liam. "I wanted to get you back. I tried for years. I never forgot you, Charlotte." That was probably true. Charlotte had a large brown envelope full of Christmas and birthday cards from Liam, which her father had always insisted on opening. "The aunts said you didn't want to see me."

"I was afraid."

"No need, no need," said Liam. He felt suddenly as familiar to Charlotte as the aunts. Underneath the strange, attractive man so formally dressed, she recognised her brother's spirit lurking.

"I never forgave you," she said. "You've no idea what it was like, being left behind."

"I can imagine," said Liam. "I used to think about you all the time. Mother told me not to write to you, she said it would be worse for you in the long run. I didn't know if that was true. I soon stopped trusting her. If I could have chosen, I'd have gone back to Father and kept you company. It was never right with Mother after you left. She couldn't bear remembering you, she felt so guilty. Then she pretended it hadn't happened. She wouldn't let me go back, she said Father wouldn't have me."

"What was Roddy like?"

"Okay. He never took to me, of course. Mother went off me, too. She wanted to forget her first marriage. She never mentions it now unless people directly ask who I am. She makes out I'm a devoted youth, dancing attendance. Not so young now. I'm thirty, isn't that amazing?"

"I'm twenty-seven. I couldn't bear to see you before now."

"I know," said Liam. "The aunts told me. I was sorry to hear about you and school – you were doing so well."

"Tessy said I was lucky to be shot of such a dreary job."

"Tessy knows nothing about it," said Liam with the old air of assurance, unbearably poignant in this suited stranger. "I'm seriously asking you to work in my company. We're expanding all the time. Tell me what you were earning and I'll add a bit."

"You're trying to impress me," said Charlotte.

"Only a little. Who else can I show off to?"

"The universe, knowing you," said Charlotte perkily. She was beginning to feel at home with him. She settled herself more comfortably on the sofa, pulled her feet up under her, hugged her knees. Liam was back. He had been there, all the time, the same person.

"Do sit down, Liam," she said.

"There's someone you must meet first. Part of my plan for you. He's waiting in the car."

The man Liam brought in was extremely flamboyant, dressed with obvious extravagance in a performing style, as if he would at any moment acknowledge the applause of his fans, grasp a microphone, perch on a stool and sing a duet with Dolly Parton. Beige cotton trousers, wide cut from a gathered waist, tapered to a puttee effect and very soft beige leather boots. His shirt was fine wool, brown and cream American checks, and over it he wore a sleeveless flying jacket of shiny brown leather with raised rolls on the shoulders. He had a large actor's head with a thick rigid mass of gelled blond hair, not visibly thinning or augmented with a wig, though his tanned and weathered face put him firmly in his forties. He was slightly shorter than Liam, heavier built.

"This is Del Busby," said Liam. "I brought him along to meet you and make arrangements about this afternoon."

"How do you do," said Charlotte, extending her hand. "What arrangements?" Del's eyes and manner made her want to keep him at a distance. He could have been an attractive man, but his eyes were dead. They looked extinguished, as if their owner was out of town, visiting; as if he had given up hope for the human race. Romantic novelists often describe these eyes as appealing but to

Charlotte they were disheartening and sinister.

He smiled at her indifferently. His gaze was fixed on her body and it made her self-conscious. She wriggled around inside the sweatshirt, trying to cover herself more completely.

"You know I own a record company," said Liam. "Del works for me. He's my right-hand man."

"His gofer," said Del, in a voice as dead as London tap water. "You may know me better under other names. I used to be Jack the Knave – of Jokers Wild."

"Oh," said Charlotte.

"And Sunning Dale," he continued. Charlotte had dimly heard of Sunning Dale, a singer of the late Sixties. She deduced that this creature was a name-changed pop star in the style of Alvin Stardust.

"Are you involved in the pop music scene at present?"

"Not as a performer," said Liam. "There's more money in agenting and promotions. He and I both think there's room in the UK market for a squeaky-clean group on the lines of Bucks Fizz and the Brotherhood of Man. A singing, dancing, glowing group with an album in every Australian home, eventually. We've got the boy and one girl ready. This afternoon, he's auditioning for the other girl. We want you to go to the auditions."

"Why?"

"I want you to work for me. General assistant. Your first task is to chaperone the group. That's going to be a selling point. Untouched amid the grime of pop – sex, drugs, punk – protected by a chaperone, lately employed at one of our top girls' schools – wander The Babes in the Wood, trilling their innocent songs, executing their nifty but unprovocative dance routines."

"That sounds dreadful," said Charlotte. "You can't seriously want me to be involved."

"Very serious, darlin'," said Del in his flat voice. "Publicity won't hurt, do you a bit of good as well. Take you out of yourself. I hear your life ain't all coke and roses. We'll soon change that, a lovely girl like you."

"Del's got to go now, haven't you, Del?" said Liam.

"Yeah, if you say so," said Del. "See you this p.m., Charlotte. Lee will tell you where."

Charlotte watched his loose-hipped stride across the room, into the hall. She breathed in relief as the front door shut behind him.

"He's not so bad when you get to know him," said Liam. He had retained his responsiveness to people's feelings, thought Charlotte, and she sat down abruptly, overwhelmed by the suddenness of his arrival and the reality of his presence.

"I expect he's worse. Tell me about him. Talk to me."

"I've got to catch a plane," he said, but joined her on the long squashy sofa with its crocheted cushions.

"Seriously," she began.

"You keep saying that."

"Seriously, what use would I be working in your company? I don't want to be employed out of kindness."

"Can you type?"

"Yes."

"Can you think?"

"I suppose so."

"That'll do to start with. It sets you head and shoulders above the other two assistants."

"You actually run a record company," said Charlotte wonderingly.

"The aunts must have told you. And don't you ever read the papers?"

She had avoided reading about Liam.

"I can't stay, Carly. I have to go to Frankfurt on the midday plane."

"When will you be back?"

"Friday. Del will look after you till then."

"I don't need looking after," said Charlotte, piqued by the implication, thinking him presumptuous. He balled his fist and tapped her cheek.

"No offence in the world," he said. "I only wish you well. Have you something better to do than work for me?"

"I have nothing to do," admitted Charlotte. "Except

clean Suki's kitchen and look for a place to live, and I've been dodging that. London frightens me."

"You can stay with us in Richmond. Joanna would love to have you."

"I doubt that," said Charlotte.

"She wouldn't mind, anyway. She's always wanted to meet you. You'll like her, Carly."

"Don't call me Carly," she said abruptly. In their childhood he had only called her that in particularly tender moments, and now she resented it. She felt at home with him, but not reconciled. She needed more time to accept him without reservation, and she didn't like to be told she'd like his wife.

"We sent you an invitation to our wedding," he said.

"I've nothing against your wife."

"Yes you have. You're jealous because we've missed so much of each other's lives. We'll talk about it when I get back from Frankfurt. Here —" he put a card in her hand — "the office address is where the auditions are being held — starting at two."

"What kind of clothes should I wear?"

"Not those shorts or Del will be all over you like a tent. You needn't look like a chaperone yet, there won't be any press, we won't launch the group for months. Wear what you like, you'll soon get the hang of the people in the record business." He heaved himself up, kissing her lightly on the cheek as he went. "It'll be all right, Charlotte, you'll see."

Liam's visit fired Charlotte with confidence. He accepted her, had even welcomed her. She couldn't imagine herself working for a record company, but its owner did, and after all competence was one of her strong points. If she was earning money then she could live without the constant anxiety of diminishing savings, she could afford a flat.

All she had in common with Suki was their shared schooldays and affection. Although Charlotte was generally opposed to nuclear weapons and had nothing in principle against the whale, she had her own more pressing concerns.

"That's all very well," objected Suki, suckling Hector. "If everybody thought like that, nobody would ever take political action and we'd all be blown up. Where would your personal problems be then?"

"Dissolved," said Charlotte.

Suki smiled at her indulgently. "I know you don't mean that, but it's nice to see you so cheerful," she said. "I wish you'd kept Liam here until I got back. What's he like now? Still as attractive?"

"How can I tell?"

"Guess."

"Still as attractive," said Charlotte. An involuntary grin kept spreading across her face. She felt buoyant, immortal. She felt as if no task was beyond her. "Advise me, Suki. What should I wear as an assistant in a record company?"

"Assistant to what?"

"Anybody."

Suki loved giving advice, even about clothes, which she high-mindedly affected to despise. Between them they kitted Charlotte out in a brightly coloured combination of summer cotton, layered and fashionably nonchalant.

"You look – amazing," said Suki finally. "You could be a model."

"Too short."

"Or an actress."

"Too self-conscious."

The office was in a tiny cul-de-sac off Wardour Street. Charlotte marked it with a large red circle in her *A to Z*. "I'll go by bus," she said.

Suki approved of buses, they were energy-conserving, but she demurred none the less. "You'll get those white trousers filthy."

"I want to be a real Londoner."

"Then go by Underground."

"Not yet, it's too stuffy and too crowded. I feel exiled from the country when I'm rattling along in artificial air."

Suki watched Charlotte bustle about in preparation. "I'm

worried about this," she said. "It's all going to be so new for you, so different from teaching. There'll be masses of men. Don't you mind about men any more?"

"No," said Charlotte. "It wasn't men I was frightened of, anyway. I just thought it was."

"What were you frightened of?"

"I think – not being wanted. Or liked. Or loved."

"Oh," said Suki, out of her depth, not ready to admit it.

"Don't worry about me."

"You could always look for a job in a country school."

"I'll manage at Broken Records."

She was wearing the right clothes. Everybody else at Broken Records was layered and trousered and cottoned. She lacked designer running shoes but her red plastic fun sandals would do. Del met her in the reception area, a capsule of moulded white plastic with the Broken Records logo on the walls, the floor, the ceiling. A painted teenager, probably male judging by its biceps, manned a large and sophisticated switchboard. Several girls stood around clutching bags, pretending not to be nervous.

"Through here, Charlotte," said Del, leading her along a white moulded passageway. "Glad you could make it." Now they were in a long room with windows looking out into the back of the house opposite, a spring wooden floor, a giant mirror behind a barre. "Used to be a dance studio, went bust," said Del. "Pull up a chair, I want you to meet Vince Hampton."

Vince Hampton was an old man who dressed and moved like a young one, slim-hipped, tall, wearing a wig and a sun-bed tan. He waved at Charlotte. "Glad you could make it," he said. He seemed to know all about her.

"First off, we go on appearance," said Del. "We've got one girl already, tallish, blonde. We could do with a small brunette."

"A black?" said Vince.

"Nah. The guy's black. Vince takes care of the movement side," he said to Charlotte. "He's in dance." Vince

executed a few tap steps in illustration, winked at Charlotte
pulled up a chair beside hers and sat astride it, flexibly.

"What about singing?" said Charlotte.

"Later. We don't worry about that till we've weeded ou
the scrawny ratbags and the popsies with three left feet."

"Have you got a list of names?" said Charlotte. "I coul
call the girls for you and make notes of what you say."

"Bit keen, aren't you? You're the boss's sister, no nee
to work. Sit back and enjoy."

"I'd rather work," said Charlotte. Del shrugged. Vinc
twinkled with shallow and slightly desperate responsive
ness.

"No list, ducky, unless you make one," said Del. "D'yo
want some paper?" He looked aimlessly around the bar
room.

Charlotte produced a clipboard and pen from he
shoulder bag. The clipboard, dating from Suki's days a
researcher on ecological TV programmes, had a pro
fessional air. Vince looked impressed. "This girl's on th
ball," he said.

"Keep it clean," said Del. Both men laughed. The tele
phone on the floor behind them gave a muted warble. De
answered it. "Yeah, yeah, right, yeah. Send the first thre
along." He replaced the receiver. "Let's have some goo
sounds, Vince."

In answer, Vince stretched out a mobile and sinewy arr
to the tape deck on a shelf beside him. Michael Jackson'
piping filled the room. Three girls entered, smiling. Char
lotte took their names, noting beside each name a characteristic so she could tell them apart. Del watched this
expressionless. When she had finished he beckoned he
over and took the list from her. "You with the frizzy hair,"
he said, reading Charlotte's description. "Let's see yo
move."

"That's Jackie Shaw," said Charlotte.

"You with the frizzy hair is easier," said Del.

The girl, under any name, was gyrating to the music.

"Sorry, dear," said Vince. "Not quite what we're after."

"That's it, then," said Del. "Ta, girls." They filed out.

Twenty-seven girls turned up for the audition. Twenty were physically unacceptable to Del, four more rejected by Vince. The remaining three, fetched back from the reception area by Charlotte, couldn't sing.

"Bloody useless cows," said Del. "The younger generation's got no talent."

Vince agreed.

"Perhaps we should have tried their voices first," said Charlotte.

"Do me a favour. Stick to what you know about," said Del. He shrugged his padded shoulders irritably.

"Two of the blondes you turned down had sung in West End shows," Charlotte said.

"How do you know?" Del was suspicious.

"I asked them."

"I told you," said Del. "I want a fuckin' brunette, don't I?"

"Bucks Fizz has two blonde girls. There's no absolute reason you should have one blonde and one brunette."

"Yes there bloody is," said Del. "It's my creative concept, how I see the group. One black guy, one blonde bird, one dark bird. That's fuckin' *it*. That's central to the marketing component as I visualise it."

"I wish you wouldn't swear," said Charlotte.

"Fan-fuckin'tastic," said Del. "You won't survive a day in this business, darlin', if you're going to get clever with me."

"You would know," said Charlotte. "With your long years of experience at the top of the charts."

Vince's face contorted. He hurriedly looked away. Del slammed his hand against the wall. "You're here as an assistant," he muttered between clenched teeth. "Assist, like to help. Not stick your bloody nose in. Keep your mush zipped unless I ask for your opinion, okay? All right?"

"Do you want me to recall the two blondes?" said Charlotte.

"You can't," said Del. "I sent them all away."

"I told those two to stay."

"Don't push me too far, girl, just don't push me," said Del, visibly trying to recover. "What's going on here? Explain. What don't you like about the set-up? What did we do to you?"

"I don't like swearing," said Charlotte, making an effort in return. "Because I am – I was – a teacher, I suppose. Also I didn't like the way you dismissed the girls without even listening to them because their hair was the wrong colour or their bodies the wrong shape. Come to think of it, they could dye their hair."

"Girl, you got some hard lessons to learn," said Del, smoothing his dyed hair defensively. "Selling records is tough. If these dollies don't like the heat, they can stay out of the fuck – er – the kitchen. We don't need 'em, they need us. They all want to be famous and they want to be rich and they haven't the faintest bleedin' idea how to do it. Isn't that right, Vince? They'd do anything."

"I still wish you didn't treat them like meat," said Charlotte. "Commenting on their bodies in front of them. 'Tits too small.' 'Sorry darlin', we're looking for a dancer today, not a reserve for the weightlifting team.'"

Del laughed. "I thought that was funny, eh Vince?"

Vince laughed towards Del and lofted an eyebrow at Charlotte.

"Anyway," said Charlotte, "I'm supposed to be chaperoning the group, aren't I? And one of the girls this afternoon might have joined the group. So I want them shown respect."

Del sighed. "You misunderstood, girl. The chaperone deal is a gimmick, right? It's for publicity, okay? It don't mean nothing, you don't need to do nothing, just be photographed with them looking like a governess. We write the press handouts all about what you do protecting them and like that, see? It's nothing to do with you."

"Yes it is," said Charlotte. "Liam hired me and until he fires me I'm going to do what I think is right." This sentiment sounded so priggish that she wanted to retract it as soon as the words were spoken, but the mention of Liam had its effect on Del. He adopted a sincere manner which was marginally more unpleasant than his previous street-wise macho character.

"See here, Charlotte," he confided. "I've got a whole lot riding on the success of this group, see? I need the money, I've got expensive tastes, so I want the group to be absolutely right for the market. Maybe you think I'm fussy. Maybe I am. But quality is what counts here, and attention to detail."

"And tits," said Vince.

"Of course, tits. And bums."

Both men looked at Charlotte as if they had given her a concise explanation of love, death and the universe.

"It can't be as simple as that," said Charlotte.

It was a long afternoon. Eventually, Del agreed to see Charlotte's two blondes again. He chose the younger one, an eighteen-year-old who could sing and dance and who claimed her natural hair colour was brown. "I'll check that out later," smirked Del.

The girl giggled complaisantly, but Charlotte thought she sensed a spark of awareness and independence lurking in the kohl-shaded eyes under the mascaraed eyelashes. She felt a pang of regret that this talented and energetic girl should be involved with Del, but she took her address and telephone number, and her agent's address and telephone number.

"Pity about the agent," said Del after she'd gone. "I prefer dealing with the artists direct."

The auditions completed, Del took Charlotte for a tour to introduce her round the office. The building was Georgian in origin and some of the rooms still retained the well-proportioned windows and elegant ceilings. Many other rooms were garnished with plastic and wilting indoor plants in a space-ship style Charlotte found sterile and dated. The employees, all of them young and brightly dressed, their manner varying in vivacity from lively to hysterical, greeted Charlotte with an effusiveness that did not attempt to mask their lack of warmth. She had felt hesitant about Liam employing her – unfair to the others, she thought, nepotism, intruding on a good working team, inappropriate. These reservations dwindled and died as she moved among them; they were so clearly not a team but a collection of creatures of a bright-plumaged, cold-blooded species.

She was relieved to escape. Outside, she took a deep breath of the stale and petrol-laden London air and walked up towards Oxford Street, past the Chinese restaurants and the strip clubs and the Adults Only bookshops, pushing her way through the crowded pavements. Don't generalise, she told herself. Don't make snap judgements. All those people may be worth knowing, they may be excellent at their jobs. Appearance is important in the record business. For Liam's sake – and her own – she should try the job. She knew it wouldn't be permanent, but it would provide experience. At least she'd meet different people. Perhaps also Liam would let her work on the business side, with the accountants, or financial directors, on the top floor where Del had so far not taken her. "I leave the money men to Lee, I'm in charge of the creative side, the artists and the music," he had said.

"Who's your most successful group?" Charlotte had asked.

Del displayed his first signs of spontaneous and deeply felt emotion. He was shocked. "You mean – you really don't KNOW? Where most of the money comes from? Where the company started?"

"No."

"Ever heard of Metropolitan Line?"

Even if she hadn't, Charlotte would have lied out of politeness. Del looked so disconcerted, almost distressed, as if he had stepped on a solid floor which gave beneath him or given a fiver to a blind man who then attacked him with his white stick. But she had heard of Metropolitan Line, and said so. They were an early Seventies' group who had taken over something of the mantle of the Rolling Stones, four youths with loud untuneful voices and a strong sense of rhythm. They were popular all over the world, seldom out of the newspapers, marrying or being arrested for drug offences or giving benefit concerts for CND.

"Lee discovered them," said Del. "That's where it all started. He saw them at a gig in Cambridge, he spotted their potential." Threading her way through the Oxford Street tourists and touts, Charlotte reflected on the gulf between her and Liam. She could no more have spotted and sponsored a pop group than climb Everest. Climbing Everest would, in fact, certainly be easier. What was it Liam had seen? The fevered, enthusiastic faces of Metropolitan Line's Cambridge audience – the talent of the group? Charlotte couldn't see their attraction even now, when their annual record sales must be counted in millions. She felt warm towards Liam, he had been kind to her; it seemed as if he cared what happened to her, as if he was glad to see her again. Tessy, on the other hand – Charlotte could almost accept it, two days later – would have preferred not to see her.

It had just rained, the pavements gently steamed in the heat. Another Indian summer. Charlotte associated London with the long hot summer days at the Reduced Gentlefolk's, partly because they had been the most suffocating, the most irksome. At least in winter she had enjoyed the warmth of the coal fire, eaten the teacakes with some semblance of appetite.

It was rush hour and the buses were full. Charlotte decided to go by Underground, fought her way down the steps, along a platform, into the train. She was pressed close to swaying bodies, many of them male. She felt pleased with herself for not minding, now, what sex people were. Perhaps the next stage would be finding an attractive man of her own, not borrowing one from Wendy Craig Stewart.

Chapter Nine

Suki found Charlotte a flat. Previously, it had been rented by the secretary of a Third World charity who embezzled the funds and disappeared. It was near the British Museum, two small rooms, a kitchen and bathroom, up three flights of rickety stairs above a shuttered and deserted second-hand book shop. Two women lived on the first and second floors, seldom appearing in the daytime, giving only their first names on the street-level bells. Charlotte went to inspect the flat and signed the furnished lease that same afternoon. She was paying more in rent than she had been at Ashcombe for her mortgage repayments, but even her fleeting acquaintance with flat-hunting in London had convinced her that she should accept this flat and be thankful.

It was furnished in the sense that all available space was occupied by hideous, stained, badly designed objects presumably bought in the contents sale of a much larger house. The wardrobe was so bulky that to open it you had to close the bedroom door and stand on the bed: the kitchen cupboard, freestanding, bright green, possessed of six doors all of which refused to stay shut, blocked access to the cooker: the double bed was a terrain of lumps and hollows, only too recognisably stained.

She devoted her energies to cleaning, to washing the walls and the ceilings and the floors, painting the walls cream and the woodwork white because those seemed the antithesis of London with its grime and fumes and ankle-deep fast-food wrappers.

On Friday evening Liam telephoned. "I'm back from Frankfurt."

"Hi. When can you help me move ghastly furniture out of my new flat?"

"Tomorrow?"

It seemed too good to be true; like having a magic

brother in a fairy-tale, glad to see you, glad to help. It *was* too good to be true, decided Charlotte, besides not being fair to Liam's wife. "Won't Joanna mind? What about spending time with her, since you've just got back?"

"I'm with her now. Besides, she's decided to go and stay with her mother for two weeks. Make the most of the good weather while it lasts."

Charlotte wished she could see his face and Joanna's. Was Joanna sulking, or was she being supremely tactful? "Where does Joanna's mother live?"

"Devon," said Liam. "The children love it there."

"Tomorrow would be ideal," said Charlotte. "I haven't done much work the last two days, by the way, Del said I wasn't needed."

"I spoke to him yesterday. He said you'd found a flat and I told him to give you time off."

All very well, Charlotte thought when the telephone call was finished and she was back with the tray of white emulsion and the paint-spattering roller, all very well to work for one's brother, but she didn't want Liam and Del taking care of the little woman behind her back.

"Don't look a gift employer in the mouth," advised Suki later when Charlotte returned to spend her last night amid Suki's high-minded jumble. "Liam wants to look after you: well and good. Take what you need. What do you owe to a rip-off like Broken Records? Peddlers of dreams, the lot of them, zombie-makers by Royal Appointment."

"I don't think the Royal Family are directly involved," said Charlotte.

"I was speaking metaphorically," said Suki. "Have a pistachio, the grocer round the corner imports them straight from the Middle East." She was blooming with contentment, her Victorian cotton nightdress delicately embroidered at neck and wrist, her bush of red hair caught in a bone clasp at the nape of her neck. Charlotte sat cross-legged at the other end of the sofa, too tired even to wash.

"No thanks, I've eaten," she said. "A sandwich at my pub on the corner." Already she was beginning to think of it as her pub, and the little general store down an alleyway between a print shop and a minicab office, as her shop.

"Besides," said Suki. "Broken Records and companies like them win awards for export, don't they? Which just means that it's okay to turn foreign brains to mush with the repetitive hypnotic pap those groups turn out, so long as there's a profit in it. It's just as bad as selling arms."

"No it isn't," said Charlotte.

"Okay, not *just* as bad," admitted Suki, who wasn't stupid. "But bad."

"Not as bad as drug-peddling."

"True, but —"

"Belt up, Suki," said Charlotte, weakly tossing a cushion at her. "Who crochets these things, anyway?"

"An amazing woman who used to sleep with Bertrand Russell in the Twenties. A socialist."

"That doesn't narrow down the field much."

"She does masses of envelopes for me. She's got terrific enthusiasm. She can't see much so I usually have to do the envelopes again but I couldn't possibly tell her. She can't really see to read so she knits and crochets and every so often they interview her on the radio."

Charlotte shuddered. She had a vision of herself forty years on, unmarried, perhaps still virgin, with not even the dubious distinction of having slept with Bertrand Russell, crocheting heroically in a cramped flat. She would not, she was sure, retain tremendous enthusiasm. In fact she might well have turned into batty Victoria or desperate Henrietta; Liam might still have to be understanding and kind, when Joanna was prepared to lend him. Her confidence took one of its lurches and she felt the old panic and the old bewilderment.

"There's a telephone message for you," said Suki, watching her curiously. "Sophie Preston rang, said would you give her a call, wanted to know your new address. I pretended I didn't know it, just in case she was a nuisance."

"That's okay," said Charlotte. "She's the girl I told you about who just left Ashcombe."

"She sounded a bit dotty, I thought. Hey, tell you who else rang tonight – your chap from school, the painter one. He'll be in London this Sunday, asked you to lunch."

"I can give him lunch at the flat," said Charlotte grandly.

The kitchen cupboard was the first to go. She and Liam sellotaped each recalcitrant door then humped it down the twisting stairs and along the pavement to perch forlornly on the builders' rubble of a nearby skip. Liam was dressed in worn jeans and a Metropolitan Line T-shirt. The hirsute group glared from his chest with the arrogance that was their stock-in-trade. Liam's face above theirs was obliging and youthful. He seemed to change personality with his clothes.

Next to go was the bed. By the time that reached the skip, the kitchen cupboard had gone. Charlotte and Liam began to giggle as they suggested why anyone should want it.

"To keep six green rabbits."

"To make a raft for a transatlantic crossing of the ancient MFI tribe."

Laughing, they collapsed onto the bed, which was obstructing the pavement. Passers-by had to squeeze past them, irritated or amused. "You're behaving very badly," said the voice of Charlotte's father, "attracting attention. In those shorts, too."

"Let's not bother to put the bed on the skip. We'll prop it up here, out of the way. Someone'll want it," said Liam. Sure enough, by the time they returned with the monster wardrobe in two parts plus the base, the bed also had disappeared. It seemed a good omen.

With both of them working, the decoration of the flat was soon finished. Charlotte had hardly even prepared the surfaces. "After all," she said when Liam protested at the skimpy workmanship of her first coat, "who knows how long I'll be here?"

"You're not planning to leave?" said Liam, dropping his paint brush in dismay then cursing at the dust and fluff it gathered. Charlotte was touched that he wanted her to stay: still more touched when he insisted, after lunch at her pub, on taking her to Heal's for new furniture.

"Habitat will do," she said firmly. "Habitat is what I want." Bookshelves, a sofa bed, towels. "Red would be fun," she said, remembering all the pastel towels in storage with her quietly suitable furniture.

"Twenty red towels," said Liam. "The largest size."

"Don't be ridiculous. I haven't storage for twenty. Make it four."

"Ten," insisted Liam. "I want to give you ten. And you'll need sheets and a duvet –"

"I've brought those –"

"A linen-basket," he said, his eye roaming round the bathroom shop. "Shelves, a mirror, bath mats –"

He wanted so much to please her, make her happy. It was evident to Charlotte, standing amid the gritted-teeth confusion of Saturday afternoon shoppers, that he had suffered from the family rupture, if not as much as she had, at least enough. Left with Tessy, he must have felt responsible both for Charlotte's misery and for his mother's happiness. Charlotte had always taken for granted, in thinking about Liam, that he was the lucky one. Now, seeing the hesitation and eagerness, the adolescent uncertainty as he offered her armfuls of best quality fluffy bath sheets, she began to imagine a thirteen-year-old boy on whom the sun had always shone, trying to shoulder, as he would have done, the burden of his flighty mother's well-being. Impossible to make Tessy happy: impossible not to be jealous of Roddy: impossible for Tessy not to feel, and Liam to know she felt, that it would have been easier to leave both children to Geoffrey. Tessy's enthusiasms were short-lived. Even her affection for Liam had been three parts vanity, one part genuine, thought Charlotte with sudden certainty. Pretty mother, charming son. Perhaps the link between Tessy and Liam had been about as fragile as that between Charlotte and Geoffrey – the reality of being left together more demanding than the relationship could bear.

Charlotte took a basket and began to pile bathroom

fittings into it. An over-equipped bathroom was a small price to pay for not crushing Liam. When the basket was full he commandeered a stock trolley and rolled it through the shop, demanding shelves and tables and rugs, until at last it was full and he was sated.

"There isn't room in the flat for this," said Charlotte, "and besides, they'll never take a cheque."

This was evidently the moment he had been building up to: taking a roll of £50 notes from his jeans pocket, he counted out the total. The roll was hardly diminished.

"Show-off," said Charlotte, and began to laugh. They were surrounded by bulky packages of self-assemble furniture; she looked at her bare dusty legs in shorts and felt her tousled hair, thought of the Governors' Meeting and Heather Noakes.

Liam was also laughing, though he didn't understand the joke. Even two of the sales assistants began to giggle.

"What are we laughing at?" said Liam finally.

"You and the money, all the things we bought – everything." It sounded lame. Charlotte didn't know the reason herself. The laughter welled up irresistibly and exultantly.

In the taxi on the way back, wedged between Liam and a box labelled "Tech Video trolley", Charlotte began to laugh again. "I haven't even got a TV in London, let alone a video, and don't say you'll buy me one or I'll –"

"What?" said Liam, punching her gently on the arm. "What'll you do to me, champ? Eh?"

"Say thank you," said Charlotte.

Next day, Nicholas arrived early for lunch. Charlotte was still unpacking books and arranging them on shelves. "My," he said, "what a thrilling life you do lead. Have you considered taking up book-handling as a vocation?"

"It's called moving house," said Charlotte, "and you're early and I haven't dressed properly yet." She was in an old pair of jeans cut off just above the knee, and a running singlet. Her hair was uncombed. She beamed at him, waved her arm around the room. "Isn't it smashing, Nicholas? This is the bedroom, through here – and a kitchen, look, just big enough – and a bathroom. Liam absolutely insisted on buying all this Italian bathroom stuff – and I painted the walls myself! Except for the second coat, Liam helped with that."

The flat looked clean, airy and spanking new. It had something of the naively meliorist quality of a colour supplement, as if an AB consumer, his *Guardian*-reading wife and 2.4 computer-using children would pop up from a Human Body book and disport themselves. Only Charlotte's books provided reminders of human suffering, age and death. *Paradise Lost, War and Peace, Decline and Fall, Memento Mori.*

"I can see you did the painting," said Nicholas. "I like the streaky effect over here."

"Don't be sarcastic," said Charlotte happily. "I think that's gone streaky because the wall's damp."

"Very likely."

"But aren't I lucky? Out of this window, if I lean out and turn my head like this, look, I can see the British Museum."

"Straight ahead, on the other hand, you have an excellent close-up of a blank wall."

"Don't be gloomy. This is only the side window. Out of the main one I can see –"

"I know what you can see, Charlotte," he said lowering himself gingerly into a high tech chair. "You can see your life ahead of you, and more power to your elbow, say I. Can I have a drink, please?"

"Lager. That's all I've got. It's not healthy to drink as much as you do, anyway."

Nicholas accepted the lager, grumbling.

"Your stereo is in the boot of my car," he said. "I thought you'd need it. Remind me to bring it up before we go to lunch."

"That was really kind," said Charlotte. "With music, this flat will be perfect. Liam's coming to dinner to-night."

"Does Liam have a wife?" said Nicholas.

"I told you, remember? In Moscow. He's got a wife and

children but they're away. He also has a record company, and I'm working for it."

"Head of English, I suppose."

"Owner's sister seems to be employment enough in itself," said Charlotte happily.

"And you don't mind that?"

"Not for a few months. The company can afford it. It'll be interesting seeing another way of life. Talking of which, tell me about Ashcombe."

"You've only been away a week," he protested. "Nothing much has happened in all the years I've worked there – apart from your escapade – so to hope for further activity within the week seems to me unrealistic. Paula Madders sent you a pot plant."

"Good. This flat could do with more plants."

"Where are yours?"

"Still with odds and ends at Suki's place – the friend I was staying with until last night."

"Well, your own plants will have to be enough. I've appropriated Paula's."

Charlotte washed, changed, went to lunch with Nicholas. His company was as pleasant as always, the restaurant in Chelsea lively and the food edible.

"So how's your mother?"

"A disappointment. A stranger."

"And Liam?"

"I can't believe how good it is to be with him. I can't believe how pleased he is to see me. And best of all, it's obviously the right time for both of us. It wouldn't have worked if I'd met him again when I was eighteen, there was too little of me formed then. I'd have been much too bitter and much too vulnerable. The same is true of him, I suppose. Now he's got a wife and children and a complete life of his own, and I've got my confidence back. Why are you smiling, Nicholas?"

"No special reason."

"Don't be provoking."

"No ma'am."

"Tell me what you were smiling at."

"This confidence you got back. Was it by post? Or in a delivery van from Harrods?"

"I don't understand." Charlotte looked hurt as well as annoyed, and Nicholas patted her hand. She withdrew it with a snap.

"Tell me plainly what you mean."

"I mean that in my experience, nothing is ever as simple as you would like it to be. Your world is a tidy place."

"That makes me sound like Heather Noakes."

"If the cap fits . . . perhaps you should also wear her shoes."

Charlotte imagined this, and smiled.

"That's better. Don't take yourself so seriously."

"I always have. The aunts used to say 'poor dear Charlotte, such a serious little thing'."

"That was *then. Now* you're a sex symbol."

"Hardly."

"According to Ashcombe gossip. You'd be amazed to find out how many other liaisons you carried on during your time there."

"With whom?"

"Me, obviously. That funny chap from the Physics Department whose mother knits him sweaters —"

"Oh, no! Stop!" said Charlotte.

"And there are also dark rumours about your carryings-on in London."

"Whereas I spend most of my evenings with Liam, and the rest with Suki."

"But it is only a matter of time."

"Until what?"

"Until you find a lover."

"Why?"

"You're beautiful, reckless, curious."

"I sound like the blurb of a pornographic video." Charlotte was pleased by his words, by his taking for granted that she would find a lover and by his tacit approval of this. "Do you realise," she said, watching him patiently watching her, "that I always talk to you and never listen?" She dipped a breadstick in her wine absent-mindedly.

"Disgusting habit," said Nicholas. "Do you dip toast in your breakfast coffee?"

"I've just realised how patient you are with me."

He shook his head, smiling. "Not patient. I enjoy watching growing things. Besides, you'll have to be patient with me this afternoon. I'm taking you to the National Portrait Gallery."

"Good," said Charlotte. "I haven't been there for years. Any particular reason? Have they bought something of yours?"

"The term is 'acquired', and they've acquired not a little of my output over the years. My callow period, starving period, hack period and alimony period are all well represented. More to the point – they've hung me." He paused. Charlotte smiled encouragingly, said nothing. "You must be one of the few people who could restrain themselves from facetious comment on that," he went on. "Do you want pudding?"

"No. I can feast my soul on your painting."

Charlotte expected work on the newly formed sub-Bucks Fizz group The Babes in the Wood (also known as Bix, also known as Nix, also known as whatever the creative meeting chaired by Del came up with) to start straight away. She was commandeered by Liam pending further development of the group, and week after week she trailed round the office, round London, then England, and twice to Frankfurt, clipboard in hand, assisting where assistance was needed, waiting for the summons from Del to resume work with him and Vince Hampton. Del vanished for two weeks, masterminding the plans for Metropolitan Line's tour of Europe.

Inside the company, Metropolitan Line were known as The Boys. Charlotte applied herself to the vocabulary of charts, air time, freebies, gigs, venues, plugs, plays, videos, cable exposure, synthesisers, tracks, session musicians, studios, and fan clubs. She listened to commercial radio, took *The Face* and *Rolling Stone*, played the top twenty albums and made notes on them. She studied the artists Broken

Records handled (she had to force herself to call them artists), looked at details of the site and turnover of the shops it owned. She went through the breakdown costings of an album, saw how the payout was distributed, and was no longer surprised at Liam's affluence. She was amazed by the money in pop: the huge fees of the top earners, the pittance paid to most one-hit groups.

Most of the time, she knew, she was no use to Liam, but he still wanted her company. She was there to be impressed, she supposed; to appreciate what he had built with his own wits. He was offering her the chance to share his working life. Nothing could recapture the loss of their shared adolescence, but he was providing what he could.

She had forgotten how charming, how funny he could be. She began to understand how his mind worked – he was not as academic as she, nor as philosophical, nor as clear-thinking. He operated on intuition and a gut-feeling for the record market. He listened to demo tapes for hours on end. To Charlotte they were indistinguishable, but she accurately logged his comments and learned to admire his skill in adapting to the world he had chosen. She noticed that with the money men he was formally dressed, decisive: in the studio and with musicians he wore flamboyant, casual clothes, and appeared street-wise and sharp. Even his vocabulary and accent adjusted to the milieu. This flexibility, verging on compliance, Charlotte recognised as an echo of herself.

She admired his expertise, deplored the business he applied it to. She couldn't imagine Broken Records as employment for a grown man.

"The money," he said. "Think of the money." In another year or two he planned to sell out and retire from work, live on his investments, buy race horses.

"What about tax?" said Charlotte.

"I may have to move abroad." It was vague. Charlotte wasn't convinced. The company seemed to her to fascinate him, like a flickering video game with a hypnotic beep compelling the player to try for ever higher scores. He also enjoyed music. With the huge padded headphones on, totally absorbed, his body would move in rhythmic jerks to a sound only he could hear.

"What'll happen to the company if you leave it?"

"God knows," said Liam. "Depends who buys it."

"In other words if the person who buys it doesn't have your talent-spotting ability, it'll go down the tubes."

"The shops should go on making a profit. And there's The Boys, of course. Even if they don't renew when the contract comes up, we own so much good stuff of theirs, people will go on buying and buying."

"You're just like the Anglo-Irish landlords," said Charlotte. "Work the land till it's exhausted and clear out, sucking the country dry."

"If you say so," said Liam. He appeared entirely amoral with no sense of public duty. Charlotte found him incomprehensible. She had the high moral sense of a lonely child instructed by a traditional school and solitary reading of the classics; had lived at Ashcombe constantly in an atmosphere where duty, service and self-sacrifice were ideals, often enunciated, sometimes carried out. Liam's only sense of morality was private. Be kind to his wife, family and friends; provide for his old age. "And I pay a pension to the aunts," he added once.

The aunts were being supported all round the shop, thought Charlotte. She didn't know what her values were, any more. What she had considered, in her own case, to be service to others, was mostly fear and ambition. She had wanted power — apparently to do good – but had that been an illusion? Whereas Liam, manipulating the taste of the public, wanted no more than to sell them raucous sounds massaged in video packaging; happy to offer them ersatz hope, romance, sex, escape, a soulmate, company and comfort.

Most of the time, however, she just enjoyed his presence. Occasionally they both had lunch with Tessy and fell into other roles, charming, accomplished grown-up children of a beautiful woman. She always took them out to restaurants, to preclude serious conversation, Charlotte supposed. Tessy smiled a lot and kissed Charlotte warmly on arrival and departure and Charlotte felt almost sorry for her. Now it was her turn to be excluded. Charlotte and Liam would catch each other's eye and smile and know what each other was thinking. They were both as sharp as monkeys and Tessy had lost her edge. Charlotte felt for her mother when she saw the helpless anxiety with which she patted her hair, repaired her make-up, preserved her youth. She seemed to be finding maturity impossible. Although she read *Vogue* with rigorous attention, checked her favourite dress shops fortnightly, and kept her sharp eye on clothes wherever she went, she hadn't kept her manner up to date and it was still the flirtatious, superficial, would-be daring style of the early Fifties. Probably, thought Charlotte, her mother behaved like that because she thought men responded to it: particularly, she believed that Roddy responded to it.

At Charlotte's first meeting with Roddy, an apparently well-intentioned man with goggling eyes and the interrogatory manner of one accustomed to a production line of strangers, she thought him a little weary of Tessy's relentless vivacity. She thought the relationship sad. Tessy wanted to please, for her own satisfaction; Roddy wanted to be pleased, for Tessy's satisfaction, and neither could manage it.

When Joanna returned with the children from her tactful visit to her mother, Charlotte went to dinner at their house in Richmond. She took to Joanna at once, could see exactly why Liam had married her. She was small, slightly plump, as silent as courtesy allowed, with a gentle manner that Charlotte found restful. She was utterly different from Tessy.

After dinner, when Liam had darted upstairs to attend to a crying child – probably over-excited from earlier romps with him – Joanna washed up and Charlotte dried.

"I'm so glad you decided to take up with Liam," she said. "Knives and forks in the basket over there, please." It was a very large kitchen. Even Liam's compulsion to buy household fittings for his women hadn't managed to fill it. "He's told me so much about you, Charlotte. I think he felt losing you like losing a part of himself. Plates in that cupboard under the window. He's much happier since you came to London."

"He seems very happy with you."

"Oh, he is. We are. We suit each other. I like the house and the children and the security of marriage. I'm not a women's libber."

"Ummm," said Charlotte. Joanna was working up to an invitation to dinner to meet a nice potential husband. "I'm not sure what I think about marriage."

"And why should you," said Joanna, with enough sense to leave it. She had long brown hair piled on top of her head, presumably to give her height. It was held by a haphazard assortment of combs, and wisps were clinging to her damp neck. "Salt and pepper things on the dresser over there."

With Joanna in London, Charlotte was alone most evenings. It was October: chill, damp. It would have been autumn in the country, with the smell of burning leaves. In London Charlotte could hardly distinguish the seasons, though she noticed the tourists had gone. Those left were often not British, but were Londoners, self-absorbed, knowing their way around, scurrying into the Underground, along the platforms, up the escalators again, with the blind certainty of well-trained laboratory rats.

Charlotte bought electric fires for the flat, put up heavy curtains, settled in for the winter. Sometimes, alone with cups of coffee and the television, she thought about Ian. The stationery cupboard incident was still blush-provoking, but it had auspicious elements. She had, after all, begun by enjoying Ian's touch, much as she had enjoyed the Pole's. Sometimes, she imagined the scene with a different outcome. In her fantasy Ian, too, took his clothes off and they made love. When they had finished she told him that, though she loved him, their affair must end there. He was so affected, he cried and clung to her, saying that he must make love to her again.

It was a satisfying fantasy, though it lacked verisimilitude.

*   *   *

Charlotte was worried about Sophie. She rang her up once a week, took her to lunch once a fortnight. The girl seemed to be getting fatter, more depressed, and more idle. She was disinclined to follow up her request for Charlotte to help her with the English course. "Don't nag me, Miss Parker, I'm getting along fine. Can I have a baked potato with this lasagne?"

"Are your parents going to be in England for Christmas?"

"No, I'm going out to Strasbourg."

"Have you heard from them recently?"

"What is this? An inquisition?"

"I'm worried about you, Sophie."

"Well, don't. I'm perfectly old enough to take care of myself, I'm sixteen now. I've got it all worked out. I'll pass the exams this time and then I'll go on to do A-levels in one year, then I'll go to Oxford."

"Why Oxford?"

"I like the look of it. You can punt there, can't you? I like punting."

"What subject do you want to study at Oxford?"

"I'm not sure. Astronomy, maybe. I'm really into horoscopes."

"What grade do you expect for O-level Maths?"

"I'll pass, I'm sure I'll pass."

"That isn't good enough. Modern astronomy is all mathematical. You'll need Double Maths at A-level. Besides, I don't even think Oxford has a course in Astronomy."

"So what? I'll do something else then."

Charlotte often spent the evening with Suki, whose cheerful energy was gradually seeping away. She had been alone with Hector for four months, she missed her husband. Most of her London acquaintances were even worse off than she was, since she sought out the underprivileged, the single parent family, the disabled, the neurotic.

"I bit off more than I can chew," she confessed to Charlotte one night when Hector at last agreed to be put to bed. "When Ollie knew he'd have to be away so much he wanted us to buy a flat in Oxford, so I could see Ma and Pa and everyone else."

"Why didn't you?"

"Oxford's so middle-class. I thought I could do some good in Kilburn, actually help people. I enjoyed London while I worked in television, but most of my media mates are too busy now. Besides, I don't want to hang around like a discontented wraith."

"Wraith! Ho-ho!" teased Charlotte. Suki was indifferent to observations on her size: she seldom thought of herself as anything other than delightful and lovable.

"A Rubens wraith," she amended. "But it really opened my eyes, Charlotte. It's so handy to have a man about. It's lonely without."

"That's why they invented marriage, I suppose."

"I only got married because Ollie set his heart on it. I think it's an outmoded institution."

"I'll make you some herb tea," said Charlotte. "Put your feet up. You're just tired." She arranged the crocheted cushions behind Suki's back. "You're not going to be lonely for long, think of that. You have Ollie and when he comes back, think how much you'll enjoy it."

"Whereas you don't have a man at all," said Suki bluntly. "Does that worry you?"

Yes, was the true answer. Charlotte had begun to look about her, to notice attractive men at the office. "No," she said. "And aren't you betraying all your feminist principles, have'?" me that?"

"Certainly not. I'd ask a man the same about women. It's not feminist to pretend sex and love don't exist, you know."

Love. Charlotte thought about Ian, how convinced she had been of her love for him. Now, her behaviour seemed incomprehensible. It was as if another person had dreamed away the Russian trip. She went to make the herb tea. When she came back, Suki was crying silently. Tears meandered down her broad cheeks and plopped onto the cushion she was hugging.

"Suki, do you like Metropolitan Line?"

"On the Underground?"

"No. The pop group, you know. The ones who sing Death Row."

"Oh, Metropolitan Line. They're not bad. At least their songs have some ideological content."

"Tomorrow Liam's taking me to watch them filming a video for their new single. Come along, it'll be fun. You've been wanting to see Liam for weeks . . ."

"Years," said Suki.

"Years. And you can see Metropolitan Line. And meet Del."

"He sounds too revolting to miss."

Charlotte rang Liam, later that night. "Of course, bring Suki," said Liam enthusiastically. "She used to have a crush on me. I remember her trailing round the Norham Gardens house about a yard behind me, suggesting a game of sardines. She was all of ten. Is she attractive now?"

"She's married with a small baby."

"What kind of answer is that?"

"The only one you're getting."

"I'd like to see her anyway."

"So she can say, 'My, Liam, how successful and rich and powerful you are, and what a big record company you have?'"

"No. I'd like to see her because you want to bring her along and because I want to please you."

"Umm," said Charlotte.

"You'll have to get used to being cherished."

"I doubt if I can."

Charlotte and Suki were in the reception area of Broken Records waiting for Liam. Charlotte was chatting to the receptionist, a dim ambitious youth who wanted to be rich and who waited by his switchboard to become so. Every time she spoke to him Charlotte was reminded of Del's remarks about the auditioning girls, that they deserved what they got. She was still not wholly in sympathy with those sentiments, but she could see why he held them. So many people in the pop world combined pretensions with idleness.

"Hi, girl," said Del, sauntering in from the street wearing jodhpurs, knee-boots, spurs, and several layers of cotton shirts slashed in different places, under a full-length military-style leather coat. He ignored Suki completely.

"This is Suki Holland, a friend of mine. Suki, Del Busby."

"Yeah," said Del. "It's all sorted out with The Boys."

"Why do you assume that whoever you talk to shares your information and preoccupations?" said Charlotte.

"Yer what?"

"What was the problem with The Boys?"

"A minor pharmaceutical furore." He waved his hand, set off up the stairs.

"What does he mean?" Charlotte appealed to the receptionist.

"Drugs," said the receptionist. "Harry was busted in Paris. It was all a misunderstanding. The Paris police let him go. There's your car outside now."

Liam stood by the door of the Mercedes, Broken Records's top rank company car. He was wearing jeans, soft leather boots and a distressed leather flying jacket over a black wool shirt. He looked pleased with himself and greeted Suki with an exuberant kiss.

"I'll go in front with the driver," said Charlotte.

"Plenty of room on the back seat," said Liam.

"Why the Mercedes?" said Charlotte.

"I just felt like it," said Liam. "Every now and then I enjoy being rich."

"Hear hear," said the driver. He had just retired, aged twenty-eight, from the most unsuccessful group Broken Records promoted.

The car headed north towards the studio in Hertfordshire. Suki and Liam gossiped about Suki's elder brothers and about the video business. Suki found she knew the production company they would be watching at work that day. One of her friends from the BBC had joined them.

Recently they had been filming in Rome; before that, in Brazil.

"I could be doing that kind of work, I suppose," said Suki. "If I hadn't had Hector."

"And if you hadn't been so high-minded," said Charlotte.

"There's something about travel," said Suki wistfully. "I get so tired of London, especially in winter. My last year at the Beeb we went to the Holy Land for three weeks. I do miss it."

"If I was still at Ashcombe I'd be teaching the Lower Fourth some grammar. It would be apples for break, and stew, swedes and potatoes for lunch."

"You'll hardly be missing that," said the driver. "This is the life, eh? None of that grammar and stew rubbish. I mean, it stands to reason, dunnit?"

It took nearly an hour to reach the studios. They were a collection of anonymous buildings surrounded by a wire fence. A stocky, taciturn Welshman was on guard at the gate. He was in his late twenties and looked to be fresh from the army, with highly polished shoes and clipped hair. He checked the car thoroughly, checked their names against a list, waved them through.

"Why the security?" said Suki.

"The Boys. Ever since Lennon, they've been jumpy. You wouldn't believe what their fans get up to."

"So who provides the security here?" said Charlotte. "Is it the studios, or Broken Records?"

"We hire them and The Boys pay. There's normal studio security as well, of course. We just hired a new outfit. The last lot made a major cock-up last month in Holland. Excessive use of force. Broke a fan's arm and put three others in hospital. These are all ex-army. The top man sounds quite normal, for a change."

The day was damp, chill, overcast. There was another security check, and then they were allowed into the largest barnlike building, into the warmth. Most of the huge area was in shadow: one end, a beach set, was blazing bright. In this stood the four members of Metropolitan Line. They were dressed in silver leotards. All visible skin was painted silver, and their hair sprayed with glitter. They were practising a synchronised routine of pelvic thrusts, with their right arms punching the air.

"There's people I must see," said Liam. "Will you two be all right? Have a look round."

"We'll be fine," said Suki. She looked at home picking her way over cables and round cameras.

"Explain," said Charlotte. "Who's doing what? Is it like a TV studio?"

Suki explained. As she spoke Charlotte watched Liam move round, talking to the director, then The Boys, then to a tall man about Liam's age with a battered inexpressive face.

There was a disturbance at the door, raised voices, a scuffle, a shout: "Lee! Lee!" Del was being held by the security guard, one arm twisted behind his back.

Liam was out of earshot. Charlotte and Suki were the only denizens of the studio to pay attention to Del's plight.

"Shit, man, I'm Del Busby," he kept saying. The security man was unmoved.

"Sorry, sir, I'm sure you are, but you're not on my list. If you'll hold still a minute I can get on the walkie-talkie and check with my boss."

"Charlotte, for Christ's sake, tell him."

"Just hold still, sir," said the security man, giving Del's arm what Charlotte suspected was a vicious little tweak.

"That is Del Busby," she said. "He works for Broken Records. Please let him go." She smiled and tilted her head appealingly. The security man loosened his hold and Del stepped away, shrugging and patting his dishevelled clothes, smoothing his hair. "If you lot are going to look after The Boys, you'd better sharpen up," he said. "You'd better get on the ball."

Liam and his companion were approaching. "Lee, tell 'em. Tell 'em who I am."

"We weren't expecting you, Del," said Liam. His companion was strongly built, wearing a grey suit that hadn't been cut to disguise the ridge of muscle behind his neck. His face was bony, his nose crooked, as if it had been broken several times. He had dark red hair cut close to his head and round his flat ears. Charlotte found herself fluffing up her hair.

"Charlotte, this is Patrick Rendell," said Liam. "He was just telling me he knows the aunts."

"I also know Charlotte," said Patrick.

"Good God," said Charlotte, jolted. "It's the red-haired boy."

"Do you mind?" said Del, tired of being ignored. "I see a clock on the wall telling me it's time to wind it up."

Liam went on with introductions, then he, Del and Suki moved towards the set, where there was a renewed bustle of activity. Charlotte was left with Patrick, who seemed at ease and entirely sure of himself. She remembered him trying to reassure the aunts. Was he still as kind?

"Why are you here?" she said.

"I'm with Metropolitan Line. In charge of security. Liam just said that."

"I wasn't listening. Is it a coincidence that Liam hired you?"

Patrick stopped his methodical scanning of the studio for long enough to raise an eyebrow at her. "Why should it not have been?"

"I wondered if the aunts . . ."

Patrick laughed. "Are they still match-making for you?"

Charlotte was offended, moved away. He was laughing at her. She felt embarrassed, exposed, undesirable. Patrick stretched out and caught her arm. "I meant, it would be self-evidently absurd. That you should need them to."

"WHAM BAM
THANK YOU
THANK YOU
MA'AM"

The playback tape was very loud. The silver Boys strutted.

The attention of everyone in the studio, except the door guard, was focussed on the lighted set. Charlotte pretended to watch The Boys. Patrick stood close beside her. "Is this your kind of music?" he said.

"No."

"Why do you work for Broken Records?"

"I was sacked from my job," said Charlotte, surprising herself. Patrick had something of Nicholas's imperturbable quality.

"Oh!" he said.

"I was a teacher."

"What went wrong?"

"Hard to explain."

"But you'd be prepared to try? For instance, if I asked you to dinner?" said Patrick. He wasn't smiling, but she felt he was amused. She glanced at him from under her lashes, enjoying the game.

"Tomorrow night?" he said.

"I'm not sure . . ."

"The night after?"

"Tomorrow night would be possible."

"Eight o'clock? I'll pick you up."

"Whaddya think, girl?" said Del, approaching. "Ain't The Boys amazin? Some kinda talent, eh?"

"WHAM BAM," howled the playback tape. Two of the silver Boys were lying on the sand, writhing in simulated ecstasy. The other two were being winched up on wires.

"What's the point of this scene?" said Charlotte.

Del sniggered. "Can't you guess?"

"The song is apparently about sex."

"Got it in one."

"What does the beach have to do with sex?"

"WHAM BAM THANK YOU MA'AM TAKE IT ANY WAY YOU CAN UH UH UH UH."

Del sniggered again. "Good place to have it away, you know what I mean?"

"No," said Charlotte. "You could have sex anywhere."

"It's the visual impact, see? The art director's great on

visual impact. That's essential to the creative components, visual impact."

"So it doesn't matter what it means, so long as it looks good?"

"Nah. It's the *visual impact*," said Del.

"But that's what I just said."

"I wish you'd speak English," said Del. "Sodding teachers. Anyhow, I come to tell you we got lift-off."

"Sorry?"

"Babes in the Wood. All go-go-go, from tomorrow. Creative meeting, eleven o'clock, my room. Unless Lee wants you, of course."

"I'll be there," said Charlotte.

"Well played that girl," said Del in his public school voice. He often did imitations, had a talent for them. "Bye for now." Then, to Patrick, "So long. Keep your shirt over it."

"I wish you'd speak English," said Charlotte.

The creative conference in Del's office, a medium-sized room with walls papered with pictorial evidence of his modest achievements in the entertainment field, started badly because only two-thirds of the projected group turned up: Sharon, the blonde, now brunette, whose audition Charlotte had been present at, and the black youth, Elliot Simson. The original blonde was nowhere to be found.

A secretary was despatched to make inquiries. She returned with the news that the blonde had tired of waiting for the call to stardom that never came, and had gone on a tour of Middle East night clubs.

The meeting was cast into gloom. Vince frowned in sympathy with Del and twinkled at Charlotte. Del slapped his forehead. "Oh, shit. I mean – shit. What kind of loyalty is that? The Middle East, I ask you. Now we've got to start over."

"If you're going to audition again, maybe you could look for a brunette and I could go back to being blonde," said Sharon hopefully. "It's been murder trying to adapt my wardrobe to the brown hair."

"Mebbe *I* should go blonde," said Elliot, and laughed loudly. No one else did.

"Coffee, let's have some coffee here," said Del. The secretary left again. Charlotte looked at the pattern she was doodling on her clipboard. Patrick, Patrick, Patrick, it said. She hastily began ornamenting the letters into a design. Of course he won't ring, she told herself.

The phone rang. Charlotte answered it. "Mr Busby's in conference," she said automatically. Everyone answering Del's phone had to say that: Del believed it impressed people.

"Miss Parker?" said the receptionist. "There a girl down here asking for you, says it's urgent, name of Miranda Chalker."

"I'll be down," said Charlotte.

"Oh, wait! wait!" came as a muffled wail through the receiver, then the boy spoke to Charlotte again: "I'm sorry, but she's coming on up. I couldn't stop her."

Before Charlotte could explain to Del, Miranda was in the room, all long legs in red stockings, a red mini-skirt, and a fantastically elaborate top with padded shoulders which clearly outlined the shape of her breasts. She looked breathtaking, Charlotte acknowledged even through her mingled anxiety and irritation. "Miss Parker, oh Miss Parker, I'm so relieved to have found you. It's Sophie. She's taken an overdose and she called me. I fetched an ambulance and now she's in hospital."

"What did she take?" said Del.

"Paracetamol, I think."

"Terrible on the stomach lining, paracetamol," said Del.

"True," agreed Vince.

"Aspirins are better than paracetamol," said Del.

"What about Valium?" suggested the secretary.

"That's right," said Vince. "You can't o.d. on Valium."

"Depends on whether she wanted to die," said Del. "I mean, some suicides want to die. In that case there's nothing to beat yer actual barbs."

"Oh yes," said Vince feelingly. "I had a dear friend

who passed over with barbiturates. Nembutal, I think. H[
choked, poor love."

"Miranda," interrupted Charlotte, "how is Sophie[
How many pills did she take?"

"She's okay now," said Miranda. "They pumped he[
stomach out. She didn't even lose consciousness. Sh[
reckons she took ten but I think she's exaggerating."

"Ten's a lot of paracetamol," said Del. The topic evidently excited him, and he was also eyeing Miranda. "Si[
down, girl," he said. "Coffee's coming. It must have been
a shock. Friend of Charlotte's are you?"

"Miss Parker taught at my old school," said Miranda,
with a knowing glance in Charlotte's direction which Charlotte was too preoccupied to mind.

"And what are you doing now?" pursued Del.

"I'm at a college of music."

"Oh yeah?" said Del. "Sing, do you?"

"Yes," said Miranda. "I've got my grade eight in voice."

"Oh yeah?" Del unwrapped a piece of gum, nonchalantly popped it into his mouth. He usually did this,
Charlotte noticed, when he wanted to appear suave.

"Grade eight is the highest grade," said Miranda help-
fully. She couldn't resist showing off, even when it might
damage her own interests.

"I know," lied Del. "What about dancing?"

"I learnt modern expressive dance at school."

Vince shuddered. "Never mind, ducky, we'll soon cure
that."

Charlotte was absorbed in thought of Sophie. The child
was in hospital being taken care of: no hurry to visit
her immediately, then. But something must definitely be
arranged for the future. Her parents must be made to
understand how unsatisfactory the tutorial college and the
flat were proving to be. Sophie needed a school.

"Ever thought of performing, girl? Singing, like?"

"No," said Miranda, eyes downcast. "I've led a very
sheltered life."

Del seemed to inflate like a rubber macho doll. "Sheltered, eh? Just right for The Babes in the Wood."

"Oh, Miss Parker, it was terrible!" gloated Sophie, tucked up in a high bed. "I felt so depressed. I was all alone in the flat, the other girls had left me alone, they said they had to go to college no matter how bad I felt. I just couldn't go on. I took masses and masses of paracetamol and then I realised how upset my parents would be – and I knew my duty was to live. So I rang you but they said you were in conference and then I rang Miranda. And the ambulance came and they pumped my stomach out and it really hurt and the nurses aren't a bit sympathetic."

"They probably think you were very silly," said Charlotte, "deliberately making yourself ill and taking up valuable time while other people need doctors and nurses."

It was a huge modern ward, built in the expansionist Seventies for a glorious future of funding which hadn't materialised. Already the window frames were buckling, the plaster beneath them cracking, like the hotel in Moscow. The end of the ward was screened off: not enough staff to man it. And one bed was being occupied by poor useless Sophie.

"Have you telephoned your parents?"

"Oh, I hoped you'd do that," said Sophie. "They'll be terribly upset."

"Don't look so pleased about it."

"Aren't you glad I didn't die?"

"Of course I'm glad you didn't die," said Charlotte. "But I'd be gladder still if you hadn't taken an overdose."

"Will you come to fetch me when they let me out?"

"When will that be?"

"Tomorrow morning," said Sophie. She made a face. "They want me to talk to a psychiatrist, can you imagine?"

"Don't you think that would be a good idea?"

"I'm not round the bend," said Sophie. "There's nothing wrong with me."

It was towards the end of visiting hours. All round them awkward people sat staring at each other, constrained by the public nature of the place and the absence of a flickering television screen to authorise their silence.

"Wouldn't you like to talk to someone about why you're so depressed?"

Sophie thought about this. "Yes," she said. "But I could talk to you."

"It wouldn't be the same. Psychiatrists are trained, they know what to do."

"You don't need training just to talk."

"What about your parents, Sophie? Shouldn't you talk to them?"

"I don't think they'd want to hear." She plucked agitatedly at the sheet. "Is there a shop in the hospital, Miss Parker? Could you bring me something to eat?"

"Haven't you had supper?"

"It wasn't very nice," said Sophie sulkily. "Where's Miranda? Why hasn't she come to visit me? I want to thank her for saving my life."

"She's busy tonight."

"What's she doing?"

"Having dinner with some people from my record company. They're forming a new group and they want her to be in it."

"Oh, she can't do that, can she, Miss Parker? She's still at college."

"I shouldn't have thought so."

"Mrs Preston? Hello, is that Mrs Preston?"

The long-distance line twanged and echoed. "Yes?" said the voice cautiously.

"This is Charlotte Parker here. I used to be a teacher at Ashcombe, we met once or twice at Open Days. It's about Sophie. She's quite all right now, but she's in hospital, recovering from a small overdose of pills that she took in a mock suicide attempt."

"What nonsense is this?" demanded Mrs Preston. Even over the telephone Charlotte could imagine her discontented face with its deep lines from nose to chin and downturned mouth. "There must be some mistake. Sophie couldn't possibly have made a suicide attempt, mock or otherwise. She's loving it in London, learning to stand on her own two feet. I had a letter from her only last week. There must be confusion here. Perhaps a misunderstanding. Let me speak to a doctor."

"I'm not at the hospital. They'll be ringing you separately. They've tried on and off all afternoon but the lines to Strasbourg were busy."

"What part have you played in this?" said the woman suspiciously.

"I am an acquaintance of Sophie's, we meet for lunch occasionally. She asked for me when she was taken to hospital," said Charlotte coolly. She was beginning to feel sorry for Sophie again. "She'll be allowed out of hospital tomorrow. Will you be able to get here in time? I could tell the ward sister when to expect you."

Mrs Preston spluttered. She spluttered about flights from Strasbourg being heavily booked, about commitments to important political functions, about her husband's career, about how if Sophie was well enough to leave hospital so quickly she must be quite all right, and how it was all a mistake.

"What shall I tell the ward sister?" said Charlotte implacably. "And what arrangements will you make for Sophie after this?"

"What arrangements? That is none of your business, Miss Parker. My husband and I are perfectly capable of looking after our own daughter without any help from you, and I'll thank you to remember that."

"Very well, Mrs Preston," said Charlotte, furiously angry. "Just tell me when I should remember it. When visiting Sophie in hospital, perhaps? When taking her back to a flat in which she lives without responsible adult supervision? When visiting her in hospital after yet another abortive suicide attempt? When identifying her body in the mortuary after a successful one?"

Charlotte was shaking with futile anger. The other woman slammed her phone down. Charlotte replaced hers with care. She knew already that it had been a mistake, as far as Sophie's welfare was concerned, to lose her temper, but the combination of Sophie's grizzling and her mother's self-righteousness had been too much. Deprived children always touched Charlotte deeply, particularly when the parents pretended that any family problem was the child's alone.

"Would you like coffee?" said Patrick.

"Yes, please." Charlotte was aware of the momentous nature of the occasion. Suki had called it her first date, had been full of advice, none of which Charlotte had listened to.

She was enjoying herself. The restaurant was French, very expensive (either he was well off, or he was complimenting her), and quiet. He didn't talk to waiters about food (a change from Liam). He listened when she spoke, asked intelligent questions. His questions led her to tell him more about herself than she had intended to, and she suspected that he had guessed the rest. He was physically attractive. She was delighted by her own composure and calculating what to do when dinner was over. Should she ask him in when he drove her home? Would he kiss her?

"Charlotte! What are you thinking about?"

"Sorry," she said, pulling herself back. "I'm rather prone to trances. Nicholas is always teasing me about it." As soon as the words were out, she regretted her gaucherie. Why drag Nicholas into this?

"Who is Nicholas?"

She explained.

"Are you and he . . ."

"Oh, *no!*" she said. "No, no. Nothing like that. He was just the first man I got to know. I explained all that earlier." He nodded. "And Nicholas was so kind, so . . ."

"Does Nicholas have a woman of his own?"

"I don't think so." The suggestion was unwelcome. "He's quite old."

Patrick nodded again. "Seventy or so?"

"Of course not, he couldn't still be teaching. He's fifty-ish."

"I see."

He stopped the car outside the flat. Now she was nervous, her confidence ebbing. "Would you like to come in for some coffee?"

"Not tonight," he said.

"Oh. Oh, I see," said Charlotte, bewildered. She had been convinced he found her attractive.

It was warm in the car. She decided to get out, searched the door for a handle to open it. He stretched across her to open it and his arm brushed against her breast. It was a stimulating, pleasurable sensation. She waited for him to touch her again. It was hardly a first date after all, she thought. They had known each other for ten years. He was certainly entitled to kiss her.

She lay in bed, awake, for hours. He hadn't kissed her. He hadn't touched her. Quite right, she thought. We need to progress slowly. But her impulse was for haste. She was sure he desired her. She desired him. She was frightened and excited at the same time. He was taller and stronger than Ian had been, more powerful, and though closer to her own age, he seemed more masculine, more exotic. She stretched her limbs, wriggled against the bedclothes, imagined.

The telephone woke her at half-past seven. He's coming round for breakfast, she guessed muzzily. Good.

It was Liam. "How's your friend?"

"Thanks for ringing, Liam. She's fine."

"You don't sound very cheerful."

"I'm okay. Just a bit tired. How did you hear about Sophie?"

"The office was buzzing with it. And the dramatic appearance of The Red Queen, new member of Del's projected group."

"You mean Miranda, I suppose? That's ridiculous, Liam. She can't be in a group, she's at a college of music."

"I expect she'll fiddle it somehow. She seemed to me a determined young lady."

"You were with them at dinner?"

"Yes. Del was very keen on her artistic potential."

"On her tits and bum, I suppose," snapped Charlotte.

"Good grief," said Liam. "What's eating you?"

"I don't like Del. I don't like his attitude to women, his ridiculous appearance, his poses, his gum-chewing, his swearing, his jargon, his selfishness, his stupidity, and his hair-spray. Besides, I'm upset about Sophie."

"Why, particularly?"

"Because she's got useless parents."

"Don't take it personally. She'll probably survive."

"I hope so."

"It was fun seeing Suki again."

"Thanks for letting her come along."

"Isn't it a coincidence about Patrick Rendell?"

"Isn't it just," said Charlotte. "I'm not going to tell you anything about our dinner last night, so there."

"As if I'd want to know."

"Are you jealous?" said Charlotte. There had been an edge in Liam's voice that was best acknowledged.

"No. Yes. Perhaps," said Liam.

"If you weren't my brother I'd be after you like a shot," said Charlotte.

"No you wouldn't. Not if you fancy Rendell the Incredible Hulk."

"Don't be bitchy."

"Is he still there?"

"Certainly not."

"Be careful, Charlotte. I don't want you to be hurt. I want to keep you happy."

Chapter Ten

It was late November. Charlotte was having tea in the Reduced Gentlefolk's Club. The aunts were excited. Henrietta was in full voice. "Patrick Rendell, such a nice boy. Liam's told us. We're so pleased for you, Charlotte."

"There's nothing much to be pleased about, yet," said Charlotte, and ate her chocolate cake with unnecessary attention.

The aunts exchanged knowing glances.

"If you'd rather we didn't *talk* about it . . ." said Henrietta, "we'll respect your wishes, of course."

She coughed. Victoria winked, and nodded.

"Isn't it fun that Liam's given you the task of looking after those charming young people," said Henrietta. "We read all about it in the *Express* and the *Mail*. We saw the photographs. Liam sent us clippings. Wasn't it lucky that Liam found Sharon, Elliot and Miranda?"

"How do you know their names?"

"It was all in the papers. About how eager they are to learn and improve their music and how you look after them and raise the standard of their English and discuss Eastern philosophy. It does sound worthwhile."

"The dress you were wearing in the photograph looked a bit dowdy," said Victoria. "A ruffle down the front would have helped."

"I wasn't sure why you discussed Eastern philosophy," said Henrietta. She looked expectantly at Charlotte. She was normally level-headed, thought Charlotte, how could she not see through the Babes in the Wood charade? How could she be so naive?

"Publicity handouts aren't always quite accurate," said Charlotte.

"You mean it isn't *true*?" Henrietta was almost wailing.

"It sounded such a happy arrangement. Those innocent young people, determined to preserve the traditional values even in the tinsel glitter of the world of popular music; and you, dedicated to the task of educating and protecting them. You were always such a responsible little girl, Charlotte, I knew the task would appeal to you. Bringing your standards to Liam's world."

"Yes, Aunt," said Charlotte.

"Everyone had a great weekend, right?" said Del. The occupants of the studio nodded, grunted, smiled.

"Piss-artist," said Sharon under her breath. The Babes in the Wood were sitting on the floor at one end of the studio, leaning against the wall in a row like dolls at a toy maker. Charlotte stood beside them, waiting for an order from Del.

Del in the studio was in his element. He understood the environment and dominated it, giving orders in a peremptory voice to the singers, the engineers, the secretaries and Charlotte. The setting suited him with its matt black walls, the abundance of oblique glass panels, the concealed lighting and deadened sound. In the real world he looked artificial: in the studio he was at home.

He and the chief engineer were conferring, the troops could stand at ease. Elliot was moaning. "What a party! What a party!"

"Spare us the details," said Sharon, moving away. "You stink, Elliot."

"Yeah. Haven't washed, have I?"

"Christ, Elliot," said Miranda. "Go and wash. Go now."

"I met a girl. Lips like a vacuum cleaner." He rolled his eyes. "You wouldn't *believe* it."

"We don't. Go wash," said Sharon.

Elliot moved away. Miranda leant against the wall, closed her eyes.

"Did you have a good weekend?" Charlotte asked Sharon.

"Terrible. I went home, didn't I? Talk about mistakes. I had to see my dad."

"Don't you get on with him?"

"Hard to say, really. Whether I get on with him. He fucked me, see. Since I was eight. Mum looked the other way." Sharon delivered this information without emotion.

"Sharon, how awful!" said Charlotte. "What a dreadful thing!"

"It's not so bad now. The Social Services took me away and I had to go to a self-help group. I got to understand about why he did it. Inadequate and that. I still hate the bastard."

"Oh," said Charlotte. "I'm sorry."

"'S okay. Incest's quite common, you know. That's what I found out at the self-help group. Lots of parents fuck their children."

"I read a novel about it the other day," offered Charlotte, out of her depth. "About a girl who lived near Heathrow."

"That's funny," said Sharon. "P'raps it's something to do with airports. We live near Gatwick."

"What a sordid conversation," said Miranda. "I'll add to it. Did you know that Del is impotent?"

All three looked at Del, still absorbed in technical discussion at the mixing desk.

"I'd be surprised if he could buy a stiff carrot," said Sharon.

"I didn't know what to do," said Miranda.

"You tried a blow job?" said Sharon.

"Yes."

"Jerking him off?"

"Yes."

"Offer your bum?"

"Yes."

"You did the best you could," said Sharon.

Charlotte, listening to them, remembered Henrietta's naive belief in the publicity Liam's PR department churned out. "I'm supposed to protect you lot from the big bad world," she said.

"We *are* the big bad world," said Miranda. "I felt almost sorry for Del. He was so pathetic."

"You're pathetic to let him anywhere near you," said Sharon robustly. "You *can't* fancy him."

"Boy and girls, into the booth," called Del. "Singing time."

They filed into the booth, adjusted their headphones, looked expectantly at Del. He flicked the microphone switch and gave them instructions.

Charlotte stopped listening. She felt battered by the ugliness all round her. She could almost understand Henrietta's belief in The Babes in the Wood: it was tempting to turn away from what actually happened to somebody else's Disney version of what might happen.

"We come to bring you happiness," sang the group, "we come to bring you joy."

"Oh shit, sorry," said Miranda. "Let's take it again. I always miss that note."

"So much for grade ten in voice," said Del.

"Grade eight, actually."

"What d'you think to that?" Del asked the engineer.

"The boy could come up a touch."

"Leave it for now. We'll fix it later if need be. Okay, here we go."

"We come to bring you happiness
We want to bring you joy
Light of day and laughter
To build and not destroy
La la
la la
la la
la la."

"Get those lyrics," said Del. "Whaddya think, teacher?"

"Amazing," said Charlotte.

"Bloody marvellous. I wrote them myself." He was sweating into his hair, she could see damp at the roots. Close up, his face was blunt and brutish. "You gotta be positive. Emphasise the positive, that's my creative concept for this group. Put a little happiness into people's lives, that's how I see it."

"Yes," said Charlotte.

"What d'you think to the sound?"

"It sounds just like Abba."

"Isn't it great?" He shifted a wad of gum from one tanned cheek to the other. "Isn't it fantastic? Unbelievable? Aren't they lovely?" He waved a braceleted arm at the group. They were sitting morosely on high stools, their faces largely obscured by microphones, their heads helmeted with metal and foam rubber.

"Miranda was supposed to be at a college of music," said Charlotte. "She's given that up. Do you think it's a good thing?"

"That's down to her, ain't it. I'm not my brother's fuckin' keeper."

"I'm supposed to be looking after them."

"That's down to you, then. Talk to her."

"I have. She doesn't listen."

Del shrugged. "She's a tough little slag. She can take care of herself."

"Hey, Del," called the engineer. "A word." Del sauntered over to him with an ironic salute to Charlotte. The group, dismissed for ten minutes, filed out of their booth.

"Stay away from us, Elliot," said Sharon. "I nearly fainted in there."

"It's the smell of a real man," said Elliot. "I'm just too masculine for you."

"Call it what you like, so long as you move."

Elliot lay on the floor, arms folded. The girls moved away from him.

"Seen Sophie recently?" Charlotte asked Miranda.

"Too much," said Miranda. "She hangs round all the time. She's got a crush on Del, you know."

"Yuck," said Sharon. They all looked at Del, flushed with enthusiasm, hot in discussion with the engineer.

"We could stretch the reverb on that," he said.

"How much?" said the engineer.

"Just a gnat's cock."

"He's more interested in this than he was in me," said Miranda.

"I've got an idea," said Sharon. "Where did you try to make it with him?"

"Does it matter?"

"Yeah. Was it in bed?"

"Yes," said Miranda.

"I bet he could make it in the studio."

"In here?"

"Yeah. I bet he could get it up in here. Not that I'd ever want to find out."

Suki had gone to stay with her parents in Oxford until Ollie returned from the Gulf. She went soon after the day at the studios. Charlotte missed her. She wanted to talk about Patrick. Not only did she want to recite the lovers litany of what he said, what he implied, what he did; she wanted advice, and advice of the kind that cannot be given over the telephone. He had taken her for six dinners, four drinks at the pub, one breakfast, one Sunday walk. He had kissed her twice, both in his car. Charlotte wanted to know if he desired her; if he was homosexual; if she appeared offputting; if he disapproved of sex before marriage; if he was progressing slowly out of consideration for her. Or was he progressing slowly? Judging by television plays, certainly. But then again television plays were so manifestly inaccurate in their depiction of all aspects of life that she was familiar with that they could not be a guide.

It was not a subject to be discussed with a man. Not even Nicholas. But Sharon — a girl who declared that she had been fucked by her father opened up unusual avenues of discourse.

After the recording session Charlotte gave Sharon a lift back to the Broken Records office.

"Sharon —"

"Yeah?"

"Would you mind if I asked you something?"

"Go ahead," said Sharon. Her feet were on the dashboard; she was working on her toes. The smell of nail polish remover filled the car.

"It's about a man."

"It always is. If he never takes you out he's married, if he only takes you out he's bent. He won't get you an audition or a recording contract – that doesn't apply to you, of course, you wouldn't want 'em. If he says he's had a vasectomy, check the scar."

"What a suspicious girl you are."

"Nah. Just been looking after myself a while now. Tell me your problem, see if I can help."

"There's a man who's invited me out quite often." She paused, reluctant to go on.

"Yeah," said Sharon, intelligent eyes gleaming. "You fancy him?"

"I think so. I did at first. I do when I'm not with him. But when I am – I freeze up. When he kisses me, I go cold and wish he'd stop."

"Ah," said Sharon. "Forgive me if I'm out of line . . ."

"Go on."

"I get the impression you're not amazingly, like, experienced."

"Not at all."

"Yeah, well. Teachers – I mean, all that marking. Must have cut down your social life. And all the studying at college. Stands to reason. So now it's unfamiliar. Men and that. Nerves are great passion-killers."

"What do you suggest I do?"

"Relax, don't think about it. You'll stop worrying soon enough."

"Isn't there anything I can *do*?" said Charlotte, baffled.

"You could drink a bit. Not too much, mind."

"Umm," said Charlotte.

"It's natural. Sex. Just what you feel like doing. Don't go thinking about it. Do you like green nail varnish?"

"No."

"Neither do I." She started to paint her toenails bright red.

*　　*　　*

"So you think you've got your life sorted out now?" said Nicholas. It was a frosty Sunday in early December. They were walking along the South Bank, two isolated figures against the concrete starkness of the buildings. It was low tide and the Thames mud was dotted with plastic bottles, wrappers, driftwood. Charlotte's feet were so cold that each step jarred. She burrowed her face further into her red scarf and blew warm breath up to her nose.

"More or less," she said defensively. "Why do you think I haven't?"

"What you say about Patrick."

"Which is what?"

"Ambivalent."

"No it isn't," lied Charlotte crossly. "I know exactly what I feel about Patrick."

"Ah," said Nicholas.

"Anything else?"

"Have you seen your father recently?"

"Don't be so ridiculous. Of course I haven't. You know I haven't. Why should I?"

Nicholas didn't answer. He leant on the river rail and looked east, towards St Paul's.

"Why should I, Nicholas? Answer me, damn it!"

"I could give you a lift down to Oxford one day. There are probably still some of your things at his house, aren't there?"

Charlotte thought. "Clothes and books. And my bicycle. And my sledge. All my photographs and letters, my exercise books, my American posters. Nothing valuable."

"You could pick them up. And see your father."

Charlotte thought again. She had never intended to return to the house, to her father. But if Nicholas was there . . . "I don't want the sledge and bicycle," she resisted faintly, and started to walk away. Nicholas followed.

Two black boys on skateboards waltzed past and round them.

"We could go next Sunday," said Nicholas. "Have lunch

on the way. You could send a postcard to warn your father. Is he likely to be there?"

"Term's just finished. He's bound to be."

"I'll be up in London next Friday. You can reach me at the usual number."

"Your friend's flat," said Charlotte, glad to change the subject.

"Yes."

"Is your friend male or female?"

"Do you want to know?"

"Not if you don't want to tell me," said Charlotte, though she felt excluded.

"My friend is female. She's Austrian and forty-five and we are lovers."

"Oh," said Charlotte, and stopped walking. Tears oozed from her eyes, into the scarf. "Why didn't you tell me before?"

"You didn't ask."

"How long . . .?"

"Six or seven years."

"Six or seven *years*! You didn't *tell* me!"

"You didn't ask."

"What a fool you must have thought me. Asking you to . . . asking you . . ."

"Not a fool. I was flattered, and touched."

"You were feeling sorry for me. You didn't want me." She felt reft, bereft, and betrayed. It was no comfort to know that she was being unreasonable. Knowing she was unreasonable increased her distress. She felt abandoned.

"Charlotte," said Nicholas trying to take her hand. She slapped his arm away.

"I hate you," she said miserably. "I hate you. I hate all of you. I don't understand." She was crying helplessly. "I didn't know you had a woman. You didn't tell me. All that time, I thought – I thought you loved me."

"I do," said Nicholas.

"You do?"

"Oh, yes."

The black boys skated up, swerved, spun round and whirled away.

"Well then . . ." said Charlotte. "I don't understand. I don't understand anything. What Sharon says about sex, what Elliot's talking about, half the things Del says. I don't understand what I feel or what Patrick feels or why the Prestons don't look after Sophie or how my mother can be so silly or why my father didn't love me."

Nicholas opened his heavy overcoat and pulled her to him, surrounding her with the thick cloth.

"The beginning of wisdom," he said.

"What is?"

"Acknowledging you don't understand."

She held herself rigid. He stroked her back and she shrugged irritably. "I don't *like* not understanding. I want things to *make sense*."

"You can only understand when you stop thinking about it," said Nicholas.

"Why does everyone talk to me in code?" said Charlotte, beginning to enjoy the sensation of his arms around her, feeling safe.

The black boys swept past, whistling and cat-calling.

"That's exactly the kind of thing Sharon said. About sex. She told me to stop thinking about it."

"I like the sound of Sharon."

"You'd like the sight of her, too. She's lovely."

He produced a handkerchief blotched over with paint stains, and wiped her face.

"Next Sunday, we go to see your father."

"Now then now then what's all this?" said Del, crashing into his office.

"Babes in the Wood publicity conference, Del," said the secretary. There were two PR men, the secretary, and Charlotte waiting. Del looked sly and lasciviously triumphant; Charlotte wondered if Miranda had found an effective aphrodisiac for him.

"We've been waiting an hour," said Charlotte.

"That's rock 'n 'roll," said Del, and smiled reminiscently.

The chief PR man summarised the progress they had made. Charlotte, on a chair by the window, watched the street, didn't listen, thought about Patrick. He was in Surrey with The Boys. Tomorrow, they would spend the day together.

"Charlotte," said Del. "Charlotte, how about givin' us the honour of your ladyship's attention?"

"Mmm?"

"Great gimmick. We found a coma victim, little girl."

"I don't understand."

"I told you last week, we wanted human interest, right? Somethin' for the group to do, help their image as caring and clean. Well, we got it. Little girl in the West Country, loved the Babes's first single, loved the video."

"Surprising, really," said the second PR man. "That video was dead cheap, and dull with it."

"Not dull," said Del huffily. "Mostly shot up Miranda's skirt, hardly dull. Any way up, this little girl's a fan. Last week she was hit by a truck."

"How terrible," said Charlotte, still not certain whether Del was inventing the whole anecdote.

"Yeah, well, she's been in a, like, coma, ever since. Her parents sit by her bedside day and night talking to her, you know the kinda stuff, but she don't respond. The hospital said they should make a tape of her favourite sounds. The father rang us yesterday, asked us to help. Great opportunity! We mustn't sit on this one. The local TV station will play ball when we let'm know what's going on. I want you to go down there tomorrow, suss it out, what the parents are like, get them sorted to meet The Babes. And get the girl fixed up so the viewers won't puke up their tea when they see her. Cut down on the tubes. Viewers don't like tubes."

"What if she needs tubes?"

"See what you can do with camouflage."

"What do you suggest? Christmas streamers, wound round the tubes?"

"Great," said Del.

"I don't go along with that a thousand per cent," said the first PR man.

"Whatever," said Del. "You got taste an' breedin', Charlotte, you deal with it."

"When is the TV crew coming?"

"If you can get it sorted, day after tomorrow. The Babes can mime to playback, that should help the poor little bleeder. Wake her up, like."

"No," said Charlotte.

"Whaddya mean?"

"How many people work here, Del?"

"About half," said Del, and laughed. The others laughed too. Charlotte ignored him.

"How many people could you send instead of me?"

"Some," he admitted.

"Well, send them."

"Too squeamish? Scared of hospitals?"

"I don't like the idea."

"We'll do it whether you like it or not. So will you help or won't you?"

"If I don't handle it, who will?"

Del thought. He looked cunning. "I will," he said. "With a whole lot less taste."

Patrick didn't mind being driven. He didn't mind spending the day accompanying Charlotte down to the hospital in the West Country. He didn't mind listening to her fulminations about Del. So far, he hadn't appeared to mind her inability to respond sexually.

"Are you always this patient?" she asked. They were travelling along the M4 in driving rain.

"It depends," he said.

"On what?"

"On what I stand to gain. Take The Boys, for instance. I'm patient with them because it's my living. A dispro-portionately good living."

"You were patient with my aunts. All those years ago."

"I liked your aunts. When can I go to tea with them again?"

"You don't mean it."

"I do."

"Why are you so patient with me?"

"What are we talking about?"

"Kisses and things."

"That's not patience. That's guile."

She glanced at him, then back to the road. He was looking amused again. He was too big for the car: his shoulders bulked out the light.

"And affection," he went on.

There was silence inside the car. Outside, the water swish-swished under the wheels, drowning the hum of the engine.

"What do you mean, guile?"

"Biding my time."

"Until what?"

"Until you get used to me."

"What if that never happens?"

"We will see," said Patrick.

"You seem very confident."

"Not unpleasantly so, I trust."

Charlotte shivered. His certainty was stimulating.

The hospital was a collection of huts and Portakabins huddled around an Edwardian Tudor house. Water had pooled in sheets on the canopied concrete walkways between the buildings. Charlotte and Patrick, heads down against the sleet, found Ward E. "Follow me," said the Sister, a tall, thin woman whose features softened when she heard their errand. "TV," she said, rubber-soled shoes squeaking on the linoleum. "Well, well. We've never had TV cameras in here. I hope it helps Lisa, poor little scrap." She shouldered through swing doors to a four-bed ward.

Three beds were empty. In the fourth a child lay so still that at first Charlotte thought her part of the bed.

Del would be pleased. There were few tubes, none to her face, all attached to equipment on the far side of the bed.

Her face was grey, her eyes closed and sunken. Her

mother sat on one side of the bed, her father on the other. They were both in their forties and they looked, most of all, bewildered. The mother was clutching a large purple mock-leather handbag that went with her purple shoes.

"Now then, Lisa," she said with the forced tone of one asked to speak naturally into a tape recorder. "This is Mum. Come on, Lisa, time to wake up. You've got to wake up, Lisa. Listen to Mum."

"Say about breakfast," prompted the father. "Go on."

"I can't, Jack, I'd feel stupid."

"Breakfast time, Lisa," said the father. "Time for your Coco-Pops."

"She'd gone off Coco-Pops."

All three seemed wrapped in a time-warped ritual. Charlotte imagined the parents talking so to their daughter for the last week.

She introduced herself and Patrick, as gently as she could. The man rose to his feet, a fierce hope in his eyes. "By God you've come. I knew you would. Janice didn't reckon to it. But I spoke to that Mr Busby and I could tell he was an important man. He said you'd be here today, and tomorrow he'd bring those singers. God bless them. Lisa loved that song, she taped the video when it was on Breakfast Telly, she played it again and again and again."

"All the time," said the mother.

"She loved all those singers, but the blonde one was her favourite. Her friends said she, Lisa that is, looked like the blonde one."

Charlotte looked at the face on the hospital pillow. It looked nothing like Miranda. It looked like death.

"We play her the video," the father said. "We brought our video in, the hospital have been very good." He nodded at the TV and equipment on a trolley at the foot of the bed.

"They were so *humble*," said Charlotte. "They're so grateful for Del's tawdry circus. I feel ashamed."

She had been silent almost all the way back to London.

"You needn't. Surely this is one of the rare occasions on which everyone wins. Del and the group have their publicity; the girl – who knows? It may help. The parents feel something's happening, so they're pleased."

"What if Del says something dreadful, tomorrow?"

"Odds on the parents won't understand a word he says. They wouldn't believe it, either. He'll be like a Martian to them."

"I'm glad you came with me."

"So am I."

It was past five. The rain had stopped but there was still damp in the air, shimmering in the stream of headlights leaving London. Patrick's presence seemed massively comforting.

"I wish we could spend the evening together."

"So do I," said Patrick.

"I suppose security men don't call in sick."

"Hardly. Not to a Wembley concert. Not if they want to stay in business."

"Will The Boys be straight enough to perform?"

"Should be."

"I'll drive you home," said Charlotte.

"Don't bother. I'll take a taxi from your flat."

She parked the car in Russell Square, switched off the engine, leant back with a sigh. "Lisa looked so ill."

"I've seen worse recover," said Patrick bracingly. "All the noise and fuss will probably do her good."

They walked together to the door of Charlotte's flat. "I want you to come in with me," she said.

"I wish I could," said Patrick. "What time are you leaving tomorrow?"

"Very early. The TV crew will be there at ten."

"I'll see you next week, then."

"Next *week*?"

"I'm going to the States, remember. Talking to various security people about handling the European end of their American clients' needs."

"Oh. Oh, damn," said Charlotte. She felt cheated. "I'm going to see my father on Sunday."

"You didn't tell me. That's a change, isn't it?"

"Nicholas thought it'd be a good idea."

"He could be right." He hugged her close. Her head tucked in neatly under his chin. A nearby public address system played Silent Night very loudly.

"Do you think . . ." began Charlotte, then tailed away; started again. "Do you think it'll be difficult, seeing my father?"

"Probably not as difficult as you expect. The worst part is always before you get into action."

"We're not talking about the SAS here," said Charlotte. "We're talking about a delicate emotional matter."

"Same principle."

Del insisted on travelling with Charlotte and the group in the Mercedes. He sat in the front with the driver. Charlotte and Sharon took the flip-down seats; Miranda, groaning with a hangover, lay across the back seat with her feet on Elliot's lap.

"Great concert last night," said Del. "Amazin'. Incredible."

"Yeah," said the driver. "When The Boys step on stage, you know you're in the presence of greatness."

Charlotte slept most of the way down. The ex-rock singer-chauffeur was better at driving than at singing. It was a smooth ride.

"You all got it straight, then," said Del as they reached the hospital. "This kid liked Miranda so Miranda gets to do most of the talking."

"I don't like hospitals," said Elliot.

"Shut it, son," said Del. "We're none of us exactly creaming ourselves. You do your bit to the parents about acceptance and being at one with the universe."

"I dunno how I got landed with this fuckin' Oriental shit. Can't Miranda do it?"

"Please, Elliot," said Charlotte.

"Sorry, sorry. I don't know why it has to be me, that's all. I never been anythin' but Baptist. I know nuthin' about the East."

"The PR boys like it," said Del.

"Okay, okay. I still don't get it why it has to be me. The nearest I ever come to Oriental philosophy, I watched that series, about the bald git who believed in peace and tolerance and if anyone disagreed with him he kicked the shit out of them."

"Kung Fu," said Sharon.

"Yeah, well," said Del impatiently. "You all do your bit talkin' and that, then you mime to playback. That's it unless the TV guys want other. Got it?"

The parents again looked bewildered, as well they might. The ward was crowded. From the TV station there was a director/presenter, a cameraman, a sound man. From Broken Records there was Del, two PR men, The Babes in the Wood, a secretary, two sound engineers, a make-up girl hired by Del for the occasion, and Charlotte. From the hospital there was an administrator, a doctor, the ward sister, two nurses, three cleaners. From the local paper there was a reporter and a photographer.

In the bed lay Lisa. Her mother stood beside her holding one of the pale, inanimate hands. "Look who's come to see you," she said.

"This is bloody useless," said the cameraman. "Everything's white. White walls, white sheets."

"Do your best, Mike," said the director/presenter. He was a handsome man with false teeth and a wig very like Del's hair. He moved towards Sharon and nearly tripped over the sound recordist who was bent over, threading tape into his machine.

"Not a whole lot of room in here," the sound recordist said with a morose nod at the crowd. "Couldn't we lose any of these, like now?"

All the hospital staff except the ward sister were persuaded to leave by the second PR man, who left to wait outside in the corridor. Everyone else stayed.

"Oh my," said the mother weakly. "If my girl only knew how much trouble everyone was going to for her sake."

"Could you move over, please," said the cameraman. He was setting lights up around the bed.

"Careful," said the ward sister. He gave her a weary glance.

"Okay, okay, I know what I'm doing. Got any blinds for those windows?"

"Why?"

"I want less light from those windows, okay? Got anything we can screen them with?"

Sharon and Miranda were in the far corner changing behind a screen.

"Above all, we want this to be utterly, utterly natural," said the presenter, fixing the parents with a piercing plastic smile. "Let's just run over one or two questions I might ask you."

"I'm gonna throw up," Elliot confided to Charlotte. "I hate the smell in hospitals, 'n the sick people, 'n all."

"Try repeating a mantra," said Charlotte.

"Take a pull at this," said Del, producing a flask of brandy.

"How much are your kids going to move, Del?" said the cameraman.

"Not a lot. They stand on the same spot and waggle their butts."

"This area do?" He indicated a space on the other side of the bed from the medical paraphernalia.

"That'll be fine."

"Fine, that's just fine," said the presenter, making notes on his clipboard. "Now have you any little anecdotes about Lisa before the accident? Do you have a family pet, for instance?"

"We have a goldfish," said the father, bewilderment intensifying. "I'm not sure –"

"Not to worry, not to worry."

"It was just that she so wanted to meet Miranda," said the mother doggedly. "She kept writing in to see if The Babes in the Wood were appearing live. She really wanted to meet Miranda."

"Good, that's very good."

"She wanted to look like Miranda when she grew up."

"And she will, I'm sure," said the presenter heartily. "I'm sure we all hope that."

Miranda appeared from behind the screen in a tiny red mini-skirt, silver sequined top cut away under her breasts, hair spiked and sprayed with red highlights.

"She's so beautiful," said the mother, and burst into tears.

"I don't suppose the girl recovered, did she?" said Nicholas. He had listened to Charlotte's account of Broken Records' excursion into schmalz, patiently, all through lunch. Now, as Charlotte could no longer pretend she wanted more coffee, they were driving towards Oxford and her father.

"Not recovered, no. But the extraordinary thing was, she did seem more conscious. She was muttering and crying out by the time we left, and her father rang on Friday to say she was saying 'Mum' and squeezing her mother's hand."

"That's good," said Nicholas. "Hey, before I forget – I have a message for you." He coaxed the rattling old estate car up to sixty miles an hour, and Charlotte averted her eyes from the road. "From Paula Madders. I had to give you the message word for word."

"Let's have it."

"I'll have to mention the Headmaster," Nicholas warned.

"Mention away," said Charlotte. Ian was no longer a concern.

"At a Head of Departments Meeting the other day –"

"Heads of Department," corrected Charlotte.

"At a meeting the other day the Headmaster announced that he had decided to amalgamate the English, History, Geography and Religious Studies Departments."

"Humanities!" said Charlotte. "Incredible! Nora got her own way after all. It must have been blackmail."

"Wait. And the Head of Humanities was to be – Paula Madders."

Charlotte laughed. "Excellent. Nora outmanoeuvred. How did she take it?"

"Venomously, according to Paula. She's away on sick leave now. A mysterious back complaint."

Nicholas went on talking but Charlotte didn't listen. She hugged her knees, watched the flat countryside unroll, dreaded her father. The expensive lunch Nicholas had treated her to had been entirely wasted. Her throat had closed up when she tried to eat.

Perhaps he won't be there, she thought. She imagined herself going up to the front door, ringing the bell, eventually – blissfully – retreating. No answer, Nicholas, she would say. He can't have got my postcard in time. Shall we go for a walk in Christ Church meadow, then to Woodstock for tea?

The postcard, sent on Monday, had been hard to write. The final version read:

"Would like to call in next Sunday (16th) at 2.30 to collect some of my things. Any chance of seeing you? Let me know at the above address if you can't manage it. Yours, Charlotte."

There had been no answer. The likelihood was that he would be there.

She had lain awake the night before, thinking about her father, trying to understand the relationship she had failed to have with him. Getting to know Tessy had, in a way, helped. Tessy's comments on Geoffrey – "Darling, he was so cold, he just didn't know how much *care* and *attention* a woman needs. Half the time I might as well have been a piece of furniture. I'd have been much better off as a book. At least he'd have *picked* me *up* occasionally" – together with what Charlotte knew of them both, made the failure of their marriage entirely comprehensible. Geoffrey had undertaken a woman who, like a listed building, needed skilful attention and maintenance, but was too narcissistic to give it. He thought wives should be like his mother, a devoted shadow of her husband. Having married a woman

236

different in every respect from his mother, he expected the merits of his mother with Tessy's charms added.

Tessy languished, untended. She cast round for a second husband, a strong, rich, attentive man. Eventually she found Roddy. He wanted to be Prime Minister one day: couldn't risk a messy divorce, so Geoffrey had been able to strike his vindictive bargain. It was hard, looking back, for Charlotte to blame her mother. She had to have a man, the right man. She was of the last generation of men-centred women. To her a woman only existed if she belonged to a successful man, like a dehydrated foodstuff attending on a kettle.

Charlotte understood all this. She was beginning to understand her father's revenge: his disappointment, his jealousy. She had found twinges of these emotions in herself when Nicholas had told her about his Austrian. But her father as a personality eluded her. Her mind glanced away when she tried to comprehend him, like a small boa-constrictor confronted with an over-large donkey to digest.

"Which end of Norham Gardens?" said Nicholas.

"Oh, God," said Charlotte. She was appalled. "Are we there already?"

"What number, Charlotte?"

"That house. On the right."

Nicholas stopped the car. It was a typical North Oxford house, late Victorian, grey stone and stained glass, with peculiar little turrets sprouting out like the eyes of an elderly potato. The study light was on: Geoffrey was sitting at his desk, working.

"Come on," said Nicholas briskly.

"Wait a minute."

"Now," said Nicholas. He opened the car door, took her elbow, hurried her across the road and up the front steps.

"Won't be long," he said, ringing the bell.

Geoffrey answered the door. His hair was thin, his face lined, his body stooped. He looked, thought Charlotte in astonishment, insignificant.

"Charlotte," he said, in his edgy voice. "Come in."

Charlotte introduced Nicholas, made no attempt to kiss her father or even shake hands.

"Do you want to get your things first? Would you like a cup of coffee?" said Geoffrey, as if he saw her every day.

"Coffee would be nice," said Charlotte.

"Why don't you and Mr Embrey start packing your things. I'll make the coffee. You don't need me to show you your room."

"I'm not sure how much I want to take," said Charlotte.

"Ah. Well, I'll have to ask you to arrange to take anything you want to keep by the end of the year. I'm putting the house on the market."

"Goodness," said Charlotte.

"It's much too big for one person, and I've been letting rooms to undergraduates, but it wasn't entirely satisfactory."

Charlotte led Nicholas upstairs. "He always used to say that about me. 'You're not entirely satisfactory, Charlotte, I'm afraid.'"

"Who the hell is?" said Nicholas with unaccustomed vigour. "I'd like to punch his teeth in."

Charlotte laughed. She was beginning to feel the oppression of her spirits lift. With Nicholas there, the house and her father were demythologised.

She opened the door to her room, expecting to find her possessions stored away in the wardrobe and cupboards. But everything was as she had left it, the posters on the walls, her second best hairbrush on the dressing table, her cut-glass bowl of slides and hairgrips and spare buttons next to it, her bed made up with clean sheets.

"Why America?" said Nicholas, looking at the posters.

"I *told* you all about that," said Charlotte. "What America means to me. Freedom and space –"

"I remember now."

"How could you have forgotten?" said Charlotte, a little serious.

"Because I'm not entirely satisfactory," said Nicholas. "Let's not stay long here."

Charlotte began stacking the things she wanted to take in piles on the bed. "I wouldn't bother," said Nicholas. "Since you'll have to move them all anyway. Get a removal firm to do it all at once. Let's go and drink the unwanted coffee and lay the ghost of your father once and for all."

"Sugar, Mr Embrey?"

"No thank you."

They were sitting in the conservatory. It was very hot, full of plants. It seemed smaller than Charlotte remembered, more conventional, less exotic.

"And are you and Charlotte – er –"

"Nicholas is a colleague of mine from school," said Charlotte.

"But you're no longer at that school."

"No. I got the sack." She felt irresponsible, light-headed. Her father diminished by the minute.

"What a pity. Has it ruined your career?"

"I don't think so. I'm working for Liam at the moment but I expect to go back to teaching eventually."

"And how are your mother's pathetic aunts?"

"Very well," said Charlotte staunchly. "Liam's looking after them."

"Mmmm. Do you always dress like that?"

Charlotte was wearing a red jumpsuit, yellow belt, multicoloured scarves rolled and knotted round her neck, a yellow cashmere sweater tied bandolier-style across her back.

"Most of the time."

"How extraordinary."

"It suits the record business."

"It would."

"I'll arrange for a removal firm to clear my room."

"Kindly give me plenty of notice. It wasn't at all convenient to be here today."

"Where else would you have been?" said Charlotte, undaunted.

The front door of the house closed behind them. Charlotte

and Nicholas walked soberly to the car, got in, drove away. After a few seconds they looked at each other and began to laugh. "The man's a prat," said Charlotte. "A twit, a wally, a wimp."

"A bastard," said Nicholas.

"Let's go for a walk in Christ Church meadow and then for tea in Woodstock," said Charlotte.

After seeing her father again Charlotte felt confident, almost smug. Patrick was still away in America. She decided to ask Sophie to dinner.

It was an unmitigated disaster. Sophie was due to arrive at seven but turned up at eight, so doped from sleeping pills that she could hardly articulate; aggressive, self-pitying and weepy by turns. She ate little food, drank as much wine as she could when Charlotte wasn't looking, and finally went to sleep on the sofa.

Charlotte dialled the Prestons' number in Strasbourg. This time she got a man. "Mr Preston? This is Charlotte Parker here, I used to be . . ."

"Oh yes, Miss Parker," said Preston. "I know who you are." He sounded guarded, indifferent. He was more intelligent than his wife, less transparent.

"It's about Sophie."

"I had supposed it would be."

"She's here at the moment, asleep on my bed. I'm worried about her."

"Why?"

"Because she seems so unhappy, she isn't attending her tutorial college, and she's taking too many sleeping pills."

"Where does she get those from?"

"I have no idea," said Charlotte. "Possibly her doctor."

"That would be irresponsible, wouldn't it, prescribing sleeping pills for Sophie?"

Irresponsible? thought Charlotte, confused momentarily by the Alice in Wonderland world of the Prestons where everyone except themselves was to blame.

"These medical people are all the same," continued Preston. "The hospital doctors behaved most unethically, turning an accident into a suicide attempt. The girl made a simple mistake. She hasn't been the same since they spoke to her at that hospital about suicide and psychiatrists. There was nothing wrong with her mind until she went in there. Ever since, she's been quite different. She won't even spend Christmas with us, even though we're coming back to England specially."

"I know," said Charlotte. "She told me."

"Well, that can't be right, can it?" said Preston. "That just shows you something's wrong."

"That's my point," said Charlotte. "She needs some proper care. She needs to talk to someone."

"There's nothing wrong with Sophie that time won't cure," said Preston, and Charlotte couldn't budge him from that position.

Chapter Eleven

Patrick came back from America and took Charlotte out to dinner. She told him about her father and about Sophie: he told her about America. She asked him up to her flat for a drink when he took her home and as she unlocked the flat door, she lost her nerve. She imagined him making love to her, then going away. The two events seemed inextricably connected.

On a more superficial level there were the practicalities. How did the matter proceed? The stationery cupboard incident had illustrated the pitfalls of undressing herself for a sexual encounter, but she shrank from the awkwardness of waiting while he unpeeled her like an artichoke – even though she had dressed carefully from the skin out.

They were inside the flat. Patrick removed his thick dark blue overcoat, sat down in one of the Habitat chairs, stretched his legs out in front of him. She was bustling about: turning up the heating, twitching the curtains still more firmly closed, pouring the drinks.

At last she stood, at a loss.

"You could water the plants," he suggested, smiling.

His chair was a steel and canvas structure, chosen by Liam, elegant and stylish when he sat in it, dwarfed and made insignificant by Patrick's large and muscular body.

"Why didn't you sit on the sofa?" said Charlotte, annoyed by his amusement.

"I thought it would make you more nervous," said Patrick.

"Why did you think I was nervous?"

"Because you won't sit down, because you won't meet my eye, because your hands are shaking. I thought you were nervous of me, and that if I sat on the sofa you might think I expected you to join me."

Charlotte clasped her hands together to stop them shaking. All the desire and sexual curiosity she felt for him in his absence had seeped away; the evening was splintering round her.

"I'm sorry," she said.

Patrick stood up, put his arms round her. She pulled away but he made no move to let her go. "I won't kiss you," he said. "I won't make love to you. Not while you're frightened."

"I'm not entirely frightened," she said cautiously. She liked the sensation of his hands on her back. "Perhaps . . ."

"Not yet," said Patrick. "You're trembling."

"I could be trembling with desire," said Charlotte, more confident by the second.

"But you're not," said Patrick.

"Hello? Hello? Sophie?"

"Hello?" said a voice, drowsy, hardly articulating. "Who is this?"

"Charlotte. Charlotte Parker."

"I'm not at home," said Sophie, and rang off.

Charlotte looked, baffled, at the buzzing receiver in her hand.

She was in Liam's office. It was shiny, with elegant Italian steel and leather chairs, Italian white tiles on the floor and halfway up the walls. The rest of the walls were covered with blow-ups of publicity photographs, now also featuring The Babes in the Wood, whose single Happiness was number five in the charts. The group looked set for success: all Charlotte's attempts to persuade Miranda back to her college of music were puny indeed compared to the pull of video-making and appearances on *Top of the Pops*.

She pressed one of the buttons on Liam's telephone console. The undiscovered star of the switchboard answered.

"Is Sharon in the building?" she asked.

"Yeah. She's working on a routine with Vince. In the rehearsal room."

"Warn him I'm coming down," she said.

"Hello, ducky," said Vince. "Glad you could make it." He smiled winsomely.

"This isn't a social call, Vince. I want to speak to Sharon. If you'd excuse me."

"Okay," he said. "I'll take ten." He hung a towel round his neck, smiled again, left.

Sharon, sweating, panting slightly, squatted down next to the only chair, which Charlotte sat in. "I'm worried about Sophie Preston," said Charlotte. "You know, the fat girl who trails round with Miranda and Del."

"I know Sophie. What about her?"

"I just spoke to her on the phone. She was right out of it, half-asleep."

"It figures. She pops downers all the time."

"What kind of downers?"

"Whatever Del gives her."

"Whatever *Del* gives her?" Charlotte found herself shaking with rage. "What on earth . . ."

"She's having a hard time. She's unhappy, you know? She's lonely."

"But pills don't help."

"You know that. I know that. But Sophie doesn't know that. Sophie doesn't know she's born, poor kid."

"But how can Miranda *let* him?"

"Miranda's sharp when it comes to the main chance, but considerate she's not." Sharon's little terrier face was alive with intelligence. "You don't know the half of what's been goin' on."

"So tell me."

"Remember when Miranda was tryin' to make it with Del? She tried everything – the studio and all, but he still couldn't get it up. So then she noticed that Sophie was mooning round about wanting to meet Del, so she thought it would cheer Sophie up – and help Del – if she arranged a meeting."

"They'd already met," said Charlotte, dreading the explanation.

"Yeah, well, not like Miranda arranged it, if you get my meaning. She thought it would be easier for Del with

Sophie. Her bein' a virgin and not expecting too much."

"And what happened?"

"Del got it up," said Sharon. "Which just goes to show."

"Which goes to show *what*?"

"That it's a sick old world."

"Why the hell didn't you tell me?"

Sharon looked at her consideringly. "I thought of it," she admitted. "I didn't see what good it would do. Apart from upsetting you. An' Sophie didn't want you to know."

"That's why she's been avoiding me?"

"She knew you'd disapprove. Of Del. And the pills. And her parents forbade her to see you. They said you were a bad influence. After the fuss at your school, an' all."

"I've wondered what was the matter with Sophie," said Charlotte, wretchedly raking through her memory for clues missed, hints ignored.

"Don't take it too hard. Maybe it's just a stage she's goin' through," said Sharon. "I was a bit wild at her age."

I was absorbed in Patrick, thought Charlotte. I spent all my time thinking about him, like an adolescent. Meanwhile Sophie was a victim of Miranda's heartlessness and Del's crass indifference.

"She's not under age," said Sharon, trying to console. "The law thinks she's old enough to decide for herself."

"What do you think?"

"I think Del's the pits. I think Miranda should know better. I don't think it's your fault, Charlotte. Miranda's one of those there's no telling, believe me, I know. I got sisters like her. You can tell them and tell them and all they hear is money and success and FAME. It just shows how little she knows about anything if she thinks Del's important."

"Have you ladies finished your hen talk?" said Vince. "We've got work to do, Sharon."

It was the evening of that day. Charlotte visited Sophie's flat, was let in by one of Sophie's flatmates, found the girl asleep. She couldn't, or wouldn't, be woken but she was breathing normally. Both flatmates, pleasant silly girls of seventeen, agreed they were worried about Sophie. Charlotte bullied one of them into ringing Sophie's parents. She could hear the conversation:

"She's not been at all well –"

"What's the matter with her?" Mr Preston was peremptory. "Have you called a doctor?"

"She's taking pills –"

"What kind of pills? Who prescribed them?"

"I'm not sure . . . Perhaps if you took her home . . ."

"It's up to her. She refuses to come . . . She's been very rude to us . . . She must apologise to her mother . . . She's just being silly and trying to blackmail us, and we won't be blackmailed. She's got to learn . . ."

It was no use. Charlotte could hear how little use it was being. The pleasant girl made apologetic faces.

"The Prestons will be back in England tomorrow," she said.

"We'll keep an eye on her," they both promised as Charlotte left. "We'll do what we can."

In the long term, Charlotte thought as she jerked the Golf into gear, she could get the flatmates' parents to put pressure on Sophie's parents. Meanwhile she would try Del, and Liam must help.

Liam and Del were at the studio in St John's Wood. It was rush hour traffic. Each time Charlotte seemed to choose the wrong lane and she nearly screamed with frustration as the minutes ticked by. Liam was having dinner with American visitors that night and she wanted to catch him before he left.

The studio was in a converted church. Over the door, neatly lettered, was a placard:

"We're more famous than
Jesus Christ" – (John Lennon)

The entrance hall was deserted, a carpeted waste of cigarette ends and peeling paint. The studio, by contrast

246

was full. Liam and his secretary; Del; two creative assistants from Broken Records; two engineers; three visiting Americans, men in expensive casual clothes.

"I want to talk to you, Del," she interrupted. Two of the Americans looked at her appreciatively, the third had his eyes fixed on Liam.

"Does it have to be right now?" Del was torn between the prestige of being needed urgently and the demands of the visitors.

"Yes."

"Over here," he said, taking her arm, leading her to the far corner. Even as she started to explain her worries about Sophie, the need for him to persuade her to see a doctor, she could see his eyes glaze over with indifference. Behind her with half her mind she could hear snatches of the Americans' conversation. They had West Coast accents and seemed to be speaking a language of their own:

". . . of course he pendulates, artistically . . ."

". . . to my mind it's only his perpetual aggravation that stimulates a negative block . . ."

"Please, Del," she concluded. "I'm very worried about her. I don't think she's ready for a relationship with anyone." Charlotte used the word "relationship" deliberately; it was a favourite of Del's. Now, however, he merely guffawed.

"Relationship? Ya gotta be jokin'! The kid's a groupie. Maybe I did give it to her once or twice. She asked for it. She ain't doin' me no favours."

"At least don't give her drugs."

"Don't give her drugs!" He mimicked Charlotte's voice and accent. "Those aren't 'drugs', just pills to make her feel better. Like you take for headaches or period pains. Bye, Charlotte, I got work to do."

"I don't see what I can do about it," said Liam. It was later that evening after the American visitors had gone. Charlotte and Liam were walking from the Soho restaurant to the Mercedes.

"Don't you think it's sick?" Charlotte was upset,

prepared to find opposition everywhere. Liam put his arm around her, guided her round overflowing dustbins, past the puddles with their reflections of neon signs. ADULTS ONLY flickered red and green amid soggy take-away cartons and cabbage stalks. It was raining.

"There are always kids hanging around in this business," said Liam. "They think it's glamorous. Kids with their heads full of sand."

"But actually . . . For Del to actually . . ." Charlotte was near tears and Liam stopped walking and hugged her. It was warm inside his arms.

"I could speak to him about it, but I don't reckon he'd listen."

"The sex doesn't matter so much," said Charlotte. "It's the pills. I don't know what he's giving her and I bet she doesn't either. She could kill herself. She's very self-destructive. If he doesn't stop giving her pills, I'll go to the police."

Liam smoothed her hair back from her forehead. "That would make all kinds of trouble and you wouldn't be able to prove it. They might not even take action. Come on, I'll take you home."

"Will you speak to him about it?"

"Yes."

"Promise?"

"Promise. Scout's honour." He held his fingers up in the childhood sign.

Patrick took her out to breakfast at the Italian café round the corner. "What do you think I should do about Sophie?" worried Charlotte.

"Her doctor?"

"Tried him. No dice."

"Parents?"

"Same."

"Why do you feel guilty?"

"Because I've been thinking about you and neglected Sophie."

"That's unreasonable. You've a right to your own

emotional life. Sophie's just a girl you used to teach."

"She needs protection, you don't. You earn your living looking after other people, come to that."

"Only their physical safety."

"But my work was teaching and helping girls to grow up undamaged, not calculating the quickest route out of Wembley arena. I'm one of those who should help to stop those ridiculous girls tearing the clothes off The Boys by giving them something better to think about."

"Single handed, by teaching them English, you're going to protect these girls from their own foolishness? Come off it, Charlotte."

"I should have made a better job of Sophie."

"Her parents should have made a better job of Sophie."

"I've decided to resign," said Charlotte. Miranda, in the middle of warm-up exercises, continued to stretch but peered up at Charlotte from between her legs.

"Any particular reason?" she asked casually.

"Yes. I won't go on working with Del if he gives Sophie drugs."

"Oh, is *that* all?" said Miranda. Sharon and Elliot were at the other end of the rehearsal room with Vince's nasal voice drilling them.

". . . and one and two and three and four and step and kick . . ."

"I thought you had more sense, Miranda. That poor child."

". . . to the right, hip swing, and forward and STOMP. Okay, take five, you two. Miranda, get over here."

Sharon and Elliot stretched out at Charlotte's feet.

"I'm shattered," Elliot moaned. "What a party last night! What a girl! Wheew!"

"I'm resigning," said Charlotte.

"Hey! You got a better job?" said Elliot.

"Shit," said Sharon. "How come?" She looked shocked and upset.

"Sophie," said Charlotte. "I won't work with Del."

"Liam won't like it," said Sharon. "He relies on you."

"Hardly."

"*I* rely on you," said Sharon. "*I* don't like it. You're the only person round here who talks sense."

"What about me?" said Elliot.

"You're the worst."

"And one and two and three and turn," said Vince, "AND one AND two hip SWING and STOMP." He sighed gustily. "God knows what that progressive dance teacher did to you, Miranda. Try to crisp it up, ducky. *Count* to yourself. Copy Sharon. Sharon, over here."

Sharon took Charlotte's hand, squeezed it. "I'll talk to you later, okay?"

Charlotte watched her cross the rehearsal room, all spring and energy, hair perky over a sweatband, long legs muffled in tattered leg-warmers. She felt much more affection for this product of the Social Services and the incest self-help group than for elegant Miranda, Ashcombe's finest.

On the way up to Liam's office she met Del. He pushed past her without a word, clattered on down the stairs, spurs jingling as he went.

"I came to resign," she said. Liam was at his desk, feet propped on the leather blotter. He was wearing cotton trousers and a T-shirt. His hair was ruffled and he looked reckless and boyish.

"Let's go to California," he said. "This afternoon."

"Be serious, Liam. I'm resigning."

"I am serious. I just spoke to Del. I told him, hands off Sophie, no drugs, leave her alone. Or else."

"Or else what?"

"Or else I sack him."

"Do you think it'll work?" She sank into a chair. "I think I should resign anyway. I can't go on working with Del. It's time I got another job."

"I don't want you to leave."

"I'm going to," she said decisively. It seemed the right course of action. Now the idea was expressed she saw that it had been simmering below the threshold of consciousness for weeks.

"What will you do?"

"I don't know."

"Come to California," he said again. "London's depressing in winter. You always wanted to go to America."

That was true. She didn't tell Liam that the most important part of her fantasy trip to America was that she made it alone.

"I can't leave Sophie," she said. "Not now."

Eventually, Sophie answered the doorbell. She looked ravaged, puffy and pathetically young. She had been crying. She tried to shut Charlotte out.

"I don't want to see you," she said, trailing back to her nest of grubby blankets on the sofa. "Del just called. He told me what you made Liam do. I think it's despicable. I think you're jealous, that's what it is, you want him for yourself."

"I want you to be all right, Sophie. Believe me, I'm thinking of you."

"Then don't interfere. Leave me alone. Go away. I hate you." Sophie was working herself up to an impotent rage, her fists with their gnawed and bleeding nails drumming against the sofa.

"Let me call a doctor. He can give you something to make you feel calmer."

"I thought you didn't approve of feeling calmer. No more pills, that's what Del said."

It was impossible to reason with her, though Charlotte tried. Eventually Sophie sobbed herself exhausted and fell into a light doze. Charlotte tried a last phone call to the Prestons.

This time it was Mrs Preston and she sounded anxious. "I wasn't at all happy with Sophie last time I spoke to her," she admitted. "Do you really think she needs a doctor, Miss Parker? I want to do my duty. I want to do what's right. But my husband was so sure, we have to let Sophie find her own feet, she has to grow up."

"Please, Mrs Preston. She needs you."

"She was a lovely baby," said the woman wistfully.

"She cried a lot. My husband said we should train her, you know, teach her not to cry, but I wanted to pick her up and cuddle her. She was so lovely."

"She needs cuddling now."

"Oh, but she should have grown out of that. She's nearly seventeen."

"Could you come and fetch her? Take her home?"

"My husband's got the car."

"Take a taxi."

"All the way to Sevenoaks?"

Chapter Twelve

"You did what you could," said Patrick for the twentieth time. It was a month later. They were sitting in an Italian restaurant in Covent Garden. Charlotte was crying.

"I thought she'd be safe with her parents," she said.

"Of course you did."

"Poor kid."

"You did your best."

"She must have been so miserable. Imagine how she must have felt."

"It wasn't your fault."

"What does it matter whose fault?"

"Those parents of hers must be cretins," said Patrick irritably. "Leaving her alone for the evening with enough sleeping pills to stun an elephant."

Charlotte sniffed, blew her nose, wiped her eyes. "Poor Sophie. Poor, poor Sophie. I keep remembering her in Russia, telling me all about the Impressionist paintings in the Hermitage. She wanted to do an art course."

"Was she any good?"

"Not specially. She wanted to be an astronomer as well. She had no idea . . . They buried her yesterday."

"I know."

Charlotte sniffed again, tried to pull herself together. Patrick had been remarkably patient.

"I have to leave for Paris tomorrow," he said.

"I know."

"Will you be all right?"

"Oh yes. I'll probably go away myself."

"The famous trip to America?" he teased, gently.

"Yes."

"How long for?"

"A month or two."

"Promise you'll come back?"

"I promise."

London was almost home for Charlotte. Even unemployed, with no office hours to keep and no occupation, she was happy in her flat. But a month was more than enough to be idle. Three job interviews at small country schools had been unproductive: she suspected she was overqualified. Never mind. She would find something. Meanwhile, with Patrick often away, The Babes in the Wood out of London on their first tour ("Packing them in by the dozen," Sharon had said chirpily, "going down a bomb in Doncaster"), Tessy in South Africa, the aunts in Ireland, and now Sophie dead, it was a good time to choose for the American trip.

Liam took her to lunch. In the reception area at Broken Records, she saw Del. His eyes flickered away from hers and then back in a glance of triumph. She knew he hadn't forgiven her for Liam's threats: according to Sharon, he was planning revenge. She couldn't guess what it was.

Next morning she knew. Liam rang. "Have you see the papers?"

"No."

"Charlotte . . . Carly . . ."

"Come on, Liam. Whatever it is, it can't be as bad as Sophie."

"It's the Ashcombe business. With you and the Headmaster and the stationery cupboard. In detail. With photographs."

"Not photographs of the stationery cupboard, surely," said Charlotte. She felt untouched, unworried. It was sad for Ashcombe: she hoped the school would ride the storm. This, presumably, was Del's revenge working on information supplied by Miranda. He had miscalculated, if so. Everyone who mattered to Charlotte already knew what had happened. The public at large, consumers of Broken Records' products and fast food, would forget the scandal in twenty-four hours.

"Are you all right? Carly? I'm coming round. Wait there for me. Don't go out, don't buy the papers. Wait for me."

"Bring a plane ticket," she said, suddenly decided. "I'll go to America."

"Good move," said Liam after a pause. "I'll come with you."

"No. I'll go by myself, Liam. I must. You can't leave the office for weeks, you know you can't."

He hesitated. "Are you sure?"

"Ultra-treble-positive," she said, using a catch-phrase from their childhood.

"Okay. Where do you want to go?"

"Phoenix, Arizona," she said. "An afternoon flight, if you can get one."

Liam drove her to the airport. He was being cheerful, encouraging, providing dollars and addresses, telling jokes. Charlotte didn't have the heart to tell him she wasn't as upset as he expected her to be. It was a relief when she went through passport control into the VIP lounge he insisted she use. She was wearing jeans, a sweatshirt, and trainers, her idea of American clothes. She accepted the fussing of the stewardess with the same tolerance as she had accorded to Liam: obviously the airline staff had been well tipped.

Once the plane took off and she had listened carefully to the lifejacket demonstration and noted the position of the emergency exits, she settled down to writing letters. There were so many people to be told she was visiting America. She checked the list, added more names.

A note to Joanna would be civil.

The aunts, of course.

Tessy, Liam.

Heather Noakes – difficult, but should be done.

A postcard of encouragement to the coma girl, Lisa, who was now at home, slowly re-learning all the accomplishments it had taken her childhood to acquire.

Sharon.

Suki, now back in Kilburn with Ollie.

"Champagne?" said the stewardess. She was breathtakingly pretty.

"Orange juice, please," said Charlotte. Should she write a postcard to her father? Now that it no longer mattered, why not?

A long letter to Patrick. She would save that up till last.

But first, and most important. She took a blank sheet of paper, headed it:

In the plane, on the way to America, Wednesday, 18th February.
THIS IS A THANK YOU LETTER.

Then she paused, pen in hand. The plastic shelf in front of her juddered slightly with vibration. Next to her, a businessman sipped his whisky, eyed her. She looked away, not frightened, not even apprehensive. The sheet of paper still waited. She knew what she had to say; knew also that she could not express it. Poor dear Charlotte was gone. She nearly loved Patrick. It was only a matter of time. Her life stretched ahead like a Grand Canyon of opportunity.

"Dear Nicholas," she began